PENGUIN BOOKS

MEN AT ARMS

Evelyn Waugh was born in Hampstead in 1903, second son of the late Arthur Waugh, publisher and literary critic, and brother of Alec Waugh, the popular novelist. He was educated at Lancing and Hertford College, Oxford, where he read Modern History. In 1927 he published his first work, a life of Dante Gabriel Rossetti, and in 1928 his first novel, *Decline and Fall*, which was soon followed by *Vile Bodies* (1930), *Black Mischief* (1932), *A Handful of Dust* (1934), and *Scoop* (1938). During these years he travelled extensively in most parts of Europe, the Near East, Africa, and tropical America. In 1939 he was commissioned in the Royal Marines and later transferred to the Royal Horse Guards, serving in the Middle East and in Yugoslavia. In 1942 he published *Put Out More Flags* and then in 1945 *Brideshead Revisited*. *When the Going was Good* and *The Loved One* were followed by *Helena* (1950), his historical novel. *Men At Arms*, which came out in 1952, is the first volume in 'The Sword of Honour' trilogy, and won the James Tait Black Prize; the other volumes *Officers and Gentlemen* and *Unconditional Surrender*, were published in 1955 and 1961. Evelyn Waugh was received into the Roman Catholic Church in 1930 and his earlier biography of the Elizabethan Jesuit martyr, *Edmund Campion*, was awarded the Hawthornden Prize in 1936. In 1959 he published the official *Life of Ronald Knox*. For many years he lived with his wife and six children in the West Country. He died in 1966.

EVELYN WAUGH

MEN AT ARMS

PENGUIN BOOKS

Penguin Books Ltd, Harmondsworth, Middlesex, England
Penguin Books, 625 Madison Avenue, New York, New York 10022, U.S.A.
Penguin Books Australia Ltd, Ringwood, Victoria, Australia
Penguin Books Canada Ltd, 2801 John Street, Markham, Ontario, Canada L3R 1B4
Penguin Books (N.Z.) Ltd, 182–190 Wairau Road, Auckland 10, New Zealand

—

First published by Chapman & Hall 1952
Published in Penguin Books with *Officers and Gentlemen* and
Unconditional Surrender as The 'Sword of Honour' trilogy 1964
Reprinted 1965, 1967, 1970, 1971, 1973, 1974, 1975,
1976, 1978, 1979, 1980, 1981, 1982 (twice)

—

—

Made and printed in Great Britain by
Hazell Watson & Viney Ltd,
Aylesbury, Bucks
Set in Intertype Times

CONTENTS

Sword of Honour

1

WHEN Guy Crouchback's grandparents, Gervase and Hermione, came to Italy on their honeymoon, French troops
manned the defences of Rome, the Sovereign Pontiff drove out
in an open carriage and Cardinals took their exercise side-
saddle on the Pincian Hill.

Gervase and Hermione were welcomed in a score of frescoed
palaces. Pope Pius received them in private audience and
gave his special blessing to the union of two English families
which had suffered for their Faith and yet retained a round
share of material greatness. The chapel at Broome had never
lacked a priest through all the penal years and the lands of
Broome stretched undiminished and unencumbered from the
Quantocks to the Blackdown Hills. Forbears of both their
names had died on the scaffold. The City, lapped now by the
tide of illustrious converts, still remembered with honour its
old companions in arms.

Gervase Crouchback stroked his side-whiskers and found a
respectful audience for his views on the Irish question and the
Catholic missions in India. Hermione set up her easel among
the ruins and while she painted Gervase read aloud from the
poems of Tennyson and Patmore. She was pretty and spoke
three languages; he was all that the Romans expected of an
Englishman. Everywhere the fortunate pair were praised and
petted but all was not entirely well with them. No sign or hint
betrayed their distress but when the last wheels rolled away
and they mounted to their final privacy, there was a sad gap
between them, made by modesty and tenderness and innocence,
which neither spoke of except in prayer.

Later they joined a yacht at Naples and steamed slowly up
the coast, putting in at unfrequented harbours. And there, one

night in their state room, all at last came right between them
and their love was joyfully completed.

Before they fell asleep they felt the engines stop and heard
the rattle of the anchor-chain, and when Gervase came on deck
at dawn, he found that the ship lay in the shelter of a high peninsula. He called Hermione to join him and so standing together hand-in-hand, at the moist taffrail, they had their first
view of Santa Dulcina delle Rocce and took the place and all
its people into their exulting hearts.

The waterfront was thronged as though the inhabitants had
been shaken from bed by an earthquake; their voices came
clearly across the water, admiring the strange vessel. Houses
rose steeply from the quay; two buildings stood out from the
ochre and white walls and rusty pantiles, the church domed,
with a voluted façade, and a castle of some kind comprising
two great bastions and what seemed a ruined watch-tower.
Behind the town for a short distance the hillside was terraced
and planted, then above broke wildly into boulders and briar.
There was a card game which Gervase and Hermione had
played together in the schoolroom in which the winner of a
trick called, 'I claim.'

'I claim,' cried Hermione, taking possession of all she saw
by right of her happiness.

Later in the morning the English party landed. Two sailors
went first to prevent any annoyance from the natives. There
followed four couple of ladies and gentlemen; then the servants carrying hampers and shawls and sketching materials.
The ladies wore yachting caps and held their skirts clear of the
cobbles; some carried lorgnettes. The gentlemen protected
them with fringed sunshades. It was a procession such as
Santa Dulcina delle Rocce had never seen before. They sauntered through the arcades, plunged briefly into the cool twilight
of the church and climbed the steps which led from the piazza
to the fortifications.

Little remained. The great paved platform was broken everywhere with pine and broom. The watch-tower was full of
rubble. Two cottages had been built in the hillside from the
finely cut masonry of the old castle and two families of peas-

ants ran out to greet them with bunches of mimosa. The picnic luncheon was spread in the shade.

'Disappointing when you get up here,' said the owner of the yacht apologetically. 'Always the way with these places. Best seen from a distance.'

'I think it's quite perfect,' said Hermione, 'and we're going to live here. Please don't say a word against our castle.'

Gervase laughed indulgently with the others but later, when his father died and he seemed to be rich, the project came to life. Gervase made inquiries. The castle belonged to an elderly lawyer in Genoa who was happy to sell. Presently a plain square house rose above the ramparts and English stocks added their sweetness to the myrtle and the pine. Gervase called his new house the Villa Hermione, but the name never caught the local fancy. It was cut in large square letters on the gate-posts but honeysuckle spread and smothered it. The people of Santa Dulcina spoke always of the 'Castello Crouchback' until eventually that title found its way to the head of the writing-paper and Hermione, proud bride, was left without commemoration.

Whatever its name, however, the Castello kept the character of its origin. For fifty years, until the shadows closed on the Crouchback family, it was a place of joy and love. Guy's father and Guy himself came there for their honeymoons. It was constantly lent to newly married cousins and friends. It was the place of Guy's happiest holidays with his brothers and sister. The town changed a little but neither railway nor high road touched that happy peninsula. A few more foreigners built their villas there. The inn enlarged itself, installed sanitation of a sort and a café-restaurant, took the name of 'Hotel Eden' and abruptly changed it during the Abyssinian crisis to 'Albergo del Sol'. The garage proprietor became secretary of the local Fascists. But as Guy descended to the piazza on his last morning, he saw little that would have been unfamiliar to Gervase and Hermione. Already, an hour before midday, the heat was fierce but he walked as blithely as they on that first morning of secret jubilation. For him, as for them, frustrated love had found its first satisfaction. He was packed and dressed for a long journey, already on his way back to his own country to serve his King.

Just seven days earlier he had opened his morning newspaper on the headlines announcing the Russian-German alliance. News that shook the politicians and young poets of a dozen capital cities brought deep peace to one English heart. Eight years of shame and loneliness were ended. For eight years Guy, already set apart from his fellows by his own deep wound, that unstaunched, internal draining away of life and love, had been deprived of the loyalties which should have sustained him. He lived too close to Fascism in Italy to share the opposing enthusiasms of his countrymen. He saw it neither as a calamity nor as a rebirth; as a rough improvisation merely. He disliked the men who were edging themselves into power around him, but English denunciations sounded fatuous and dishonest and for the past three years he had given up his English newspapers. The German Nazis he knew to be mad and bad. Their participation dishonoured the cause of Spain, but the troubles of Bohemia, the year before, left him quite indifferent. When Prague fell, he knew that war was inevitable. He expected his country to go to war in a panic, for the wrong reasons 'or for no reason at all, with the wrong allies, in pitiful weakness. But now, splendidly, everything had become clear. The enemy at last was plain in view, huge and hateful, all disguise cast off. It was the Modern Age in arms. Whatever the outcome there was a place for him in that battle.

Everything was now in order at the Castello. His formal farewells were made. The day before he had visited the Arciprete, the Podestà, the Reverend Mother at the Convent, Mrs Garry at the Villa Datura, the Wilmots at the Castelletto Musgrave, Gräfin von Gluck at the Casa Gluck. Now there was a last piece of private business to transact. Thirty-five years old, slight and trim, plainly foreign but not so plainly English, young now, in heart and step, he came to bid good-bye to a life-long friend who lay, as was proper for a man dead eight hundred years, in the parish church.

St Dulcina, titular patroness of the town, was reputedly a victim of Diocletian. Her effigy in wax lay languorously in a glass case under the high altar. Her bones, brought from the Greek islands by a medieval raiding party, lay in their rich casket in the sacristy safe. Once a year they were carried shoulder high through the streets amid showers of fireworks, but except on her feast day she was not much regarded in the town to which she had given her name. Her place as benefactor had been usurped by another figure whose tomb was always littered with screws of paper bearing petitions, whose fingers and toes were tied in bows of coloured wool as *aides-mémoire*. He was older than the church, older than anything in it except the bones of St Dulcina and a pre-Christian thunderbolt which lay concealed in the back of the altar (whose existence the Arciprete always denied). His name, just legible still, was Roger of Waybrooke, Knight, an Englishman; his arms five falcons. His sword and one gauntlet still lay beside him. Guy's uncle, Peregrine, a student of such things, had learned some of his story. Waybroke, now Waybrook, was quite near London. Roger's manor had long ago been lost and over-built. He left it for the second Crusade, sailed from Genoa and was ship-wrecked on this coast. There he enlisted under the local Count, who promised to take him to the Holy Land but led him first against a neighbour, on the walls of whose castle he fell at the moment of victory. The Count gave him honourable burial and there he had lain through the centuries, while the church crumbled and was rebuilt above him, far from Jerusalem, far from Waybroke, a man with a great journey still all before him and a great vow unfulfilled; but the people of Santa Dulcina delle Rocce, to whom the supernatural order in all its ramifications was ever present and ever more lively than the humdrum world about them, adopted Sir Roger and despite all clerical remonstrance canonized him, brought him their troubles and touched his sword for luck, so that its edge was always bright. All his life, but especially in recent years, Guy had felt an especial kinship with 'il Santo Inglese'. Now, on his last day, he made straight for the tomb and ran his finger, as the fishermen did, along the knight's sword. 'Sir Roger, pray for me,' he said, 'and for our endangered kingdom.'

The confessional was occupied that morning, for it was the

day when Suora Tomasina brought the schoolchildren to their duties. They sat on a bench along the wall, whispering and pinching one another, while the sister flapped over them like a hen leading them in turn to the grille and thence to the high altar to recite their penance.

On an impulse, not because his conscience troubled him but because it was a habit learned in childhood to go to confession before a journey, Guy made a sign to the sister and interrupted the succession of peasant urchins.

'*Beneditemi, padre, perche ho peccato ...*' Guy found it easy to confess in Italian. He spoke the language well but without nuances. There was no risk of going deeper than the denunciation of his few infractions of law, of his habitual weaknesses. Into that wasteland where his soul languished he need not, could not, enter. He had no words to describe it. There were no words in any language. There was nothing to describe, merely a void. His was not an 'interesting case', he thought. No cosmic struggle raged in his sad soul. It was as though eight years back he had suffered a tiny stroke of paralysis; all his spiritual faculties were just perceptibly impaired. He was 'handicapped' as Mrs Garry of the Villa Datura would have put it. There was nothing to say about it.

The priest gave him absolution and the traditional words of dismissal: '*Sia lodato Gesù Cristo,*' and he answered '*Oggi, sempre.*'* He rose from his knees, said three 'Aves' before the waxen figure of St Dulcina and passed through the leather curtain into the blazing sunlight of the piazza.

Children, grandchildren, great-grandchildren of the peasants who first greeted Gervase and Hermione still inhabited the cottages behind the Castello and farmed the surrounding terraces. They grew and made the wine; they sold the olives; they kept an almost etiolated cow in an underground stable from which sometimes she escaped and trampled the vegetable beds and plunged over the low walls until she was, with immense drama, recaptured. They paid for their tenancy in produce and service. Two sisters, Josefina and Bianca, did the work of the house. They had laid Guy's last luncheon under the orange trees. He

---

* 'Jesus Christ be praised.'   'Today, always.'

ate his spaghetti and drank his *vino scelto*, the brownish, heady
wine of the place. Then with a fuss Josefina brought him a
large ornamental cake which had been made in celebration of
his departure. His slight appetite was already satisfied. He
watched with alarm as Josefina carved. He tasted it, praised it,
crumbled it. Josefina and Bianca stood implacable before him
until he had finished the last morsel.

The taxi was waiting. There was no carriage drive to the
Castello. The gates stood in the lane at the bottom of a flight
of steps. When Guy rose to leave, all his little household,
twenty strong, assembled to see him go. They would remain
come what might. All kissed his hand. Most wept. The children
threw flowers into the car. Josefina put into his lap the remains
of the cake wrapped in newspaper. They waved until he was
out of sight, then returned to their siestas. Guy moved the cake
to the back seat and wiped his hands with his handkerchief. He
was glad that the ordeal was over and waited resignedly for the
Fascist secretary to start a conversation.

He was not loved, Guy knew, either by his household or in
the town. He was accepted and respected but he was not *simpatico*. Gräfin von Gluck, who spoke no word of Italian and
lived in undisguised concubinage with her butler, was *simpatica*. Mrs Garry was *simpatica*, who distributed Protestant
tracts, interfered with the fishermen's methods of killing octo-
puses and filled her house with stray cats.

Guy's uncle, Peregrine, a bore of international repute whose
dreaded presence could empty the room in any centre of
civilization – Uncle Peregrine was considered *molto simpatico*.
The Wilmots were gross vulgarians; they used Santa Dulcina
purely as a pleasure resort, subscribed to no local funds, gave
rowdy parties and wore indecent clothes, talked of 'wops' and
often left after the summer with their bills to the tradesmen
unpaid; but they had four boisterous and ill-favoured daughters whom the Santa-Dulcinesi had watched grow up. Better
than this, they had lost a son bathing from the rocks. The Santa-Dulcinesi participated in these joys and sorrows. They observed with relish their hasty and unobstrusive departures at the
end of the holidays. They were *simpatici*. Even Musgrave who

had the Castelletto before the Wilmots and bequeathed it his name, Musgrave who, it was said, could not go to England or America because of warrants for his arrest, 'Musgrave the Monster', as the Crouchbacks used to call him – *he* was *simpatico*. Guy alone, whom they had known from infancy, who spoke their language and conformed to their religion, who was open-handed in all his dealing and scrupulously respectful of all their ways, whose grandfather built their school, whose mother had given a set of vestments embroidered by the Royal School of Needlework for the annual procession of St Dulcina's bones – Guy alone was a stranger among them.

The black-shirt said: 'You are leaving for a long time?'

'For the duration of the war.'

'There will be no war. No one wants it. Who would gain?'

As they drove they passed on every windowless wall the lowering, stencilled face of Mussolini and the legend '*The Leader is always right*'. The Fascist secretary took his hands off the wheel and lit a cigarette, accelerating as he did so. '*The Leader is always right*' . . . '*The Leader is always right*' flashed past and was lost in the dust. 'War is foolishness,' said the imperfect disciple. 'You will see. Everything will be brought to an arrangement.'

Guy did not dispute the matter. He was not interested in what the taxi-driver thought or said. Mrs Garry would have thrown herself into argument. Once, driving with this same man, she had stopped the cab and walked home, three hot miles, to show her detestation of his political philosophy. But Guy had no wish to persuade or convince or to share his opinions with anyone. Even in his religion he felt no brotherhood. Often he wished that he lived in penal times when Broome had been a solitary outpost of the Faith, surrounded by aliens. Sometimes he imagined himself serving the last mass for the last Pope in a catacomb at the end of the world. He never went to communion on Sundays, slipping into the church, instead, very early on weekdays when few others were about. The people of Santa Dulcina preferred Musgrave the Monster. In the first years after his divorce Guy had prosecuted a few sad little love affairs but he had always hidden them from the village. Lately he had fallen into a habit of dry and negative chastity which even the priests felt to be unedifying. On the lowest, as on the highest plane, there was no sympathy between him and his fellow men. He could not listen to what the taxi-driver was saying.

'History is a living force,' said the taxi-driver, quoting from an article he had lately read. 'No one can put a stop to it and say: "After this date there shall be no changes." With nations as with men, some grow old. Some have too much, others too little. Then there must be an arrangement. But if it comes to war, everyone will have too little. *They* know that. *They* will not have a war.'

Guy heard the voice without vexation. Only one small question troubled him now: what to do with the cake. He could not leave it in the car; Bianca and Josefina would hear of it. It would be a great nuisance in the train. He tried to remember whether the Vice-Consul, with whom he had to decide certain details of closing the Castello, had any children to whom the cake might be given. He rather thought he had.

Apart from this one sugary encumbrance, Guy floated free; as untouchable in his new-found contentment as in his old despair. *Sia lodato Gesù Cristo. Oggi, sempre.* Today especially; today of all days.

2

THE Crouchback family, until quite lately rich and numerous, was now much reduced. Guy was the youngest of them and it seemed likely he would be the last. His mother was dead, his father over seventy. There had been four children. Angela, the eldest; then Gervase, who went straight from Downside into the Irish Guards and was picked off by a sniper his first day in France, instantly, fresh and clean and unwearied, as he followed the duckboard across the mud, carrying his blackthorn stick, on his way to report to company headquarters. Ivo was only a year older than Guy but they were never friends. Ivo was always odd. He grew much odder and finally, when he was twenty-six, disappeared from home. For months there was no news of him. Then he was found barricaded alone in a lodging in Cricklewood where he was starving himself to death. He was carried out emaciated and delirious and died a few days later stark mad. That was in 1931. Ivo's death sometimes seemed to Guy a horrible caricature of his own life, which at just that time was plunged in disaster.

Before Ivo's oddness gave real cause for anxiety Guy had married, not a Catholic but a bright, fashionable girl, quite unlike anyone that his friends or family would have expected. He took his younger son's share of the diminished family fortune, and settled in Kenya, living, it seemed to him afterwards, in unruffled good-humour beside a mountain lake where the air was always brilliant and keen and the flamingos rose at dawn first white, then pink, then a whirl of shadow passing across the glowing sky. He farmed assiduously and nearly made it pay. Then unaccountably his wife said that her health required a year in England. She wrote regularly and affectionately until one day, still affectionately, she informed him that she had fallen deeply in love with an acquaintance of theirs named Tommy Blackhouse; that Guy was not to be cross about it; that she wanted a divorce. '*And, please,*' her letter ended, '*there's to be no chivalrous nonsense of your going to Brighton and playing "the guilty party". That would mean six months separation from Tommy and I won't trust him out of my sight for six minutes, the beast.*'

So Guy left Kenya and shortly afterwards his father, widowed and despairing of an heir, left Broome. The property was reduced by then to the house and park and home farm. In recent years it had achieved a certain celebrity. It was almost unique in contemporary England, having been held in uninterrupted male succession since the reign of Henry I. Mr Crouchback did not sell it. He let it, instead, to a convent and himself retired to Matchet, a near-by watering-place. And the sanctuary lamp still burned at Broome as of old.

No one was more conscious of the decline of the House of Crouchback than Guy's brother-in-law, Arthur Box-Bender, who had married Angela in 1914 when Broome seemed set unalterably in the firmament, a celestial body emanating tradition and unobstrusive authority. Box-Bender was not a man of family and he respected Angela's pedigree. He even at one time considered the addition of Crouchback to his own name, in place of either Box or Bender, both of which seemed easily dispensable, but Mr Crouchback's chilling indifference and Angela's ridicule quickly discouraged him. He was not a Catholic and he thought it Guy's plain duty to marry again, preferably someone with money, and carry on his line. He was not a sensitive man and he could not approve Guy's hiding himself away. He ought to take over the home farm at Broome. He ought to go into politics. People like Guy, he freely stated, owed something to their country; but when at the end of August 1939 Guy presented himself in London with the object of paying that debt, Arthur Box-Bender was not sympathetic.

'My dear Guy,' he said, 'be your age.'

Box-Bender was fifty-six and a Member of Parliament. Many years ago he had served quite creditably in a rifle regiment; he had a son serving with them now. For him soldiering was something that belonged to extreme youth, like butterscotch and catapults. Guy at thirty-five, shortly to be thirty-six, still looked on himself as a young man. Time had stood still for him during the last eight years. It had advanced swiftly for Box-Bender.

'Can you seriously imagine yourself sprinting about at the head of a platoon?'

'Well, yes,' said Guy. 'That's exactly what I did imagine.'

Guy usually stayed with Box-Bender in Lowndes Square when he was in London. He had come straight to him now from Victoria but found his sister Angela away in the country and the house already half dismantled. Box-Bender's study was the last room to be left untouched. They were sitting there now before going out to dinner.

'I'm afraid you won't get much encouragement. All that sort of thing happened in 1914 – retired colonels dyeing their hair and enlisting in the ranks. I remember it. I was there. All very gallant of course but it won't happen this time. The whole thing is planned. The Government know just how many men they can handle; they know where they can get them; they'll take them in their own time. At the moment we haven't got the accommodation or the equipment for any big increase. There may be casualties, of course, but personally I don't see it as a soldier's war at all. Where are we going to fight? No one in his senses would try to break either the Maginot or the Siegfried Lines. As I see it, both sides will sit tight until they begin to feel the economic pinch. The Germans are short of almost every industrial essential. As soon as they realize that Mr Hitler's bluff has been called, we shan't hear much more of Mr Hitler. That's an internal matter for the Germans to settle for themselves. We can't treat with the present gang of course, but as soon as they produce a respectable government we shall be able to iron out all our differences.'

'That's rather how my Italian taxi-driver talked yesterday.'

'Of course. Always go to a taxi-driver when you want a sane, independent opinion. I talked to one today. He said: "When we are at war then it'll be time to start talking about war. Just at present we aren't at war." Very sound that.'

'But I notice you are taking every precaution.'

Box-Bender's three daughters had been dispatched to stay with a commercial associate in Connecticut. The house in Lowndes Square was being emptied and shut. Some of the furniture had gone to the country; the rest would go into store. Box-Bender had taken part of a large brand-new luxury flat, going cheap at the moment. He and two colleagues from the House of Commons would share these quarters. The cleverest of his dodges had been to get his house in the constituency accepted as a repository for 'National Art Treasures'. There would be no trouble there with billeting officers, civil or military. A few minutes earlier Box-Bender had explained these provisions with some pride. Now he merely turned to the wireless and said: 'D'you mind awfully if I just switch this thing on for a moment to hear what they're saying? There may be something new.'

But there was not. Nor was there any message of peace. The evacuation of centres of population was proceeding like clockwork; happy groups of mothers and children were arriving

punctually at their distributing centres and being welcomed
into their new homes. Box-Bender switched it off.

'Nothing new since this afternoon. Funny how one keeps
twiddling the thing these days. I never had much use for it before. By the way, Guy, that's a thing that might suit you, if
you really want to make yourself useful. They're very keen to
collect foreign language speakers at the B.B.C. for monitoring
and propaganda and that sort of rot. Not very exciting of
course but someone has to do it and I think your Italian would
come in very handy.'

There was no great affection between the two brothers-in-
law. It never occurred to Guy to speculate about Box-Bender's
view of him. It never occurred to him that Box-Bender had any
particular view. As a matter of fact, which he freely admitted
to Angela, Box-Bender had for some years been expecting Guy
to go-mad. He was not an imaginative man, nor easily impres-
sionable, but he had been much mixed up in the quest for Ivo
and his ghastly discovery. That thing had made an impression.
Guy and Ivo were remarkably alike. Box-Bender remembered
Ivo's look in the days when his extreme oddness still tottered
this side of lunacy; it had not been a wild look at all; something rather smug and purposeful; something 'dedicated';
something in fact very much like the look in Guy's eyes now as
he presented himself so inopportunely in Lowndes Square talking calmly about the Irish Guards. It could bode no good.
Best get him quickly into something like the B.B.C., out of
harm's way.

They dined that night at Bellamy's. Guy's family had always
belonged to this club. Gervase's name was on the 1914–18 Roll
of Honour in the front hall. Poor crazy Ivo had often sat in the
bay window alarming passers-by with his fixed stare. Guy had
joined in early manhood, seldom used it in recent years, but
kept his name on the list notwithstanding. It was an historic
place. Once fuddled gamblers, attended by linkmen, had felt
their way down these steps to their coaches. Now Guy and
Box-Bender felt their way up in utter blindness. The first glass
doors were painted out. Within them in the little vestibule was

a perceptible eerie phosphorescence. Beyond the second pair
of doors was bright light, noise, and a thick and stagnant fog
of cigar-smoke and whisky. In these first days of the black-out
the problem of ventilation was unsolved.

The club had only that day re-opened after its annual cleaning. In normal times it would have been quite empty at this
season. Now it was thronged. There were many familiar faces
but no friends. As Guy passed a member who greeted him,
another turned and asked: 'Who was that? Someone new,
isn't it?'

'No, he's belonged for ages. You'll never guess who he is.
Virginia Troy's first husband.'

'Really? I thought she was married to Tommy Blackhouse.'

'This chap was before Tommy. Can't remember his name.
I think he lives in Kenya. Tommy took her from him, then
Gussie had her for a bit, then Bert Troy picked her up when
she was going spare.'

'She's a grand girl. Wouldn't mind having a go myself one of
these days.'

For in this club there were no depressing conventions against
the bandying of ladies' names.

Box-Bender and Guy drank, dined and drank with a group
which fluctuated and changed throughout the evening. The conversation was briskly topical and through it Guy began to
make acquaintance with this changed city. They spoke of domestic arrangements. Everyone seemed to be feverishly occupied
in disencumbering himself of responsibilities. Box-Bender's
arrangements were the microcosm of a national movement.
Everywhere houses were being closed, furniture stored, children transported, servants dismissed, lawns ploughed, dower-
houses and shooting lodges crammed to capacity; mothers-in-
law and nannies were everywhere gaining control.

They spoke of incidents and crimes in the black-out. So-and-
so had lost all her teeth in a taxi. So-and-so had been sand-
bagged in Hay Hill and robbed of his poker-winnings. So-and-
so had been knocked down by a Red Cross ambulance and left
for dead.

They spoke of various forms of service. Most were in uniform. Everywhere little groups of close friends were arranging to spend the war together. There was a territorial searchlight battery manned entirely by fashionable aesthetes who were called 'the monstrous regiment of gentlemen'. Stockbrokers and wine salesmen were settling into the offices of London District Headquarters. Regular soldiers were kept at twelve hours' notice for active service. Yachtsmen were in R.N.V.R. uniform growing beards. There seemed no opportunity for Guy in any of this.

'My brother-in-law here is looking for a job,' said Box-Bender.

'You've left it rather late, you know. Everyone's pretty well fixed. Of course things will start popping once the balloon goes up. I should wait till then.'

They sat on late, for no one relished the plunge into darkness. No one attempted to drive a car. Taxis were rare. They made up parties to walk homeward together. At length Guy and Box-Bender joined a group walking to Belgravia. They stumbled down the steps together and set out into the baffling midnight void. Time might have gone back two thousand years to the time when London was a stockaded cluster of huts down the river, and the streets through which they walked, empty sedge and swamp.

In the following fortnight Guy came to spend most of the day in Bellamy's. He moved to an hotel and immediately after breakfast daily walked to St James's Street as a man might go to his office. He wrote letters there, a thick batch of them every day, written shamefacedly with growing facility in a corner of the morning-room.

'Dear General Cutter, Please forgive me for troubling you at this busy time. I hope you remember as I do the happy day when the Bradshawes brought you to my house at Santa Dulcina and we went out together in the boat and so ignominiously failed to spear pulpi ...'

'Dear Colonel Glover, I am writing to you because I know you served with my brother Gervase and were a friend of his ...'

'Dear Sam, Though we have not met since Downside I have

23

followed your career with distant admiration and vicarious pride...'

'Dear Molly, I am sure I ought not to know, but I *do* know that Alex is Someone Very Important and Secret at the Admiralty. I know that you have him completely under your thumb. So do you think you could possibly be an angel ...'

He had become a facile professional beggar.

Usually there was an answer; a typewritten note or a telephone call from a secretary or aide-de-camp; an appointment or an invitation. Always there was the same polite discouragement. 'We organized skeleton staffs at the time of Munich. I expect we shall expand as soon as we know just what our commitments are' – from the civilians – 'Our last directive was to go slow on personnel. I'll put you in our list and see you are notified as soon as anything turns up.'

'We don't want cannon-fodder this time' – from the Services – 'we learned our lesson in 1914 when we threw away the pick of the nation. That's what we've suffered from ever since.'

'But I'm not the pick of the nation,' said Guy. 'I'm natural fodder. I've no dependants. I've no special skill in anything. What's more I'm getting old. I'm ready for immediate consumption. You should take the 35s now and give the young men time to get sons.'

'I'm afraid that's not the official view. I'll put you on our list and see you're notified as soon as anything turns up.'

In the following days Guy's name was put on many lists and his few qualifications summarized and filed in many confidential registers where they lay unexamined through all the long years ahead.

England declared war but it made no change in Guy's routine of appeals and interviews. No bombs fell. There was no rain of poison or fire. Bones were still broken after dark. That was all. At Bellamy's he found himself one of a large depressed class of men older than himself who had served without glory in the First World War. Most of them had gone straight from school to the trenches and spent the rest of their lives forgetting the mud and lice and noise. They were under orders to await orders and spoke sadly of the various drab posts that awaited them at railway stations and docks and dumps. The balloon had gone up, leaving them on the ground.

Russia invaded Poland. Guy found no sympathy among these old soldiers for his own hot indignation.

'My dear fellow, we've quite enough on our hands as it is. We can't go to war with the whole world.'

'Then why go to war at all? If all we want is prosperity, the hardest bargain Hitler made would be preferable to victory. If we are concerned with justice the Russians are as guilty as the Germans.'

'Justice?' said the old soldiers. 'Justice?'

'Besides,' said Box-Bender when Guy spoke to him of the matter which seemed in no one's mind but his, 'the country would never stand for it. The socialists have been crying blue murder against the Nazis for five years but they are all pacifists at heart. So far as they have any feeling of patriotism it's for Russia. You'd have a general strike and the whole country in collapse if you set up to be just.'

'Then what are we fighting for?'

'Oh we had to do that, you know. The socialists always thought we were pro-Hitler, God knows why. It was quite a job in keeping neutral over Spain. You missed all that excitement living abroad. It was quite ticklish, I assure you. If we sat tight now there'd be chaos. What we have to do now is to limit and localize the war, not extend it.'

The conclusion of all these discussions was darkness, the baffling night that lay beyond the club doors. When the closing hour came the old soldiers and young soldiers and the politicians made up their same little companies to grope their way home together. There was always someone going Guy's way towards his hotel, always a friendly arm. But his heart was lonely.

Guy heard of mysterious departments known only by their initials or as 'So-and-so's cloak and dagger boys'. Bankers, gamblers, men with jobs in oil companies seemed to find a way there; not Guy. He met an acquaintance, a journalist, who had once come to Kenya. This man, Lord Kilbannock, had lately written a racing column; now he was in Air Force uniform.

'How did you manage it?' Guy asked.

'Well, it's rather shaming really. There's an air marshal whose wife plays bridge with my wife. He's always been mad keen to get in here. I've just put him up. He's the most awful shit.'

'Will he get in?'

'No, no, I've seen to that. Three blackballs guaranteed already. But he can't get me out of the Air Force.'

'What do you do?'

'That's rather shaming too. I'm what's called a "conducting officer". I take American journalists round fighter stations. But I shall find something else soon. The great thing is to get into uniform; then you can start moving yourself round. It's a very exclusive war at present. Once you're *in*, there's every opportunity. I've got my eye on India or Egypt. Somewhere where there's no black-out. Fellow in the flats where I live got coshed on the head the other night, right on the steps. All a bit too dangerous for me. I don't want a medal. I want to be known as one of the soft-faced men who did well out of the war. Come and have a drink.'

So the evenings passed. Every morning Guy awoke in his hotel bedroom, early and anxious. After a month of it he decided to leave London and visit his family.

He went first to his sister, Angela, to the house in Gloucestershire which Box-Bender bought when he was adopted as Member for the constituency.

'We're living in the most frightful squalor,' she said on the telephone. 'We can't meet people at Kemble any more. No petrol. You'll have to change and take the local train. Or else the bus from Stroud if it's still running. I rather think it isn't.'

But at Kemble, when he emerged from the corridor in which he had stood for three hours, he found his nephew Tony on the platform to greet him. He was in flannels. Only his close-cropped hair marked him as a soldier.

'Hullo, Uncle Guy. I hope I'm a pleasant surprise. I've come to save you from the local train. They've given us embarkation leave and a special issue of petrol coupons. Jump in.'

'Shouldn't you be in uniform?'

'Should be. But no one does. It makes me feel quite human getting out of it for a few hours.'

'I think I shall want to stay in mine once I get it.'

Tony Box-Bender laughed innocently. 'I should love to see you. Somehow I can't imagine you as one of the licentious soldiery. Why did you leave Italy? I should have thought Santa Dulcina was just the place to spend the war. How did you leave everyone?'

'Momentarily in tears.'

'I bet they miss you.'

'Not really. They cry easily.'

They bowled along between low Cotswold walls. Presently they came into sight of the Berkeley Vale far below them with the Severn shining brown and gold in the evening sun.

'You're glad to be going to France?'

'Of course. It's hell in barracks being chased round all day. It's pretty good hell at home at the moment – art treasures everywhere and Mum doing the cooking.'

Box-Bender's house was a small, gabled manor in a sophisticated village where half the cottages were equipped with baths and chintz. Drawing-room and dining-room were blocked to the ceiling with wooden crates.

'Such a disappointment, darling,' said Angela. 'I thought we'd been so clever. I imagined us having the Wallace Collection and luxuriating in Sèvres and Boulle and Bouchers. Such a cultured war, I imagined. Instead we've got Hittite tables from the British Museum, and we mayn't even peep at them, not that we want to, heaven knows. You're going to be hideously uncomfortable, darling. I've put you in the library. All the top floor is shut so that if we're bombed we shan't panic and jump out of the windows. That's Arthur's idea. He's really been too resourceful. He and I are in the cottage. I know we shall break our necks one night going to bed across the garden. Arthur's so strict about the electric torch. It's all very idiotic. No one can possibly see into the garden.'

It seemed to Guy that his sister had grown more talkative than she had been.

'Ought we to have asked people in for your last night, Tony? I'm afraid it's very dull, but who is there? Besides there really isn't elbow room for ourselves now we eat in Arthur's business-room.'

'No, Mum, it's much nicer being alone.'

'I so hoped you'd say that. We like it of course, but I do think they might give you two nights.'

'Have to be in at reveille on Monday. If you'd stayed in London ...'

'But you'd sooner be *at home* your last night?'

'Wherever you are, Mum.'

'Isn't he a dear boy, Guy?'

The library was now the sole living-room. The bed already made up for Guy on a sofa at one end consorted ill with the terrestrial and celestial globes at its head and foot.

'You and Tony will both have to wash in the loo under the stairs. He's sleeping in the flower-room, poor pet. Now I must go and see to dinner.'

'There's really not the smallest reason for all this,' said Tony. 'Mum and Dad seem to enjoy turning everything topsy-turvy. I suppose it comes from having been so very correct before. And of course Dad has always been jolly close about money. He hated paying out when he felt he had to. Now he thinks he's got a splendid excuse for economizing.'

Arthur Box-Bender came in carrying a tray. 'Well, you see how we're roughing it,' he said. 'In a year or two, if the war goes on, everyone will have to live like this. We're starting early. It's the greatest fun.'

'You're only here for week-ends,' said Tony. 'I hear you're very snug in Arlington Street.'

'I believe you would sooner have spent your leave in London.'

'Not really,' said Tony.

'There wouldn't have been room for your mother in the flat. No wives. That was part of the concordat we made when we decided to share. Sherry, Guy? I wonder what you'll think of this. It's South African. Everyone will be drinking it soon.'

'This zeal to lead the fashion is something new, Arthur.'

'You don't like it?'

'Not very much.'

'The sooner we get used to it the better. There is no more coming from Spain.'

'It all tastes the same to me,' said Tony.

'Well, the party is in your honour.'

A gardener's wife and a girl from the village were now the only servants. Angela did all the lighter and cleaner work of the kitchen. Presently she called them in to dinner in the little study which Arthur Box-Bender liked to call his 'business-room'. He had a spacious office in the City; his election agent had permanent quarters in the market town; his private secretary had files, a typewriter and two telephones in South-West London; no business was ever done in the room where they now dined, but Box-Bender had first heard the expression used by Mr Crouchback of the place where he patiently transacted all the paper work of the estate at Broome. It had an authentic rural flavour, Box-Bender rightly thought.

In the years of peace Box-Bender often entertained neat little parties of eight or ten to dinner. Guy had memories of many candle-lit evenings, of a rather rigid adequacy of food and wine, of Box-Bender sitting square in his place and leading the conversation in humdrum topical subjects. Tonight with Angela and Tony frequently on their feet moving the plates, he seemed less at his ease. His interests were still topical and humdrum but Guy and Tony had each his own preoccupation.

'Shocking thing about the Abercrombies,' he said. 'Did you hear? They packed up and went to Jamaica bag and baggage.'

'Why shouldn't they?' said Tony. 'They couldn't be any use here. Just extra mouths to feed.'

'It looks as though I am going to be an extra mouth,' said Guy. 'It's a matter of sentiment, I suppose. One wants to be with one's own people in war time.'

'Can't see it,' said Tony.

'There's plenty of useful work for the civilian,' said Box-Bender.

'All the Prentices' evacuees have gone back to Birmingham

in a huff,' said Angela. 'They always were unnaturally lucky. We've got the Hittite horrors for life, I know.'

'It's an awful business for the men not knowing where their wives and families are,' said Tony. 'Our wretched Welfare Officer spends his whole day trying to trace them. Six men in my platoon have gone on leave not knowing if they've got a home to go to.'

'Old Mrs Sparrow fell out of the apple-loft and broke both legs. They wouldn't take her in at the hospital because all the beds are kept for air-raid casualties.'

'We have to keep a duty officer on day and night doing P.A.D. It's a ghastly bore. They ring up every hour to report "All clear".'

'Caroline Maiden was stopped in Stroud by a policeman and asked why she wasn't carrying a gas-mask.'

'Chemical Warfare is the end. I'm jolly grateful I had a classical education. We had to send an officer from the battalion on a C.W. course. They had me down for it. Then by the mercy of God a frightfully wet fellow turned up in C Company who'd just got a science scholarship, so I stood the adjutant a couple of drinks and got him sent instead. All the wettest fellows are in C.W.'

Tony was from another world; their problems were not his. Guy belonged to neither world.

'I heard someone say that this was a very exclusive war.'

'Well, surely, Uncle Guy, the more who can keep out of it the better. You civilians don't know when you're well off.'

'Perhaps we don't want to be particularly well off at the moment, Tony.'

'I know exactly what I want. An M.C. and a nice neat wound. Then I can spend the rest of the war being cosseted by beautiful nurses.'

'*Please*, Tony.'

'Sorry, Mum. Don't look so desperately serious. I shall begin to wish I'd spent my leave in London.'

'I thought I was keeping such a stiff upper lip. Only please, darling, don't talk like that about being wounded.'

'Well, it's the best one can hope for, isn't it?'

'Look here,' said Box-Bender, 'aren't we all getting a bit morbid? Take Uncle Guy away while your mother and I clear the table.'

Guy and Tony went into the library. The french windows were open on the paved garden. 'Damn, we must draw the curtains before we put on the light.'

'Let's go out for a minute,' said Guy.

It was just light enough to see the way. The air was scented by invisible magnolia flowers, high in the old tree which covered half the house.

'Never felt less morbid in my life,' said Tony, but as he and Guy strolled out into the gathering darkness, he broke the silence by saying suddenly, 'Tell me about going mad. Are lots of Mum's family cuckoo?'

'No.'

'There was Uncle Ivo, wasn't there?'

'He suffered from an excess of melancholy.'

'Not hereditary?'

'No, no. Why? Do you feel your reason tottering?'

'Not yet. But it's something I read, about an officer in the last war who seemed quite normal till he got into action and then went barking mad and his sergeant had to shoot him.'

'"Barking" is scarcely the word for your uncle's trouble. He was in every sense a most retiring man.'

'How about the others?'

'Look at me. Look at your grandfather – and your great-uncle Peregrine; he's appallingly sane.'

'He's spending his time collecting binoculars and sending them to the War Office. Is that sane?'

'Perfectly.'

'I'm glad you told me.'

Presently Angela called: 'Come in, you two. It's quite dark. What are you talking about?'

'Tony thinks he's going mad.'

'Mrs Groat is. She left the larder un-blacked-out.'

They sat in the library with their backs to Guy's bed. Quite soon Tony rose to say good night.

'Mass is at eight,' said Angela. 'We ought to start at twenty to. I'm picking up some evacuees in Uley.'

'Oh I say, isn't there something later? I was looking forward to a long lie.'

'I thought we might all go to communion tomorrow. Do come, Tony.'

'All right, Mum, of course I will. Only make it twenty-five-to in that case. I shall have to go to scrape after weeks of wickedness.'

Box-Bender looked self-conscious, as he still did, always, when religious practices were spoken of. He did not get used to it – this ease with the Awful.

'I shall be with you in spirit,' he said.

Then he left too, and stumbled across the garden to the cottage. Angela and Guy were left alone.

'He's a charming boy, Angela.'

'Yes, so military, isn't he? All in a matter of months. He doesn't mind a bit going to France.'

'I should think not indeed.'

'Oh, Guy, you're too young to remember. I grew up with the first war. I'm one of the girls you read about who danced with the men who were being killed. I remember the telegram coming about Gervase. You were just a schoolboy going short of sweets. I remember the first lot who went out. There wasn't one of them left at the end. What chance has a boy of Tony's age starting now at the very beginning? I worked in a hospital, you remember. That's why I couldn't bear it when Tony talked of a nice neat wound and being cosseted.'

'He oughtn't to have said that.'

'There weren't any nice little wounds. They were all perfectly beastly and this time there'll be all kinds of ghastly new chemicals too, I suppose. You heard how he spoke about Chemical Warfare – a hobby for "wet" officers. He doesn't know what it will be like. There isn't even the hope of his being taken prisoner this time. Under the Kaiser the Germans were still a civilized people. These brutes will do anything.'

'Angela, there's nothing I can say except that you know

very well you wouldn't have Tony a bit different. You wouldn't want him to be one of those wretched boys I hear about who have run away to Ireland or America.'

'That's quite inconceivable, of course.'

'Well, then?'

'I know. I know. Time for bed. I'm afraid we've filled your room with smoke. You can open the window when the light's out. Thank goodness Arthur has gone ahead. I can use my torch across the garden without being accused of attracting Zeppelins.'

That night, lying long awake, obliged to choose between air and light, choosing air, not reading, Guy thought: Why Tony? What crazy economy was it that squandered Tony and saved himself? In China when called to the army it was honourable to hire a poor young man and send him in one's place. Tony was rich in love and promise. He himself destitute, possessed of nothing save a few dry grains of faith. Why could he not go to France in Tony's place, to the neat little wound or the barbarous prison?

But next morning as he knelt at the altar-rail beside Angela and Tony he seemed to hear his answer in the words of the canon: *Domine non sum dignus*.

3

Guy had planned to stay two nights and go on Monday to visit his father at Matchet. Instead he left before luncheon on Sunday so as to leave Angela uninterrupted in her last hours with Tony. It was a journey he had often made before. Box-Bender used to send him into Bristol by car. His father used to send for him to the mainline station. Now all the world seemed on the move and he was obliged to travel tediously with several changes of bus and train. It was late afternoon when he arrived at Matchet station and found his father with his old golden retriever waiting on the platform.

'I don't know where the hotel porter is,' said Mr Crouchback. 'He should be here. I told him he would be needed. But everyone's very busy. Leave your bag here. I expect we'll meet him on the way.'

Father and son and dog walked out together into the sunset down the steep little streets of the town.

Despite the forty years that divided them there was a marked likeness between Mr Crouchback and Guy. Mr Crouchback was rather the taller and he wore an expression of steadfast benevolence quite lacking in Guy. '*Racé* rather than *distingué*' was how Miss Vavasour, a fellow resident at the Marine Hotel, defined Mr Crouchback's evident charm. There was nothing of the old dandy about him, nothing crusted, nothing crotchety. He was not at all what is called 'a character'. He was an innocent, affable old man who had somehow preserved his good humour – much more than that, a mysterious and tranquil joy – throughout a life which to all outward observation had been overloaded with misfortune. He had like many another been born in full sunlight and lived to see night fall. England was full of such Jobs who had been disappointed in their prospects. Mr Crouchback had lost his home. Partly in his father's hands, partly in his own, without extravagance or speculation, his inheritance had melted away. He had rather early lost his beloved wife and been left to a long widowhood. He had an ancient name which was now little regarded and threatened with extinction. Only God and Guy knew the massive and singular quality of Mr Crouchback's family pride. He kept it to himself. That passion, which is often so thorny a growth, bore nothing save roses for Mr Crouchback. He was quite without class consciousness because he saw the whole intricate social structure of his country divided neatly into two unequal and unmistakable parts. On one side stood the Crouchbacks and certain inconspicuous, anciently allied families; on the other side stood the rest of mankind, Box-Bender, the butcher, the Duke of Omnium (whose onetime wealth derived from monastic spoils), Lloyd George, Neville Chamberlain – all of a piece together. Mr Crouchback acknowledged no monarch since James II. It was not an entirely sane conspectus but it engendered in his gentle breast two rare qualities, tolerance and humility. For nothing much, he assumed, could reasonably be expected from the commonalty; it was remarkable how well some of them did behave on occasions; while, for himself, any virtue he had came from afar without his deserving, and every small fault was grossly culpable in a man of his high tradition.

He had a further natural advantage over Guy; he was fortified by a memory which kept only the good things and rejected the ill. Despite his sorrows, he had had a fair share of joys, and these were ever fresh and accessible in Mr Crouchback's mind. He never mourned the loss of Broome. He still inhabited it as he had known it in bright boyhood and in early, requited love.

In his actual leaving home there had been no complaining. He attended every day of the sale seated in the marquee on the auctioneer's platform, munching pheasant sandwiches, drinking port from a flask and watching the bidding with tireless interest, all unlike the ruined squire of Victorian iconography.

'. . . Who'd have thought those old vases worth £18? . . . Where did that table come from? Never saw it before in my life . . . Awful shabby the carpets look when you get them out . . . What on earth can Mrs Chadwick want with a stuffed bear? . . .'

The Marine Hotel, Matchet, was kept by old servants from Broome. They made him very welcome. There he brought a few photographs, the bedroom furniture to which he was accustomed, complete and rather severe – the brass bedstead, the oak presses and boot-rack, the circular shaving glass, the mahogany prie-dieu. His sitting-room was furnished from the smoking-room at Broome with a careful selection of old favourites from the library. And there he had lived ever since, greatly respected by Miss Vavasour and the other permanent residents. The original manager sold out and went to Canada; his successor took on Mr Crouchback with the other effects. Once a year he revisited Broome, when a requiem was sung for his ancestors. He never lamented his changed state or mentioned it to newcomers. He went to mass every day, walking punctually down the High Street before the shops were open; walking punctually back as the shutters were coming down, with a word of greeting for everyone he passed. All his pride of family was a schoolboy hobby compared with his religious faith. When Virginia left Guy childless, it did not occur to Mr Crouchback, as it had never ceased occurring to Box-Bender, that the continuance of his line was worth a tiff with the Church; that Guy should marry by civil law and beget an heir and settle things up later with the ecclesiastical authorities as other people seemed somehow to do. Family pride could not be served in dishonour. There were in' fact two medieval ex-communications and a seventeenth century apostasy clearly set out in the family annals, but those were among the things that Mr Crouchback's memory extruded.

Tonight the town seemed fuller than usual. Guy knew Matchet well. He had picnicked there as a child and visited his father whenever he came to England. The Marine Hotel lay outside the town, on the cliff beside the coast-guard station. Their way led down the harbour, along the waterfront, then up again by a red rock track. Lundy Island could be seen in the setting sun, beyond the brown waters. The channel was full of shipping held by the Contraband Control.

'I should have liked to say good-bye to Tony,' said Mr Crouchback. 'I didn't know he was off so soon. There's something I looked out for him the other day and wanted to give him. I know he'd have liked to have it – Gervase's medal of Our Lady of Lourdes. He bought it in France on a holiday the year the war broke out and he always wore it. They sent it back after he was killed with his watch and things. Tony ought to have it.'

'I don't think there'd be time to get it to him now.'

'I'd like to have given it to him myself. It's not the same thing sending it in a letter. Harder to explain.'

'It didn't protect Gervase much, did it?'

'Oh, yes,' said Mr Crouchback, 'much more than you might think. He told me when he came to say good-bye before going out. The army is full of temptations for a boy. Once in London, when he was in training, he got rather drunk with some of his regiment and in the end he found himself left alone with a girl they'd picked up somewhere. She began to fool about and

36

pulled off his tie and then she found the medal and all of a sudden they both sobered down and she began talking about the convent where she'd been at school and so they parted friends and no harm done. I call that being protected. I've worn a medal all my life. Do you?'

'I have from time to time. I haven't one at the moment.'

'You should, you know, with bombs and things about. If you get hit and taken to hospital, they know you're a Catholic and send for a priest. A nurse once told me that. Would *you* care to have Gervase's medal, if Tony can't?'

'Very much. Besides I hope to get into the army too.'

'So you said in your letter. But they've turned you down?'

'There doesn't seem to be much competition for me.'

'What a shame. But I can't imagine you a soldier. You never liked motor-cars, did you? It's all motor-cars now, you know. The yeomanry haven't had any horses since the year before last, a man was telling me, and they haven't any motor-cars either. Seems a silly business. But you don't care for horses either, do you?'

'Not lately,' said Guy, remembering the eight horses he and Virginia had kept in Kenya, the rides round the lake at dawn; remembering, too, the Ford van which he had driven to market twice a month over the dirt track.

'Trains de luxe are more in your line, eh?'

'There wasn't anything very luxurious about today's trains,' said Guy.

'No,' said his father. 'I've no business to chaff you. It's very nice of you to come all this way to see me, my boy. I don't think you'll be dull. There are all kinds of new people in the inn – most amusing. I've made a whole new circle of friends in the last fortnight. Charming people. You'll be surprised.'

'More Miss Vavasours?'

'No, no, different people. All sorts of quite young people. A charming Mrs Tickeridge and her daughter. Her husband is a major in the Halberdiers. He's come down for Sunday. You'll like them awfully.'

The Marine Hotel was full and overflowing, as all hotels seemed to be all over the country. Formerly when he came to visit his father, Guy had been conscious of a stir of interest among guests and staff. Now he found it difficult to get any attention.

'No, we're quite full up,' said the manageress. 'Mr Crouchback did ask for a room for you but we were expecting you tomorrow. There's nothing at all tonight.'

'Perhaps you could fix him up in my sitting-room.'

'We'll do what we can, if you don't mind waiting a bit.'

The porter who should have been at the station was helping hand round drinks in the lounge.

'I'll go just as soon as I can, sir,' he said. 'If you don't mind waiting until after dinner.'

Guy did mind. He wanted a change of shirt after his journey, but the man was gone with his tray of glasses before Guy could answer.

'Isn't it a gay scene?' said Mr Crouchback. 'Those are the Tickeridges over there. Do come and meet them.'

Guy saw a mousy woman and a man in uniform with enormous handle-bar moustaches. 'I expect they've sent their little girl up to bed. She's a remarkable child. Only six, no nannie, and does everything for herself.'

The mousy woman smiled with unexpected charm at Mr Crouchback's approach. The man with the moustaches began moving furniture about to make room.

'Cheeroh,' he said. 'Pardon my glove.' (He was holding a chair above his head with both hands.) 'We were about to do a little light shopping. What's yours, sir?'

Somehow he cleared a small space and filled it with chairs. Somehow he caught the porter. Mr Crouchback introduced Guy.

'So you're joining the lotus-eaters too? I've just settled madam and the offspring here for the duration. Charming spot. I wish I could spend a few weeks here instead of in barracks.'

'No,' said Guy, 'I'm only here for one night.'

'Pity. The madam wants company. Too many old pussycats around.'

In addition to his huge moustaches Major Tickeridge had tufts of wiry ginger whisker high on his cheekbones, almost in his eyes.

The porter brought them their drinks. Guy tried to engage him on the subject of his bag but he was off in a twinkling with 'I'll be with you in one minute, sir.'

'Baggage problems?' said the major. 'They're all in rather a flap here. What's the trouble?'

Guy told him at some length.

'That's easy. I've got the invaluable but usually invisible Halberdier Gold standing easy somewhere in the rear echelon. Let him go.'

'No, I say, please. . . .'

'Halberdier Gold has not done a hand's turn since we got here except call me too damned early this morning. He needs exercise. Besides he's a married man and the housemaids won't let him alone. It'll do Halberdier Gold good to get away from them for a bit.'

Guy warmed towards this kind and hairy man.

'Here's how,' said the major.

'Here's how,' said the mousy wife.

'Here's how,' said Mr Crouchback with complete serenity. But Guy could only manage an embarrassed grunt.

'First today,' said the major, downing his pink gin. 'Vi, order another round while I winkle out the Halberdier.'

With a series of collisions and apologies Major Tickeridge made his way across the hall.

'It's awfully kind of your husband.'

'He can't bear a man standing idle,' said Mrs Tickeridge. 'It's his Halberdier training.'

Later when they separated for dinner Mr Crouchback said: 'Delightful people, didn't I tell you? You'll see Jenifer tomorrow. A beautifully behaved child.'

In the dining-room the old residents had their tables round the wall. The newcomers were in the centre, and, it seemed to Guy, got more attention. Mr Crouchback by a long-standing arrangement brought his own wine and kept it in the hotel cellars. A bottle of Burgundy and a bottle of port were already on the table. The five courses were rather better than might have been expected.

'It's really remarkable how the Cuthbert's cope with the in-flux. It's all happened so suddenly. Of course one has to wait a bit between courses but they manage to turn out a very decent dinner, don't they? There's only one change I mind. They've asked me not to bring Felix in to meals. Of course he did take up an awful lot of room.'

With the pudding the waiter put a plate of dog's dinner on the table. Mr Crouchback studied it carefully, turning it over with his fork.

'Yes, that looks delicious,' he said. 'Thank you so very much,' and to Guy, 'D'you mind if I take it up to Felix now? He's used to it at this time. Help yourself to the port. I'll be back directly.'

He carried the plate through the dining-room up to his sit-ting-room, now Guy's bedroom, and soon returned.

'We'll take him out later,' said Mr Crouchback. 'At about ten. I see the Tickeridges have finished dinner. The last two nights they've joined me in a glass of port. They seem a little shy tonight. You don't mind if I ask them over, do you?'

They came.

'A beautiful wine, sir.'

'Oh, it's just something the people in London send down to me.'

'I wish you could come to our mess one day. We've got some very fine port we bring out for guest nights. You, too,' he add-ed, addressing Guy.

'My son, in spite of his advanced years, is making frantic efforts to join the army himself.'

'I say, not really? I call that jolly sporting.'

'I'm not seeing much sport,' said Guy, and wryly described the disappointments and rebuffs of the last fortnight.

Major Tickeridge was slightly puzzled by the ironic note of the recitation.

'I say,' he said. 'Are you serious about this?'

'I try not to be,' said Guy. 'But I'm afraid I am.'

'Because if you *are* serious, why don't you join *us*?'

'I've pretty well given up,' said Guy. 'In fact I've as good as signed on in the Foreign Office.'

Major Tickeridge showed deep concern.

'I say, that is a pretty desperate thing to do. You know, if you're really serious, I think the thing can be managed. The old corps never quite does things in the ordinary army style. I mean none of that Hore-Belisha stuff of starting in the ranks. We're forming a brigade of our own, half regulars, half temporaries, half National Service men, half long-service. It's all on bumf at present but we're starting cadre training any day now. It's going to be something rather special. We all know one another in the corps, you know, so if you'd like me to put in a word with the Captain-Commandant, just say so. I heard him saying the other day he could do with a few older chaps among the temporary officers.'

By ten o'clock that night, when Guy and his father let Felix go bounding into the blackness, Major Tickeridge had made notes of Guy's particulars and promised immediate action.

'It's remarkable,' said Guy. 'I spent weeks badgering generals and Cabinet Ministers and getting nowhere. Then I come here and in an hour everything is fixed up for me by a strange major.'

'That's often the way. I told you Tickeridge was a capital fellow,' said Mr Crouchback, 'and the Halberdiers are a magnificent regiment. I've seen them on parade. They're every bit as good as the Foot Guards.'

At eleven lights went out downstairs in the Marine Hotel and the servants disappeared. Guy and his father went up to bed. Mr Crouchback's sitting-room smelled of tobacco and dog.

'Doesn't look much of a bed, I'm afraid.'

'Last night at Angela's I slept in the library.'

'Well, I hope you'll be all right.'

Guy undressed and lay down on the sofa by the open window. The sea beat below and the sea-air filled the room. Since that morning his affairs had greatly changed.

Presently his father's door opened: 'I say, are you asleep?'

'Not quite.'

'There's this thing you said you'd like. Gervase's medal. I might forget it in the morning.'

'Thanks most awfully. I'll always wear it from now on.'

'I'll put it here on the table. Good night.'

Guy stretched out in the darkness and felt the light disc of metal. It was strung on a piece of cord. He tied it round his neck and heard his father moving about in his room. The door opened again. 'I say, I'm afraid I get up rather early and I'll have to come through. I'll be as quiet as I can.'

'I'll come to mass with you.'

'Will you? Do. Good night again.'

Soon he heard his father lightly snoring. His last thought before falling asleep was the uneasy question: 'Why couldn't I say "Here's how" to Major Tickeridge? My father did. Gervase would have. Why couldn't I?'

BOOK ONE

Apthorpe Gloriosus

1

'HERE'S how,' said Guy.

'Cheers,' said Apthorpe.

'Look here, you two, you'd better have those drinks on me,' said Major Tickeridge, 'junior officers aren't supposed to drink in the ante-room before lunch.'

'Oh Lord. I am sorry, sir.'

'My dear chap, you couldn't possibly know. I ought to have warned you. It's a rule we have for the youngsters. It's all rot applying it to you chaps, of course, but there it is. If you want a drink tell the corporal-of-servants to send it to the billiards-room. No one will mind that.'

'Thanks for telling us, sir,' said Apthorpe.

'I expect you work up quite a thirst pounding the square. The C.O. and I had a look at you this morning. You're coming along.'

'Yes, I think we are.'

'I heard from my madam today. All's well on the Matchet front. Pity it's too far for week-end leave. I expect they'll give you a week at the end of the course.'

It was early November. Winter had set in early and cold that year. A huge fire blazed in the ante-room. Junior officers, unless invited, did not sit by it; but its warmth reached the humble panelled corners.

The officers of the Royal Corps of Halberdiers, from the very fact of their being poor men, lived in great comfort. In fashionable regiments the mess was deserted after working hours by all except the orderly-officer. The Halberdiers had made this house their home for two hundred years. As Major Tickeridge often said: 'Any damn fool can make himself comfortable.' In their month in the regiment neither Guy nor Apthorpe had once been out to a meal.

They were the eldest of the batch of twenty probationary officers now under instructions in barracks. Another similar group was said to be at the Depot. Presently they would be brought together. Some hundreds of National Service recruits were in training on the coast. Eventually in the spring they would all be interjoined with the regular battalions and the Brigade would form. This was a phrase in constant use: 'When the brigade forms . . .' It was the immediate end of all their present activity, awaited like a birth; the start of a new unknown life.

Guy's companions were mostly young clerks from London offices. Two or three had come straight from public schools. One, Frank de Souza, was just down from Cambridge. They had been chosen, Guy learned, from more than two thousand applicants. He wondered, sometimes, what system of selection had produced so nondescript a squad. Later he realized that they typified the peculiar pride of the Corps, which did not expect distinguished raw materials but confided instead in its age-old methods of transformation. The discipline of the square, the traditions of the mess, would work their magic and the *esprit de corps* would fall like blessed unction from above.

Apthorpe alone looked like a soldier. He was burly, tanned, moustached, primed with a rich vocabulary of military terms and abbreviations. Until recently he had served in Africa in some unspecified capacity. His boots had covered miles of bush trail.

Boots were a subject of peculiar interest to Apthorpe.

He and Guy first met on the day they joined. Guy got into the carriage at Charing Cross and found Apthorpe seated in the corner opposite to him. He recognized the badges of the Halberdiers and the regimental horn buttons. His first thought was that he had probably committed some heinous breach of etiquette by travelling with a senior officer.

Apthorpe had no newspaper or book. He stared fixedly at his own feet for mile after mile. Presently by a process of furtive inspection Guy realized that the insignia of rank on Apthorpe's shoulders were not crowns but single stars like his

44

own. Still neither spoke, until after twenty minutes Apthorpe took out a pipe and began carefully filling it from a large rolled pouch. Then he said: 'This is my new pair of porpoises. I expect you wear them too.'

Guy looked from Apthorpe's boots to his own. They seemed very much alike. Was 'porpoise' Halberdier slang for 'boot'?

'I don't know. I just told the man I always go to, to make me a couple of pairs of thick black boots.'

'He may have given you cow.'

'Perhaps he did.'

'A great mistake, old man, if you don't mind my saying so.'

He puffed his pipe for another five minutes, then spoke again: 'Of course, it's really the skin of the white whale, you know.'

'I didn't know. Why do they call it "porpoise"?'

'Trade secret, old man.'

More than once after their first meeting Apthorpe reverted to the topic. Whenever Guy gave evidence of sophistication in other matters, Apthorpe would say: 'Funny you don't wear porpoises. I should have thought you were just the sort of chap who would.'

But the Halberdier servant who looked after them in barracks – one between four probationary officers – found great difficulty in polishing Apthorpe's porpoises and the only criticism ever made of his turn-out on parade was that his boots were dull.

Because of their age Guy and Apthorpe became companions in most things and were called 'Uncle' by the younger officers.

'Well,' said Apthorpe, 'we'd better get a move on.'

The luncheon break allowed no time for dawdling. On paper there was an hour and a half but the squad drilled in suits of privates' dungarees (battle-dress had not yet been issued) and they had to change before appearing in the mess. Today Colour Sergeant Cook had kept them five minutes after the dinner call in expiation of Trimmer's being late on parade that morning.

Trimmer was the only member of the batch whom Guy definitely disliked. He was not one of the youngest. His large, long-lashed, close-set eyes had a knowing look. Trimmer concealed under his cap a lock of golden hair which fell over his forehead when he was bare-headed. He spoke with a slightly refined Cockney accent and when the wireless in the billiards-room played jazz, Trimmer trucked about with raised hands in little shuffling dance steps. Nothing was known of his civilian antecedents; theatrical, possibly, Guy supposed. He was no fool but his talents were not soldierly. The corporate self-esteem of the Halberdiers did not impress Trimmer, nor did the solemn comforts of the mess attract him. The moment work ended Trimmer was off, sometimes alone, sometimes with a poor reflection of himself, his only friend, named Sarum-Smith. As surely as Apthorpe was marked for early promotion, Trimmer was marked for ignominy. That morning he had appeared at the precise time stated in orders. Everyone else had been waiting five minutes and Colour Sergeant Cork called out the marker just as Trimmer appeared. So it was twelve-thirty-five when they were dismissed.

Then they had doubled to their quarters, thrown their rifles and equipment on their beds, and changed into service-dress. Complete with canes and gloves (which had to be buttoned before emerging. A junior officer seen buttoning his gloves on the steps would be sent back to dress) they had marched in pairs to the Officers' House. This was the daily routine. Every ten yards they saluted or were saluted. (Salutes in the Halberdiers' Barracks were acknowledged as smartly as they were given. The senior of the pair was taught to count: 'Up. One, two, three. Down.') In the hall they removed their caps and Sam-Brownes.

Theoretically there was no distinction of rank in the mess 'Except, Gentlemen, the natural deference which youth owes to age', as they were told in the address of welcome on their first evening; Guy and Apthorpe were older than most of the regular captains and were, in fact, treated in many ways as seniors. Together they now went into the mess at a few minutes after one.

Guy helped himself to steak-and-kidney pie at the sideboard and carried his plate to the nearest place at the table. A mess orderly appeared immediately at his elbow with salad and roast potatoes. The wine butler put a silver goblet of beer before him. No one spoke much. 'Shop' was banned and there was little else in their minds. Over their heads two centuries of commanding officers stared dully at one another from their gilt frames.

Guy had joined the Corps in a mood of acute shyness born of conflicting apprehension and exultation. He knew little of military life save stories he had heard from time to time of the humiliations to which new officers were liable; of 'subalterns' courts martial' and gross ceremonies of initiation. He remembered a friend telling him that in his regiment no one noticed him for a month and that the first words spoken to him were: 'Well, Mr Bloody, and what may your name be?' In another regiment a junior officer said 'Good morning' to a senior and was answered: 'Good morning, good morning, good morning, good morning, good morning, good morning, good morning. Let that last you for a week.' There had been nothing at all like that in the hospitable welcome he and his fellows received from the Halberdiers. It seemed to Guy that in the last weeks he had been experiencing something he had missed in boyhood, a happy adolescence.

Captain Bosanquet, the adjutant, coming cheerfully into the mess after his third pink gin, stopped opposite Guy and Apthorpe and said: 'It must have been pretty bloody cold on the square this morning.'

'It was rather, sir.'

'Well, pass the word to your chaps to wear great-coats this afternoon.'

'Very good, sir.'

'Thank you, sir.'

'Oh, you two poops,' said Frank de Souza, the Cambridge man, opposite. 'That means we'll have to let out all our equipment again.'

So there was no time for coffee or a cigarette. At half past one Guy and Apthorpe put on their belts, buttoned their gloves, looked in the glass to see that their caps were straight, tucked their canes under their arms and strode off in step to their quarters.

'Up. One, two, three. Down.' They acknowledged a fatigue party called to attention as they passed.

At their steps they broke into a run. Guy changed, and began hastily adjusting his webbing equipment. Blanco got under his fingernails. (This was the time of day which, all his life since school, Guy had spent in an easy chair.) It was permissible to double in drill suits. Guy arrived on the edge of the barrack square with half a minute in hand.

Trimmer looked terrible. Instead of buttoning his great-coat across the chest and clipping it tight at the throat, he had left it open. Moreover he had made a mess of his equipment. He had let one side-strap down at the back, the other in front with monstrous effect.

'Mr Trimmer, fall out, sir. Go to your quarters and come back here properly dressed in five minutes. *As you were.* One pace *back* from the rear rank, Mr Trimmer. *As you were.* On the command "Fall out" you take one pace back with the left foot. About turn, quick march. *As you were.* Swing the right arm level with the belt as the left foot goes forward. Now get it right. Fall out. And let me not see any laughter, Mr Sarum-Smith. There's not an officer in this squad so smart as he can laugh at another. Any officer I see laughing at another officer on parade will find himself up before the adjutant. All right. Stand easy. While we wait for Mr Trimmer, we'll just run through a little Corps history. The Royal Corps of Halberdiers was first raised by the Earl of Essex, for service in the Low Countries in the reign of Queen Elizabeth. It then bore the name of the Earl of Essex's Honourable Company of Free Halberdiers. What other sobriquets has it earned, Mr Crouchback?'

'"The Copper Heels", and the "Applejacks", Sergeant.'

'Right. Why the "Applejacks", Mr Sarum-Smith?'

'Because after the Battle of Malplaquet a detachment of the Corps under Halberdier Sergeant Major Breen were bivouacked in an orchard when they were surprised by a party of

French marauders whom they drove away by pelting them with apples, Sergeant.'

'Very good, Mr Sarum-Smith. Mr Leonard, what part did the Corps play in the First Ashanti War . . .'

Presently Trimmer returned.

'Very well. Now we can get on. This afternoon we are going to the kitchens where Halberdier Sergeant Major Groggin will show you how to tell meat. Every officer must know how to tell meat. Many frauds are attempted on the military by civilian contractors and the health of his men depends on the alertness of the officer. All right? Then, Mr Sarum-Smith, will you take command. At the command, "Move", step smartly out of the ranks, about turn, face your men. Move. This is your squad now. I'm not here. I want them without arms, marched in a soldierly fashion to the kitchen yard. If you don't know where that is, follow your nose, sir. First run through the detail for piling arms, just for refreshment, and then give the executive order.'

The detail for piling arms was the most elaborate part of their education to date. Sarum-Smith faltered. Guy was called out and faltered also. De Souza ran on confidently, but incorrectly. At last Apthorpe, the safe stand-by, was called on. With an expression of strain he got it right – '. . . the odd numbers of the front rank will seize the rifles of the even numbers with the left hand crossing the muzzles, magazines turned outward, at the same time raising the piling swivels with the forefinger and thumb of both hands . . .' and the squad marched off. For the rest of the afternoon period they inspected the kitchens in great heat and the meat store in great cold. They saw vast, purple and yellow, carcasses of beef and were taught to distinguish cat from rabbit by the number of ribs.

At four they were dismissed. There was tea in the mess for those who thought it worth another change of uniform. Most lay on their beds until it was time for Physical Training.

Sarum-Smith came to Guy's room.

'I say, Uncle, have you had any pay yet?'

'Not a penny.'

'Can't we do anything about it?'

'I did mention it to the Second-in-Command. He says it always takes some time to get through. It's just a matter of waiting.'

'That's all right for those who can afford it. Some firms are making up their fellows' salaries so they don't lose by joining the army. Mine doesn't. You're quite happily placed, aren't you, Uncle?'

'Well, I'm not quite broke yet.'

'Wish I wasn't. It's jolly awkward for me. Did you realize when we joined they'd make us pay for our food?'

'Well, we don't really. We pay for what we have to supplement rations. It's very good value.'

'That's all very well, but I'd have thought the least they could do would be to feed us in war-time. It was a shock when I found my first mess bill. How do they expect us to live? I'm absolutely stony.'

'I see,' said Guy without enthusiasm or surprise, for this was not the first conversation of the kind he suffered in the last few weeks and Sarum-Smith was not a man whom he particularly liked. 'I suppose you want a loan.'

'I say, Uncle, you're a thought-reader. I would be glad of a fiver if you can spare it. Just till the Army pays up.'

'Don't tell everyone else.'

'No, of course not. A lot of us are in a bit of a fix, I can tell you. I tried Uncle Apthorpe first. He advised me to come to you.'

'Thoughtful of him.'

'Of course if it's putting *you* in a fix. . . .'

'No, that's all right. But I don't want to become banker for the whole Corps.'

'You shall have it back the moment I get my pay . . .'

Guy was owed fifty-five pounds.

Soon it was time to change into flannels and go to the gym. This was the one part of the day Guy hated. The squad of probationary officers assembled under the arc lights. Two Halberdier corporals were kicking a football about. One of them kicked it so that it smacked against the wall over their heads.

'That's damned cheek,' said a young man named Leonard. The ball came again, rather closer.

'I believe the fellow's doing it deliberately,' said Sarum-Smith.

Suddenly there was a loud authoritative shout from Apthorpe. 'You two men, there. Can't you see there's a squad of officers here? Take that ball and get out.'

The corporals looked sulky, picked up their ball and strolled out with a plausible suggestion of nonchalance. Outside the door they laughed loudly. The gym seemed to Guy to institute a sort of extra-territorial area, the embassy of an alien and hostile people, that had no part in the well-ordered life of the barracks.

The Physical Training instructor was a sleek young man with pomaded hair, a big behind and unnaturally glittering eyes. He performed his great feats of strength and agility with a feline and, to Guy, most offensive air of sang-froid.

'The purpose of P.T. is to loosen up,' he said, 'and counteract the stiffening effects of the old-fashioned drill. Some of you are older than others. Don't strain. Don't do more than you feel you can. I want to see you *enjoy* yourselves. We'll start with a game.'

These games had a deeply depressing effect even on the youngest. Guy stood in line, took a football when it came to him from between the legs of the man in front, and passed it on. They were supposed to compete, one rank against the other.

'Come on,' said the instructor, 'you're letting them get away with it. I'm backing you. Don't let me down.'

After the game came exercises.

'Make it smooth and graceful, gentlemen, as though you were waltzing with your best girl. That's the way, Mr Trimmer. That's very rhythmic. In the old days a soldier's training consisted of standing stiff at attention for long periods and stamping the feet. Modern science has shown that stamping the feet can seriously jar the spinal column. That's why nowadays every day's work ends with half an hour's limbering up.'

This man would never fight, Guy thought. He would stay in his glaring shed, rippling his muscles, walking on his hands, bouncing about the boards like an india-rubber ball, though the heavens were falling.

'At Aldershot today the advance courses are all done to music.'

There would have been no place for this man, Guy reflected, in the Earl of Essex's Honourable Company of Free Halberdiers. He was no Copper Heel, no true Applejack.

After Physical Training another change of clothes and a lecture on Military Law from Captain Bosanquet. Lecturer and audience were equally comatose. Captain Bosanquet demanded no more than silence.

'. . . The great thing to remember is to stick in all the amendments of King's Regulations as soon as they're issued. Keep your King's Regulations up to date and you can't go far wrong.'

At six-thirty they were roused, dismissed and the day's work was at last over. This evening Captain Bosanquet called Guy and Apthorpe back.

'I say,' he said, 'I looked in at your P.T. this evening. Do you think it does you any particular good?'

'I can't say I do, sir,' said Guy.

'No, it's rather rot for people like yourselves. If you like, you can cut it out. Keep clear of the ante-room. Just stay in your quarters and, if anyone asks, say you are mugging up Military Law.'

'Thanks awfully, sir.'

'You'll probably find yourself commanding companies one day. Military Law will be more use to you then than P.T.'

'I think I'll stay on in the gym, if I may,' said Apthorpe. 'I find that after the square I need limbering up a bit.'

'Just as you like.'

'I've always been used to plenty of exercise,' said Apthorpe to Guy, as they returned to their quarters. 'There's a lot of sense in what Sergeant Pringle said about jarring the spinal column. I think I may have jarred mine a bit. I've been feeling a bit off colour lately. It may be that. I don't want anyone to think I'm not as fit as the rest of the crowd. The truth is I've lived hard, old man, and it tells.'

'Talking about being different from the rest of the crowd, did you by any chance pass Sarum-Smith on to me?'

'That's right. I don't believe in borrowing or lending. Seen too much of it.'

There were two baths on every staircase. Coal fires had now been lighted in the bedrooms. Toiling old Halberdiers, recalled to the colours and put on barrack duties, kept them stoked. This was the best hour of the day. Guy heard the feet of the young officers scampering down and out to local cinemas, hotels and dance-halls. He soaked in hot water and later lay dozing in the wicker Oxford chair before his fire. No Mediterranean siesta had ever given such ease.

Presently Apthorpe came to summon him to the Officers' House. Patrol dress was optional for probationary officers. Only he and Guy had bought it and this tended to set them apart and make them more acceptable to the regulars, not because they could afford twelve guineas which the others could not, but because they had chosen to make a private investment in the traditions of the Corps.

When the two 'Uncles' in their blues arrived in the anteroom, Major Tickeridge and Captain Bosanquet were alone before the fire.

'Come and join us,' said Major Tickeridge. He clapped his hands. 'Music and dancing-girls. Four pink gins.'

Guy loved Major Tickeridge and Captain Bosanquet. He loved Apthorpe. He loved the oil-painting over the fireplace of the unbroken square of Halberdiers in the desert. He loved the whole Corps deeply and tenderly.

Dinner was formal that night. The mess-president struck the table with an ivory hammer and the chaplain said Grace. The young officers, accustomed to swifter and sparser meals, found all this rather oppressive. 'I call it a bit thick,' Sarum-Smith had remarked, 'the way they even make a drill-movement out of eating.'

The table was lit with huge many-branched candlesticks which commemorated the military history of the last century in silver palm trees and bowed silver savages. There were about twenty officers in mess that night. Many of the young were out

53

in the town; the older were in neighbouring villas with their wives. No one drank wine except on guest nights. Guy had made the mistake of ordering claret his first evening and had been rebuked with a jocular: 'Hullo, blood? Is it someone's birthday?'

'There's an Ensa show tonight. Shall we go?'

'Why not?'

'I rather thought of sticking some amendments into the King's Regulations.'

'I'm told the orderly-room clerk will do it for a pound.'

'Looks better to do it oneself,' said Apthorpe. 'Still I think I'll come for once. The Captain-Commandant may be there. I haven't spoken to him since the first day.'

'What d'you want to say to him?'

'Oh, nothing particular. Anything that crops up, you know.'

After a pause Guy said: 'You heard what the adjutant said about our probably getting companies.'

'Doesn't that verge rather on shop, old man?'

Presently the hammer sounded again, the chaplain said Grace and the table was cleared. The removal of the cloth was a feat of dexterity which never failed to delight Guy. The corporal-of-servants stood at the foot of the table. The mess orderlies lifted the candlesticks. Then with a single flick of his wrists the corporal drew the whole length of linen into an avalanche at his feet.

Port and snuff went round. The party broke up.

The Halberdiers had their own Garrison Theatre within the barrack walls. It was nearly full when Guy and Apthorpe arrived. The first two rows were kept for officers. In the centre sat the full colonel, who by an idiosyncrasy of the Corps was called the Captain-Commandant, with his wife and daughter. Guy and Apthorpe looked for places, saw only two empty seats in the centre. They hesitated, Guy seeking to withdraw, Apthorpe rather timidly advancing.

'Come along,' said the Captain-Commandant. 'Ashamed to be seen sitting with us? Meet madam and the brat.'

They took their places with the distinguished party.

'Do you go home for the week-end?' asked the brat.

'No. You see my home's in Italy.'

'Not really. Are you artistic or something? How thrilling.'

'My home used to be in Bechuanaland,' said Apthorpe.

'I say,' said the Captain-Commandant. 'You must have some interesting yarns. Well, I suppose I'd better get this thing started.'

He gave a nod; the footlights went up; he rose and climbed the steps to the stage.

'We're all greatly looking forward to this show,' he said. 'These charming ladies and accomplished gentlemen have come a long way on a cold night to entertain us. Let's see we give them a real Halberdier welcome.'

Then he returned to his place amid loud applause.

'It's really the chaplain's job,' he said to Guy. 'But I give the little fellow a rest now and then.'

A piano began playing behind the curtain. The curtain rose. Before the stage was fully revealed, the Captain-Commandant sank into deep but not silent sleep. Under the Corps crest in the proscenium there was disclosed a little concert party comprising three elderly women, over-made-up, a cadaverous old man, under-made-up, and a neuter beast of indeterminable age at the piano. All wore the costume of pierrots and pierrettes. There was a storm of loyal applause. A jaunty chorus opened the show. One by one the heads in the first two rows sank into their collars. Guy slept too.

He was awakened an hour later by a volume of song striking him from a few feet away. It came from the cadaverous man whose frail northern body seemed momentarily possessed by the ghost of some enormous tenor from the south. He woke the Captain-Commandant, too.

'I say, that's not "God Save The King", is it?'

'No, sir. "There'll always be an England".'

The Captain-Commandant collected his wits and listened.

'Quite right,' he said. 'Never can tell a tune till I've heard the words. The old fellow's got a voice, hasn't he?'

It was the last item. Soon everyone was at attention. The tenor did more. He stood at attention while company and audience joined in the National Anthem.

'On these occasions we always have the performers in for a drink. You might round up some of the young chaps to do the honours, will you? I expect you've more experience in entertaining the theatrical world than we have. And, I say, if you're here for Sunday and have nothing better to do, come and lunch.'

'Very glad to, sir,' said Apthorpe, whose inclusion in the invitation was by no means clear.

'You'll be here, too? Yes, of course, do come. Delighted.'

The Captain-Commandant did not go with them to the Officers' House. Two regulars and three or four of Guy's batch formed the reception committee. The ladies had shed all theatrical airs with their make-up and their fancy dress. They might have come in from a day's household shopping.

Guy found himself next to the tenor, who had shed his wig, revealing a few grey wisps of hair which made him appear somewhat younger, but still very old. His cheeks and nose were blotchy and bright-veined, his eyes watery in a nest of wrinkles. It was many weeks since Guy had looked into a sick man's face. He might have taken the tenor for an alcoholic, but he chose only coffee to drink.

'Find I don't sleep if I drink whisky nowadays,' he said apologetically. 'You're all wonderfully hospitable. Especially the Corps. I've always had a very warm corner for the Copper Heads.'

'Copper Heels.'

'Yes, of course. I meant Copper Heels. We were next to you in the line once in the last show. We got on very well with your chaps. I was in the Artists. Not with a commission, mind you. I wasn't the age for that, even then. Joined up in the ranks and saw it all through.'

'I only just scraped in.'

'Oh, you're young. I wonder if I might have another cup of this excellent coffee. Takes it out of one, singing.'

'You've got a fine voice.'

'D'you think it went down all right? One never knows.'

'Oh, yes, a great success.'

'Of course we aren't a No. 1 Company.'

'You were all a great success.'

They stood silent. A burst of laughter rose from the group round the ladies. Everything was going easily there.

'More coffee?'

'No more, thank you.'

Silence.

'The news looks better,' said the tenor at last.

'Does it?'

'Oh, *much* better.'

'We don't get much time to read the papers.'

'No, I suppose you don't. I envy you. There's nothing in them but lies,' he added sadly. 'You can't believe a word they say. But it's all good. Very good indeed. It helps to keep one's spirits up,' he said from the depths of his gloom. 'Something cheerful every morning. That's what we need in these times.'

Quite soon the party bowled away into the night.

'That looked a very interesting man you were talking to,' said Apthorpe.

'Yes.'

'A real artist. I should think he's been in opera.'

'I daresay.'

'Grand Opera.'

Ten minutes later Guy was in bed. In youth he had been taught to make a nightly examination of conscience and an act of contrition. Since he joined the army this pious exercise had become confused with the lessons of the day. He had failed dismally in the detail of the pile-arms ... – '... the even numbers of the centre rank will incline their muzzles to the front and place their rifles under their right arms, guards uppermost, at the same time seizing the piling swivel. ...' – He was not now certain which had the more ribs, a cat or a rabbit. He wished it had been he, not Apthorpe, who had called the impudent corporals to order in the gym. He had snubbed that decent, melancholy old man about the 'Copper Heads'. Was that the real 'Halberdier welcome' expected of him? There was much to repent and repair.

2

On Saturday at twelve there was a large exodus from bar-racks. Guy as usual remained. More than his longer and more bitter memories, his modest bank balance, his blue patrols, his boredom in the gym or any of the small symptoms of age which distinguished him from his youthful fellows, there was this recurring need for repose and solitude. Apthorpe went off to play golf with one of the regulars. It was holiday enough for Guy to change at his leisure, wear the same clothes all the after-noon, to smoke a cigar after luncheon, walk down the High Street to collect his weekly papers – the *Spectator,* the *New Statesman,* the *Tablet* – from the local newsagent, to read them drowsily over his own fire in his own room. He was thus em-ployed when, long after nightfall, Apthorpe returned from golf. He wore flannel trousers and a tweed coat much patched and bound with leather. There was a fatuous and glassy squint in his eyes. Apthorpe was tight.

'Hallo. Have you had dinner?'

'No. I don't intend to. It's a sound rule of health not to have dinner.'

'Never, Apthorpe?'

'Now, old man, I never said that. Of course not *never.* Some-times. Give the juices a rest. You have to be your own doctor in the bush. First rule of health, keep your feet dry; second, rest the juices. D'you know what the third is?'

'No.'

'Nor do I. Just stick to two rules and you'll be all right. You know you don't look well to me, Crouchback. I've been worry-ing about you. You know Sanders?'

'Yes.'

'I've been playing golf with him.'

'Good game?'

'Terrible. High wind, poor visibility. Played nine holes and knocked off. Sanders has a brother in Kasanga. I suppose you think that's near Makarikari.'

'Isn't it?'

'Just about twelve hundred miles, that's how near it is. You know, old man, for a chap who's knocked about as much as you have, you don't know much, do you? Twelve hundred bloody miles of bush and you call that near.' Apthorpe sat down and stared at Guy sadly. 'Not that it really matters,' he said. 'Why worry? Why go to Makarikari? Why not stay in Kasanga?'

'Why not indeed?'

'Because Kasanga's a perfectly awful hole, that's why. Still if you like the place, stay there by all means. Only don't ask me to join you, that's all, old man. Of course you'd have Sanders' brother. If he's anything like Sanders he plays pretty rotten golf, but I've no doubt you'd be jolly glad of his company in Kasanga. It's a perfectly awful hole. Don't know what you see in the place.'

'Why don't you go to bed?'

'Lonely,' said Apthorpe. 'That's why. It's always the same, wherever you are, Makarikari, Kasanga, anywhere. You have a good time drinking with the chaps in the club, you feel fine, and then at the end of it all you go back alone to bed. I need a woman.'

'Well, you won't find one in barracks.'

'For company, you understand. I can do without the other thing. Not, mind you, that I haven't done myself well in my time. And I will do again I hope. But I can take it or leave it. I'm above sex. You have to be, in the bush, or it gets a grip on you. But I can't do without company.'

'I can.'

'You mean you want me to go? All right, old man, I'm not as thick-skinned as you might think. I know when I'm not wanted. I'm sorry I inflicted myself on you for so long, very sorry.'

'We'll meet again tomorrow.'

But Apthorpe did not move. He sat goggling sadly. It was like watching the ball at roulette running slower and slower, trickling over the numbers. What would turn up next: Women? Africa? Health? Golf? It clicked into boots.

'I was wearing rubber soles today,' he said. 'I regret it now. Spoiled my drive. No grip.'

'Don't you think you'd better get to bed?'

It was half an hour before Apthorpe rose from the chair. When he did so, he sat heavily on the floor and continued the conversation, without apparently noticing his change of position. At last he said with a new lucidity: 'Look here, old man, I've enjoyed this talk tremendously. I hope we can go on with it some other night but at the moment I'm rather sleepy so if you don't mind I think I'll turn in.'

He then rolled over and lay silent. Guy went to bed to the sound of Apthorpe's breathing, turned off the light and slept also. He woke in the dark to hear groaning and stumbling. He turned on the light. Apthorpe was on his feet blinking.

'Good morning, Crouchback,' he said with dignity. 'I was just looking for the latrines. Must have taken a wrong turning. Good night.'

And he staggered from the room leaving the door ajar.

Next morning when Guy was called, the batman said: 'Mr Apthorpe's sick. He asked for you to go in and see him when you're dressed.'

Guy found him in bed with a japanned tin medicine chest on his knees.

'I'm a bit off colour, today,' he said. 'Not quite the thing at all. I shan't be getting up.'

'Anything I can do?'

'No, no, it's just a touch of Bechuana tummy. I get it from time to time. I know just how to take it.' He was stirring a whitish mixture with a glass rod. 'The hell of it is I promised to lunch with the Captain-Commandant. I must make a signal putting him off.'

'Why not just send him a note?'

'That's what I mean, old man. You always call it "making a signal" in the service, you know.'

'Do you remember calling on *me* last night?'

'Yes, of course. What an extraordinary question, old man. I'm not a talkative bloke as you well know, but I do enjoy a regular chinwag now and then in the right company. But I don't feel so good today. It was bloody cold and wet on the links and I'm liable to this damned Bechuana tummy if I get a chill. I wondered if you could let me have some paper and an envelope. I'd better let the Captain-Commandant know in good time.' He drank his mixture. 'Be a good chap and put this down for me somewhere where I can reach it.'

Guy lifted the medicine chest, which on inspection seemed to contain only bottles labelled 'Poison', put it on a table, and brought Apthorpe paper.

'D'you suppose I ought to begin: "Sir, I have the honour"?'

'No.'

'Just "Dear Colonel Green"?'

'Or "Dear Mrs Green".'

'That's the ticket. That's exactly the right note. Good for you, old man. "Dear Mrs Green" of course.'

One of the characteristics of the Halberdiers was a tradition of firm churchmanship. Papistry and Dissent were almost unknown among the regulars. Long-service recruits were prepared for Confirmation by the chaplain as part of their elementary training. The parish church of the town was the garrison chapel. For Sunday Mattins the whole back of the nave was reserved for the Halberdiers who marched there from the barracks behind their band. After church the ladies of the garrison – wives, widows and daughters in whom the town abounded, whose lawns were mown by Halberdiers and whose joints of beef were illicitly purchased from the Halberdier stores – assembled with hymn books in their hands at the Officers' House for an hour's refreshment and gossip. Nowhere in England could there be found a survival of a Late-Victorian Sunday so complete and so unselfconscious, as at the Halberdier barracks.

As the only Catholic officer Guy was in charge of the Catholic details. There were a dozen of them, all National Service men. He inspected them on the square and marched them to mass at the tin church in a side street. The priest was a recent graduate from Maynooth who had little enthusiasm for the Allied cause or for the English army, which he regarded merely as a provocation to immorality in the town. His sermon that morning was not positively offensive; there was nothing in it to make the basis of a complaint; but when he spoke of 'this terrible time of doubt, danger and suffering in which we live,' Guy stiffened. It was a time of glory and dedication.

After mass, as the men were waiting to fall in for their return march, the priest accosted Guy at the gate. 'Won't you just slip in to the presbytery, Captain, and pass the time of day? I've a bottle of whisky a good soul gave me, that needs opening.'

'I won't, thank you, Father Whelan. I've got to take the men back to barracks.'

'Well now and what a wonderful thing the army is to be sure, that a lot of grown lads can't walk half a mile by themselves.'

'Those are the orders, I'm afraid.'

'Now that little matter of the list of names, Captain. His Lordship wants a list of all the names of the Catholic serving men for his records as I think I mentioned to you last Sunday.'

'Very good of you to take so much interest in us. I think you get a capitation grant from the War Office, don't you, Father Whelan, when there's no Catholic chaplain?'

'Well, I do now, Captain, and isn't it me right at law?'

'I'm not a captain. You'd better write to the adjutant.'

'And how would I be telling one officer from another and me not a military man at all?'

'Just write "the Adjutant, the Royal Corps of Halberdiers". That'll get to him all right.'

'Well, if you won't help, you won't, I suppose. God bless you, Captain,' he said curtly and turned to a woman who had been standing unnoticed at his elbow. 'Well, my dear woman, and what's troubling you now?'

On the march home they passed the parish church, a lofty elaborate tower rising from a squat earlier building of flint and grey stone, with low dog-toothed arches. It stood in a well-kept graveyard behind ancient yews. Within from the hammer-beams hung the spider's-web Colours of the Corps. Guy knew them well. He often stopped there on Saturday afternoons with his weekly papers. From such a doorway as that Roger de Waybroke had stepped out on his unaccomplished journey, leaving his madam padlocked.

Less constrained than the Lady of Waybroke, the womenfolk of the Halberdiers were all over the ante-room when Guy returned. He knew most of them now and for half an hour he helped order sherry, move ashtrays and light cigarettes. One of his own batch, the athletic young man named Leonard, had brought his wife that morning. She was plainly pregnant. Guy knew Leonard little for he lodged in the town and spent his evenings there, but he recognized him as peculiarly fitted for the Halberdiers. Apthorpe looked like any experienced soldier but Leonard seemed made of the very stuff that constituted the Corps. In peace he had worked in an insurance office and had travelled every winter Saturday afternoon, carrying his 'change' in an old leather bag, to outlying football grounds to play scrum-half for his club.

In his first speech of welcome the Captain-Commandant had hinted that there might be permanent commissions for some of them after the war. Guy could imagine Leonard in twelve years' time as hairy and kindly and idiomatic as Major Tickeridge. But that was before he met his madam.

The Leonards sat with Sarum-Smith talking of money.

'I'm here because I've got to be,' Sarum-Smith was saying. 'I went to town last week-end and it cost me over a fiver. I shouldn't have thought twice of it when I was in business. Every penny counts in the army.'

'Is it true, Mr Crouchback, that they're moving you all after Christmas?'

'I gather so.'

'Isn't it a shame? No sooner settled in one place than you're off somewhere else. I don't see the sense of it.'

'One thing I won't do,' said Sarum-Smith, 'and that's buy a map-case. Or King's Regulations.'

'They say we've got to pay for our battle-dress when it comes. I call that a bit thick,' said Leonard.

'It's no catch being an officer. They're always making you buy something you don't want. The War Office is so busy suck-

63

ing up to the other ranks it hasn't time for the poor bloody officers. There was three bob on my mess bill yesterday marked "entertainment". I asked what that was for and they told me it was my share of the drinks for the Ensa party. I didn't even go to the show, let alone stand any drinks.'

'Well, you wouldn't want them to come to the Corps and not have any hospitality, would you?' asked Leonard.

'I could survive it,' said Sarum-Smith. 'And I bet half those drinks went down the throats of the regular officers.'

'Steady on,' said Leonard. 'Here's one of them.'

Captain Sanders approached. 'I say, Mrs Leonard,' he said. 'You know that the Captain-Commandant's expecting you both to luncheon today?'

'We got our orders,' said Mrs Leonard sourly.

'Grand, I'm trying to find another man. Apthorpe's chucked. You're booked for it already, aren't you, Crouchback? How about you, Sarum-Smith?'

'Spare me,' said Sarum-Smith.

'You'll enjoy it. They're grand people.'

'Oh, very well then.'

'I haven't seen Uncle Apthorpe this morning. How's he looking?'

'Terrible.'

'He had rather a load on last night. He got into a pretty hearty school at the golf club.'

'He has Bechuana tummy this morning.'

'Well, that's a new name for it.'

'I wonder what he'd call *my* tummy,' said Mrs Leonard. Sarum-Smith laughed loudly. Captain Sanders wandered away. Leonard said: 'Keep it clean, Daisy, for heaven's sake. I'm glad you're coming to lunch, Uncle. We'll have to sit on Daisy. She's in a wicked mood today.'

'Well, all I can say, I wish *Jim* had something wrong with himself. Here he is playing soldiers all the week. I never see him. They might at least give him his Sunday free. Any decent job you get that.'

'The Captain-Commandant seemed awfully nice.'

'I daresay he is, if you know him. So is my Aunt Margie. But

I don't expect the Captain-Commandant to spend his day off with her.'

'You mustn't mind Daisy,' said Leonard. 'It's just she looks forward to Sundays and she isn't one for going out and meeting people particularly at the moment.'

'If you ask me the Halberdiers think far too much of themselves,' said Mrs Leonard. 'It's different in the R.A.F. My brother's a wing commander on the catering side and he says it's just like any ordinary job only easier. Halberdiers can't ever forget to be Halberdiers even on Sunday. Look at them all now.'

Sarum-Smith looked at his brother officers and at their ladies, whose laps were full of prayer-books and gloves, their hands full of cigarettes and sherry; their voices high and happy.

'I suppose we shall find *these* drinks on the mess bill too. How much d'you suppose the Captain-Commandant charges for lunch?'

'I say, steady on,' said Leonard.

'I wish Jim had joined the R.A.F.,' said Mrs Leonard. 'I'm sure it could have been managed. You know where you are with them. You just settle down at an R.A.F. station as though it was business with regular hours and a nice crowd. Of course I shouldn't let Jim fly, but there's plenty of jobs like my brother's got.'

'Ground staff is all right in war-time,' said Sarum-Smith. 'It won't sound so good afterwards. One's got to think of peace. It'll do one more good in business to have been in the Halberdiers than the R.A.F. ground staff.'

At five minutes to one Mrs Green and Miss Green, wife and daughter of the Captain-Commandant, rose from their places and collected the guests.

'We mustn't be late,' said Mrs Green. 'Ben Ritchie-Hook is coming. He's a terror if he's kept waiting for his food.'

'I find him rather a terror always,' said Miss Green.

'You oughtn't to say that about their future brigadier.'

'Is it the man you were telling me about?' asked Mrs Leonard, whose way of showing her disapproval of the expedition was to speak only to her husband, 'the man who cuts off people's heads?'

'Yes. He sounds a regular fizzer.'

'We're all very fond of him really,' said Mrs Green.

'I've heard of him,' said Sarum-Smith as though to be known to him had some sinister connotation like being 'known' to the police.

Guy too had heard of him often. He was the great Halberdier *enfant terrible* of the First World War; the youngest company commander in the history of the Corps; the slowest to be promoted; often wounded, often decorated, recommended for the Victoria Cross, twice court martialled for disobedience to orders in the field, twice acquitted in recognition of the brilliant success of his independent actions; a legendary wielder of the entrenching tool; where lesser men collected helmets Ritchie-Hook once came back from a raid across no-man's-land with the dripping head of a German sentry in either hand. The years of peace had been years of unremitting conflict for him. Wherever there was blood and gun-powder from County Cork to the Matto Grosso, there was Ritchie-Hook. Latterly he had wandered about the Holy Land tossing hand-grenades into the front parlours of dissident Arabs. These were some of the things Guy had heard in the mess.

The Captain-Commandant inhabited a square, solid house at an extremity of the barrack area. As they approached it, Mrs Green said: 'Do any of you smoke a pipe?'

'No.'

'No.'

'No.'

'That's a pity. Ben prefers men who smoke pipes. Cigarettes?'

'Yes.'

'Yes.'

'Yes.'

'That's a pity, too. He likes you not to smoke at all if you don't smoke pipes. My husband always smokes a pipe when Ben's about. Of course he's senior but that doesn't count with Ben. My husband is rather afraid of him.'

'He's in a blue funk,' said Mrs Green. 'It's pitiful to see.'
Leonard laughed heartily.

'I don't see it's funny,' said Mrs Leonard. '*I* shall smoke if I want to.'

But no one else in the party shared Mrs Leonard's mood of defiance. The three probationary Halberdiers stood back for the ladies to pass and followed them through the garden-gate with adolescent misgivings and there before them unmistakably, separated from them only by the plate glass of the drawing-room window, stood Lieutenant-Colonel, shortly to be gazetted Brigadier Ritchie-Hook glaring out at them balefully with a single, terrible eye. It was black as the brows above it, this eye, black as the patch which hung on the other side of the lean skew nose. It was set in a steel-rimmed monocle. Colonel Ritchie-Hook bared his teeth at the ladies, glanced at his huge wrist-watch with studied pantomime and said something inaudible but plainly derisive.

'Oh dear,' said Mrs Green. 'We must be late.'

They entered the drawing-room; Colonel Green, hitherto a figure of awe, smirked at them from behind a little silver tray of cocktails. Colonel Ritchie-Hook, not so much usurping the position of host as playing the watch dog, the sentinel perhaps at one of those highly secret headquarters which Guy had visited in his search for employment, strode to meet them. Mrs Green attempted some conventional introductions but was interrupted.

'Names again, please. Must get them clear. Leonard, Sarum-Smith, Crouchback? – I can only count three. Where's Crouchback? Oh, I see. And which owns the madam?'

He flashed his huge eye-teeth at Mrs Leonard.

'*I* own *this* one,' she said.

It was braver and better than Guy would have expected, and it went down well. Leonard alone seemed put out.

'Splendid,' said Ritchie-Hook. 'Jolly good.'

'That's the way to treat him,' said Mrs Green.

Colonel Green goggled in admiration.

'Gin for the lady,' cried Colonel Ritchie-Hook. He stretched out a maimed right hand, two surviving fingers and half a thumb in a black glove, clutched a glass and presented it to Mrs Leonard. But the light mood passed and he immediately refused to take one for himself.

'Very nice if you don't have to keep awake after lunch.'

'Well, I don't,' said Mrs Leonard. 'Sunday's my day of rest – usually.'

'There are no Sundays in the firing-line,' said Colonel Ritchie-Hook. 'The week-end habit could lose us the war.'

'You're spreading alarm and despondency, Ben.'

'I'm sorry, Geoff. The Colonel here was always the brainy one,' he added, as though to explain his meek acceptance of criticism. 'He was brigade major when I only had a platoon. That's why he's sitting in this fine mansion while I'm going under canvas. Any camping experience?' he asked suddenly of Guy.

'Yes, sir, a little. I lived in Kenya at one time and did several trips in the bush.'

'Good for you. Gin for the old settler.' The black claw struck, grappled and released a second cocktail into Guy's hand. 'Did you get much shooting?'

'I bagged an old lion once who wandered into the farm.'

'Which are you? Crouchback? I knew one of my young officers came from Africa. I thought it was some other name. You'll find your African experience worth a hundred pounds a minute. There's one wretched fellow on my list spent half his life in Italy. I didn't care for the sound of that much.'

Miss Green winked at Guy and he kept silent.

'I've had fun in Africa too,' said Ritchie-Hook. 'After one of my periodical disagreements with the powers that be, I got seconded to the African Rifles. Good fellows if you keep at them with a stick but devilish scared of rhinos. One camp we had was by a lake and an old rhino used to come down for a drink every evening across the parade ground. Devilish cheek; I wanted to shoot him but the C.O. talked a lot of rot about having to get a game licence. He was a stuffy fellow, the sort of chap,' he said as though defining a universally recognized and detestable type, 'the sort of chap who owns a dozen shirts. So the next day I fixed up a flare-path right across rhino's

'drinking place, with a line of fuses, and touched it off right under his nose. I never saw a rhino move faster, smack through
the camp lines. Caught a black fellow bang through the
middle. You never heard such a yelling. They couldn't stop me
shooting him then, not when he had a sergeant stuck on his
nose.'

'Sounds like Bechuana tummy,' said Mrs Leonard.

'Eh? What's that?' said Colonel Ritchie-Hook, not so
pleased now at her cheeky ways.

'Where was this, Ben?' Mrs Green interposed.

'Somaliland. Ogaden border.'

'I didn't know there was any rhino in Somaliland,' said
Colonel Green.

'There's one less now.'

'How about the sergeant?'

'Oh, he was on parade again in a week.'

'You mustn't take all Colonel Ritchie-Hook says quite literally,' said Mrs Green.

They went into luncheon. Two Halberdiers waited at table.
Mrs Green carved. Ritchie-Hook grasped his fork in his gloved
fingers, impaled his meat, cut it rapidly into squares, laid down
his knife, changed hands with the fork and ate fast and silently,
plunging the pieces into horse-radish sauce and throwing them
back to his molars. Then he began to talk again. Had he followed any less chivalrous calling, had he worn any other uniform than a Halberdier's, it might have seemed that Colonel
Ritchie-Hook, piqued by her interruption, was seeking to discomfort Mrs Leonard, so hard did he fix her with his single,
ferocious eye, so directly aimed seemed all his subsequent
words at the hopes and susceptibilities of a bride.

'You'll be glad to hear that I've got the War House to play.
They've recognized our Special Role. I drafted the minute
myself. It went right up the line and came down again approved.
We're H.O.O.'

'What does that mean, please?' asked Mrs Leonard.

'Hazardous Offensive Operations. We've been given our
own heavy machine-guns and heavy mortars; no divisional
organization; we come direct under the Chiefs of Staff. There

was some opposition from an idiot gunner in Military Training but I soon scotched him. We've got a whizz of an area in
the Highlands.'

'Scotland? Is that where we've got to settle?'

'That is where we shall form.'

'But is that where we shall be in the summer? I've got my
arrangements to make.'

'Summer arrangements will depend on our friend the Boche.
By summer I hope to report the brigade as efficient and then
immediate action. No good hanging about. There's a limit to
the amount of training men can take. After a point they get
stale and go back. You must use them when they're on their
toes ... Use them,' he repeated dreamily, 'spend them. It's like
slowly collecting a pile of chips and then plonking them all
down on the roulette board. It's the most fascinating thing in
life, training men and staking them against the odds. You get
a perfect force. Everyone knows everyone else. Everyone
knows his commander so well they can guess his intention before they're told. They can work without orders, like sheep-
dogs. Then you throw them into action and in a week, perhaps
in a few hours, the whole thing is expended. Even if you win
your battle, you're never the same again. There are reinforcements and promotions. You have to "start all over again from
your beginnings, and never breathe a word about your loss".
Isn't that how the poem goes? So you see, Mrs Leonard, it's
no good asking where or when we shall settle. Do you all play
footer?'

'No, sir.'

'No, sir.'

'Yes,' from Leonard.

'Soccer?'

'No, sir. Rosslyn Park.'

'Pity. The men don't understand rugger, except Welshmen
and we don't get many of those. It's a great thing to play with
them. The men go for you and you go for them and there's
no hard feelings when bones get broken. In my company at
one time we had more casualties from soccer than from the
enemy and I can assure you we gave more than we took. Per-

manent injuries some of them. There was a plucky little fellow played right half for C Company lamed for life in the rest camp. You ought to follow footer even if you don't play. I remember once a sergeant of mine got his leg blown off. There was nothing to be done for the poor beggar. It had taken half his body with it. He was a goner all right but quite sensible and there was the padre one side of him trying to make him pray and me the other side and all he'd think about was football. Luckily I knew the latest League results and those I didn't know, I made up. I told him his home team was doing fine and he died smiling. If ever I see a padre getting above himself, I pull his leg about that. Of course it's different with Catholics. Their priests hold on to them to the last. It's a horrible sight to see them whispering at a dying man. They kill hundreds just with fright.'

'Mr Crouchback is a Catholic,' said Mrs Green.

'Oh, sorry. Am I talking out of turn as usual? Never had any tact. Of course it's because you live in Africa,' said Colonel Ritchie-Hook, turning to Guy. 'You get a very decent type of missionary out there. I've seen 'em myself. They don't stand any nonsense from the natives. None of that "me velly Clistian boy got soul all same as white boss". But mind you, Crouchback, you've only seen the best. If you lived in Italy like this other young officer of mine, you'd see them as they are at home. Or in Ireland; the priests there were quite openly on the side of the gunmen.'

'Eat your pudding, Ben,' said Mrs Green.

Colonel Ritchie-Hook turned his eye down to his apple-pie and for the rest of luncheon spoke mainly against air-raid precautions, an uncontroversial subject.

In the drawing-room with the coffee Colonel Ritchie-Hook showed the softer side of his character. There was a calendar on the chimney piece, rather shabby now in November and coming to the end of its usefulness. Its design was fanciful, gnomes, toadstools, hare-bells, pink bare babies and dragon-flies.

'I say,' he said. 'That's a lovely thing. My word it *is* lovely. Isn't it lovely?'

'Yes, sir.'

'Well, we mustn't stand here getting sentimental. I've a long ride ahead of me on my motor-bike. I need a stretch. Who's coming with me?'

'Not Jim,' said Mrs Leonard, 'I'm taking him home.'

'All right. Coming you two?'

'Yes, sir.'

The town where the Halberdiers lived was ill suited to walking for pleasure. It was a decent old place at the heart revealing concentric layers of later ugliness. Pleasant country had to be sought three miles out or more, but Colonel Ritchie-Hook's aesthetic appetites had been sated by the calendar.

'There's a round I always go when I'm here,' he said. 'It takes fifty minutes.'

He set off at a fast irregular lope, with which it was impossible to keep in step. He led them to the railway beside which, separated from it by a fence of black, corrugated iron, ran a cinder path.

'Now we're out of earshot of the Captain-Commandant,' he began, but a passing train put him out of earshot of his two companions. When he could next be heard he was saying '... altogether too much flannel in the Corps. Necessary in peace time. No use for it in war. You want more than automatic obedience. You want Grip. When I commanded a company and a man came up to me on a charge I used to ask him whether he'd take my punishment or go to the C.O. He always chose mine. Then I'd bend him over and give him six of the best with a cane. Court-martial offence, of course, but there was never a complaint and I had less crime than any Company in the Corps. That's what I call "Grip".' He strode on. Neither companion found any suitable reply. At length he added: 'I shouldn't try that out yourselves though – not at first.'

The walk continued mostly in silence. When Ritchie-Hook spoke it was mostly to recount practical jokes or *gaffes raisonnées*. For this remarkable warrior the image of war was not hunting or shooting; it was the wet sponge on the door, the hedgehog in the bed; or, rather, he saw war itself as a prodigious booby trap.

After twenty-five minutes Colonel Ritchie-Hook looked at his watch.

'We ought to be crossing now. I'm getting slow.'

Soon they came to an iron foot-bridge. On the farther side of the line was a similar cinder track, bounded by corrugated iron. They turned along it towards home.

'We'll have to spurt a bit if we're going to keep the scheduled time.'

They went at a great pace. At the barrack gates he looked at his watch. 'Forty-nine minutes,' he said. 'Good going. Well, glad to have got to know you. We'll be seeing plenty of each other in the future. I left my motor-bike at the guard-room.' He opened his respirator haversack and showed them a tight wad of pyjamas and hair brushes. 'That's all the luggage I carry. Best use for this damn silly thing. Good-bye.'

Guy and Sarum-Smith saluted as he drove off.

'Regular old fire-eater, isn't he?' said Sarum-Smith. 'Seems to have made up his mind to get us all killed.'

That evening Guy looked in on Apthorpe to see if he was coming to dinner.

'No, old man. Going slow today. I think I can shake this thing off but I've got to go slow. How was lunch?'

'Our future brigadier was there.'

'I'm sorry I missed that, very sorry. But it wouldn't have been much of a first impression. I shouldn't want him to see me under the weather. How did things go?'

'Not so badly. Largely because he thought I was you.'

'I don't quite get you, old man.'

'He'd heard one of us lived in Italy and the other in Africa. He thinks I'm the African one.'

'I say, old man, I don't much like that.'

'He began it. Then it had gone too far to put him right.'

'But he *must* be put right. I think you ought to write and tell him.'

'Don't be an ass.'

'But it's not a joking matter at all. It seems to me you've pulled rather a fast one, taking advantage of another chap's illness to impersonate him. It's just the sort of thing that might make a lot of difference. Did you take my name, too?'

'No, of course not.'

'Well, if you won't write, I will.'

'I shouldn't. He'd think you were mad.'

'Well, I shall have to consider what is best. The whole thing's extremely delicate. I can't think how you let it happen.'

Apthorpe did not write to Colonel Ritchie-Hook but he nursed his resentment and was never again quite off his guard in Guy's company.

3

SHORTLY before Christmas the course of elementary training came to an end and Guy and his batch were sent on a week's leave. Before they left and largely in their honour, there was a guest night. They were urged to bring guests to what, for the time being at any rate, was to be their last night in the barracks. Each felt on his mettle to provide someone creditable to himself. Apthorpe, in particular, was proud of his choice.

'Great bit of luck,' he said, 'I've got hold of "Chatty" Corner. I didn't know he was in England till I saw it in the paper.'

'Who's Chatty Corner?'

'I should have thought you would have heard of him. Perhaps it's different in the posh ranches of Kenya. If you asked that question in *Real* Africa – anywhere between Chad and Moçambique – people would think you were chaffing. He is a great character, Chatty. Queer sort of devil to look at. You wouldn't think he knew how to use a knife and fork. Actually he's a Bishop's son, Eton and Oxford and all that, and he plays the violin like a pro. He's mentioned in all the books.'

'Books on music, Apthorpe?'

'Books on gorillas, of course. And who are you bringing, old man, if one may ask?'

'I haven't found anyone yet.'

'Funny. I should have thought a chap like you would have known quite a number of people.'

He was still huffy over the affair of mistaken identity.

Guy proposed himself for Christmas to the Box-Benders. In her reply Angela said that Tony was coming on Christmas leave. Guy was able at the last moment to intercept him in London and lure him down to the Halberdiers for the night. It was the first time either had seen the other in uniform.

'I wouldn't miss seeing you masquerading as a young officer for anything in the world, Uncle Guy,' he said on arrival.

'Everyone else here calls me "Uncle", too, you'll find.'

They were walking across the gravel to the quarters where the guests had been given rooms. A Halberdier passed them at the salute and Guy shrank to see his nephew's careless flick of acknowledgement.

'I say, Tony, that may be all right in your regiment. Here we return the salute as smartly as it's given.'

'Uncle Guy, do I have to remind you that I am your superior officer?'

But that evening he was proud of his nephew, conspicuous in green patrols and black leather, as he led him up to the Mess President in the ante-room.

'Back from France, eh? I'm going to exercise my presidential privilege and put you next to me. I'd very much like a first-hand account of what's going on out there. Can't make head or tail of the papers.'

The identity of Chatty Corner was apparent to all without introduction; a brown man with grizzled hair *en brosse* stood morosely at Apthorpe's side. It was easy to see how he had gained a footing among the gorillas; easy, too, to recognize English irony in his nickname. He swung his head from side to side, gazing about him from under shaggy brows as though seeking some high path by which he could swing himself aloft and lie cradled in solitude among the rafters. Not till the band struck up 'the Roast Beef of Old England' did Chatty seem at ease. Then he beamed, nodded and gibbered confidentially into Apthorpe's ear.

The band was in the minstrels' gallery. They passed under it to enter the mess and met its full force as they took their places at the table. The Mess President was in the centre oppo-

site the Vice. Tony, next to him, began to sit down before
Grace and was hastily restrained by his uncle. The band ceased,
the hammer struck, the chaplain prayed. Band and general
conversation burst out once more together.

Drawn out by the senior officers round him, Tony began to
talk about his service in France, of field-craft, night patrols,
and booby traps, of the extreme youth and enthusiasm of the
handful of enemy prisoners whom he had seen, of the admir-
able style and precision of their raiding tactics. Guy looked
down the table to Chatty Corner to see whether he was dis-
playing any notable dexterity with his knife and fork and saw
him drink with an odd little rotary swirling motion of head and
wrist.

At length when the cloth was drawn for dessert, the brass
departed and the strings came down from the minstrel's gallery
and stationed themselves in the window embrasure. Now there
was silence over all the diners while the musicians softly bowed
and plucked. It all seemed a long way from Tony's excursions
in no-man's-land; farther still, immeasurably far, from the
frontier of Christendom where the great battle had been fought
and lost; from those secret forests where the trains were, even
then, while the Halberdiers and their guests sat bemused by
wine and harmony, rolling east and west with their doomed
loads.

They played two pieces, in the second of which a carillon
was brightly struck. Then the Captain of the Musicke presented himself in traditional form to the Mess President. Room
was made for him on a chair placed next to Tony's and a bum-
per of port brought by the corporal-of-servants. He was a
shiny, red man no more to be recognized as a man of the arts,
Guy thought, than Chatty himself.

The Mess President hammered the table. All rose to their
feet.

'Mr Vice, our Colonel-in-Chief, the Grand-Duchess Elena
of Russia.'

'The Grand-Duchess, God bless her.'

This ancient lady lived in a bed-sitting-room at Nice, but
she was still as loyally honoured by the Halberdiers as when,

a young beauty, she had graciously accepted the rank in 1902.

Smoke began to curl among the candles. The horn of snuff was brought round. This huge, heavy-mounted object was hung about with a variety of little silver tools – spoon, hammer, brush – which had to be employed ritualistically and in the right order on pain of a half-crown fine. Guy instructed his nephew in their proper use.

'Do you have all this sort of thing in your regiment?'

'Not quite all this. I'm awfully impressed.'

'So am I,' said Guy.

No one was quite sober when he left the dining-room; no one was quite drunk except Chatty Corner. This man of the wilds, despite his episcopal origin, succumbed to the advance of civilization, was led away and never seen again. Had he been competing for prestige, as Apthorpe thought he was, this would have been an hour of triumph for Guy. Instead the whole evening was one simple sublime delight.

In the ante-room there was an impromptu concert. Major Tickeridge gave an innocently obscene performance called 'The One-Armed Flautist', an old favourite in the Corps, new to Guy, a vast success with all. The silver goblets, which normally held beer, began to circulate brimming with champagne. Guy found himself talking religion with the chaplain.

'... Do you agree,' he asked earnestly, 'that the Supernatural Order is not something added to the Natural Order, like music or painting, to make everyday life more tolerable? It *is* everyday life. The supernatural is real; what we call "real" is a mere shadow, a passing fancy. Don't you agree, Padre?'

'Up to a point.'

'Let me put it another way ...'

The chaplain's smile had become set during Major Tickeridge's performance; it was like an acrobat's, a professional device concealing fear and exhaustion.

Presently the adjutant started a game of football with a waste-paper basket. They changed from soccer to rugger. Leonard had the basket. He was tackled and brought down. All the young officers began to leap on the struggling bodies. Apthorpe leapt. Guy leapt. Others leapt on them. Guy was conscious of a wrench in the knee; then the wind was knocked out of him and he lay momentarily paralysed. Dusty, laughing, sweating, panting, they disentangled themselves and got to their feet. Guy felt a remote but serious pain in his knee.

'I say, Uncle, are you hurt?'

'No, no, it's nothing.'

Somewhere the order had been given to disperse. Tony gave Guy his arm across the gravel.

'I hope you weren't too bored, Tony?'

'I wouldn't have missed it for anything. D'you think you ought to see a doctor?'

'It'll be all right in the morning. It's just a twist.'

But in the morning, when he awoke from deep sleep, his knee was swollen large and he could not walk with it.

4

TONY was driving home. He took Guy with him as they had arranged, and for four days Guy lay up at Box-Bender's with his leg bandaged stiff. On Christmas Eve they bore him to mid-night mass and then put him back on his bed in the library. There was anti-climax in Tony's return. All the stage properties remained, the crates of Hittite tablets, the improvised beds, but there was no drama. After the spacious life of his barracks Guy felt himself penned and straightened so that when after Boxing-Day his brother-in-law returned to London, Guy went with him and spent the last days of his leave in an hotel.

Those days of lameness, he realized much later, were his honeymoon, the full consummation of his love of the Royal Corps of Halberdiers. After them came domestic routine, much loyalty and affection, many good things shared, but intervening and overlaying them all the multitudinous, sad little discoveries of marriage; familiarity, annoyance, imperfections noted, dis-cord. Meanwhile it was sweet to wake and to lie on in bed; the spirit of the Corps lay beside him: to ring the bell; it was in the service of his unseen bride.

London had not yet lost its store of riches. It was the same city he had avoided all his life, whose history he had held to be mean, whose aspect drab. Here it was, all round him, as he had never seen it before, a royal capital. Guy was changed. He hobbled out into it with new eyes and a new heart.

Bellamy's, where last he had slunk in corners to write his begging letters, offered him now an easy place in the shifting population of the bar. He drank hard and happily, saying mechanically 'Cheerioh' and 'Here's how', quite unconscious of the mild surprise these foreign salutations roused.

One evening he went alone to the theatre and heard behind him a young voice say: 'Oh my prophetic soul, my uncle.'

He turned and saw immediately behind him Frank de Souza. He was dressed in what the Halberdiers called 'plain clothes' and civilians, more exotically, 'mufti'. His clothes were not particularly plain – a brown suit, a green silk shirt, an orange tie. Beside him sat a girl. Guy knew Frank de Souza little. He was a dark, reserved, drily humorous, efficient young man. He remembered vaguely hearing that Frank had a girl in London whom he visited at week-ends.

'Pat, this is my Uncle Crouchback.'

The girl smiled, without humour or welcome.

'Must you be facetious?' she said.

'Enjoying it?' Guy asked. They were at what was known as an 'intimate revue'.

'Quite.'

Guy had thought it very bright and pretty. 'Have you been in London all the time?'

'I've got a flat in Earls Court,' said the girl. 'He lives with me.'

'That must be nice,' said Guy.

'Quite,' said the girl.

Further conversation was stopped by the return of their neighbours from the bar and the rise of the curtain. The second half of the programme seemed less bright and pretty to Guy. He was conscious all the time of this cold odd couple behind him. At the end he said: 'Won't you come and have some supper with me?'

'We're going to the Café from here,' said the girl.

'Is that far?'

'The Café Royal,' Frank explained. 'Come too.'

'But Jane and Constant said they might be meeting us there,' said the girl.

'They never do,' said Frank.

'Come and eat oysters with me,' said Guy. 'There's a place just next door.'

'I hate oysters,' said the girl.

'Perhaps we'd better not,' said Frank. 'Thanks all the same.'

'Well, we'll meet again soon.'

'At Philippi,' said Frank.

'Oh God,' said the girl. 'Come on.'

On his last evening, the last day of the old year, after dinner Guy was at Bellamy's, standing at the bar, when he heard: 'Hullo, Tommy, how are the staff-officer's piles?' and, turning, found at his side a major of the Coldstream.

It was Tommy Blackhouse, whom he had last seen from his solicitor's window in Lincoln's Inn when he and Tommy's soldier-servant had been summoned to make a formal recognition during the divorce proceedings. Tommy and Virginia had come through the square laughing, had paused at the door by arrangement showing their faces, Virginia's under a bright new hat, Tommy's under a bowler, and had immediately gone on, without looking up towards the windows from one of which, they knew, they were being watched. Guy had testified: 'That is my wife.' The guardsman had said: 'That is Captain Blackhouse and the lady with him is the one I found when I called him on the morning of the 14th.' Each had then signed a statement and the solicitor had stopped Guy from giving the guardsman a ten shilling note. 'Entirely irregular, Mr Crouchback. The offer of an emolument might jeopardize the action.'

Tommy Blackhouse had had to send in his papers and leave the Brigade of Guards, but, because his heart was in soldiering, he had transferred to a line regiment. Now, it seemed, he was back in the Coldstream. Before that time Guy and Tommy Blackhouse had known one another very slightly. Now they said:

'Hullo, Guy.'

'Hullo, Tommy.'

'So you're in the Halberdiers. They're very efficient, aren't they?'

'Much too efficient for me. They nearly broke my leg the other night. I see you're back in the Coldstream.'

'I don't know where I am. I'm a sort of shuttlecock between the War House and the Lieutenant-Colonel. I got back to the Brigade all right last year – adultery doesn't matter in war-time apparently – but like an ass I spent the last two or three years at the Staff College and somehow managed to pass. So I'm called "G.2. Training" and spend all my time trying to get back to regimental soldiering. I knew one of yours at the Staff College. Awfully good chap with a big moustache. Forget his name.'

'They've all got big moustaches.'

'You're in for a pretty interesting role it seems to me. I saw a file about it today.'

'We know nothing.'

'Well, it'll be a long war. There'll be fun for us all in the end.'

It was all quite effortless.

Half an hour later the group broke up. In the hall Tommy said: 'I say you *are* going lame. Let me give you a lift.'

They drove up Piccadilly in silence. Then Tommy said: 'Virginia's back in England.'

Guy had never considered what Tommy thought about Virginia. He did not know precisely in what circumstances they had parted.

'Has she been away?'

'Yes, for quite a time. In America. She's come back for the war.'

'Typical of her – when everyone else is running the other way.'

'She's in great form. I saw her this evening in Claridge's. She asked after you but I didn't know then where you were.'

'She asked after me?'

'Well, to tell you the truth she asked after all her old boy friends – but you especially. Go and see her if you've got time. We all ought to rally round.'

'Where is she?'

'At Claridge's, I imagine.'

'I don't suppose she wants to see me really.'

'I got the impression she wants to see the whole world. She was all over *me*.'

Here they reached Guy's hotel and parted. Guy in correct Halberdier fashion absurdly saluted this superior officer in the utter darkness.

Next morning, New Year's Day, Guy awoke, as always now, at the hour when the bugles were sounding reveille in barracks; his first thought was of Virginia. He was full of overmastering curiosity, but after eight years, after all that he had felt and left unsaid, he could not pick up the telephone at his bedside and call her as, he had no doubt, she would have called him had she known where to find him. Instead he dressed and packed and settled his hotel bill with his head full of Virginia. He had until four that afternoon before setting out to his new destination.

He drove to Claridge's, asked at the desk, learned that Mrs Troy had not yet come down, and stationed himself in the hall where he could watch both lifts and staircase. From time to time people he knew passed, stopped, asked him to join them, but he kept his unwinking vigil. At length someone who might be she, came swiftly from the lift and crossed to the desk. The concierge pointed towards where Guy was sitting. The woman turned and immediately beamed with pleasure. He limped forward; she came to meet him with a skip and a jump.

'Guy, *pet*; what a treat! How lovely London is!' She hugged him; then examined him at arm's length. 'Yes,' she said. 'Very nice indeed. I was asking about you only yesterday.'

'So I heard. Tommy told me.'

'Oh, I asked absolutely everyone.'

'But it was funny hearing of it from him.'

'Yes, come to think of it, I suppose it was in a way. Why are your clothes a different colour from everyone else's?'

'They aren't.'

'Well from Tommy's and his over there and his and his?'

'They're in the Foot Guards.'

'Well, I think your colour's *much* more chic. And how it suits you. I do believe you're growing a little moustache, too. It does make you look so *young*.'

'You too.'

'Oh yes, me more than anyone. I thrive on the war. It's such heaven being away from Mr Troy.'

'He's not with you?'

'Darling, just between us two, I don't think I'm going to see much more of Mr Troy. He hasn't been behaving at all well lately.'

Guy knew nothing of this Hector Troy except his name. He knew that for eight years Virginia had floated on a tide of unruffled popularity. He willed her no evil but this prosperity of hers had stiffened the barrier between them. In destitution she would have found him at her side, but as she drifted into ever ampler felicity, Guy shrank the further into his own dry, empty place. Now in the changes of war, here she was, pretty and smart and pleased to see him.

'Are you lunching anywhere?'

'I was. I won't. Come on. I say, you're lame. Not wounded already?'

'No. Believe it or not, I've been playing football with a waste-paper basket.'

'Not true?'

'Literally.'

'Darling, how madly unlike you.'

'You know, you're the first person I've met who hasn't been surprised to find me in the army.'

'Why, wherever else would you be? Of course I've always known you were brave as a lion.'

They lunched together and afterwards went up to her room and talked continuously until it was time for Guy's train.

'You've still got the farm at Eldoret?'

'I sold it at once ; didn't you know?'

'Perhaps I did hear at the time, but you know I had such a

lot on my mind just then. First divorce, then marriage, then divorce again, before I had time to look round. Tommy didn't last any time at all, the beast. I might almost just as well have stayed put. I hope you got a big price?'

'Practically nothing. It was the year everyone went broke.'

'So it was. Don't I remember! That was another of the troubles with Tommy. The chief thing was that his regiment turned so stuffy. We had to leave London and stay in a ridiculous little town full of the dreariest people. He even talked of going to India. That was the end. I really did adore him, too. You never married again?'

'How could I?'

'Darling, don't pretend your heart was broken for life.'

'Apart from my heart, Catholics can't remarry, you know.'

'Oh, *that*. You still keep to all that?'

'More than ever.'

'Poor Guy, you did get in a mess, didn't you? Money gone, me gone, all in one go. I suppose in the old days they'd have said I'd ruined you.'

'They might.'

'Have you had lots of lovely girls since?'

'Not many, not very lovely.'

'Well, you must now. I'll take you in hand and find you something special.'

And.

'There's one thing I always did feel rather bad about. How did your father take it all? He was such a lamb.'

'He just says: "Poor Guy, picked a wrong 'un."'

'Oh, I don't like that at all. What a perfectly beastly way to speak.'

And.

'But it can't be possible just to have done *nothing* for eight years.'

It amounted to nothing. There was nothing worth the telling. When he first came to Santa Dulcina from Kenya, with the habit of farming still fixed in him, he had tried to learn viticulture, had pruned the straggling vines, attempted to introduce a system for selection among the pickers, a new French press.

The wine of Santa Dulcina was delicious on the spot but turned sour after an hour's travel. Guy had tried to bottle it scientifically. But it all came to nothing.

He had tried to write a book. It went well enough for two chapters and then petered out.

He had put a little money and much work into a tourist agency which a friend of his tried to organize. The intention was to provide first-rate aesthetic guides in Italy and to take specially deserving visitors into little-known districts and to palaces normally kept shut. But the Abyssinian crisis had cut off the flow of visitors, deserving and undeserving alike.

'No, nothing,' he agreed.

'Poor Guy,' said Virginia. 'How wretched you make it sound. No work. No money. Plain girls. Anyway you've kept your wool. Tommy's almost bald. It was quite a shock to see him again. And your figure. Augustus is as fat as butter.'

'Augustus?'

'I don't think we ever knew him in your time. He came after Tommy. But I never married Augustus. He was getting fat even then.'

And so on for three hours.

When they parted Virginia said: 'But we must *keep* meeting. I'm here indefinitely. We mustn't ever lose touch again.'

It was dark when Guy reached the station. Under the faint blue lamp he found half a dozen of his batch of Halberdiers.

'Here comes our gouty uncle,' they said as he joined them. 'Tell us all about this new course. You're always in the know.'

But Guy knew no more than was typed on his move order. It was a destination quite unknown.

5

THE Movement Order said: '*Destination, Kut-al-Imara House, Southsand-on-sea.*' It was issued on the morning of the guest night without explanation. Guy had consulted Major Tickeridge, who said: 'Never heard of the place. It must be something new the Corps has thought up,' and the adjutant,

who said: 'Not our pigeon. You'll come under the Training
Depot from now on until the brigade forms. It'll probably be
a pretty fair shambles.'

'None of the regulars from here will be coming?'

'Not on your life, Uncle.'

But to Guy sitting there with them in the ante-room among
all the trophies of the Corps, in the order and comfort of two
centuries' uninterrupted inhabitation, it seemed impossible that
anything conducted by the Halberdiers could fall short of ex-
cellence. And to him now, as the train rolled through the cold
and misty darkness, there remained the same serene confidence.
His knee was stiff and painful. He shifted his leg among the
legs that crossed and crowded in the twilight. The little group
of subalterns sat listless. High overhead their piled kitbags,
equipment, and suitcases loomed darkly and were lost in the
shadows. Faces were hilden. Only their laps were lit by shafts
too dim for easy reading. From time to time one of them
struck a match. From time to time they spoke of their leave.
Mostly they were silent. In the fog and chill Guy was full of
clear and comforting memories and he sat listening inwardly
to the repeated voices of the afternoon as though he were playing a gramophone record over and over to himself. A ghost
had been laid that day which had followed him for eight years,
lurked in every strange passage barring his way, crossing him
everywhere. Now he had met it face to face in the daylight and
found it to be kind and unsubstantial; that airy spirit could
never again block him, he thought.

For the last three quarters of an hour of the journey all
were quite silent, all save Guy asleep. At length they reached
Southsand, dragged out their gear and stood in sharper cold
on the platform. The train moved off. For long after its feeble
lamp had disappeared the sound of the engine came to them
on the east wind. A porter said: 'You from the Halberdiers?
You ought to have been on the six-eight.'

'This is the train on our orders.'

'Well, the rest of you came through an hour ago. The RTO
just locked up. You might catch him in the yard. No, that's him

driving away now. He said not to expect any more military to-night.'

'Hell.'

'Well, that's the army all over, isn't it?'

The porter moved off into the darkness.

'What are we going to do?'

'Better telephone.'

'Who to?'

Leonard pursued the porter.

'Is Kut-al-Imara House on the telephone?'

'Only the military line. That's locked up in the RTO's office.'

'Have you a telephone book?'

'You can try. Expect it's been cut off.'

In the dim office of the station-master they found the local directory.

'Here's Kut-al-Imara House Preparatory School. Let's try it.'

After a time a hoarse voice answered: 'Ullo, yes; what, who? Can't hear a thing. This line's supposed to be cut off. This is a military establishment.'

'There are eight officers here waiting for transport.'

'Are you the officers what's expected?'

'We thought so.'

'Well, 'old on, sir. I'll try and find someone.'

After many minutes a new voice said: 'Where are you?'

'Southsand station.'

'Why the devil didn't you get on the bus with the others?'

'We've only just arrived.'

'Well, you're late. The bus has gone back. We haven't any transport. You'll have to find your own way here.'

'Is it far?'

'Of course it's far. You'd better hurry or there won't be anything left to eat. There's bloody little now.'

They managed to find one taxi, and then a second, and so drove huddled and laden to their new home. Nothing was visible. There was no impression of anything until twenty minutes later they stood beside their bags in a hall quite devoid of furniture. The floor-boards had recently been washed and were still damp and reeking of disinfectant. An aged Halberdier, much decorated for long years of good conduct, said: 'I'll get Captain McKinney.'

Captain McKinney, when he came, had his mouth full.

'Here you are,' he said, chewing. 'There seems to have been a balls-up about your move order. I daresay it's not your fault. Everything's rather a shambles. I'm acting camp-commandant. I didn't know I was coming here at all till nine o'clock this morning, so you can imagine how much I know about anything. Have you had dinner? Well, you'd better come and get something now.'

'Is there anywhere to wash?'

'In there. But there's no soap I'm afraid and the water's cold.'

They followed him unwashed through the door by which he had come to greet them, and found a dining-room, soon to become familiar in every horrid aspect but now affording merely a glare of nakedness. Two trestle tables were laid with enamel plates and mugs and the grey cutlery they had seen in the mess-rooms during one of their conducted tours of barracks. There were dishes of margarine, sliced bread, huge bluish potatoes and a kind of drab galantine which Guy seemed to remember, but without relish, from his school-days during the First World War. On a side table an urn stood in a pool of tea, dripping. Beetroot alone gave colour to the spread.

'What price Dotheboys Hall?' said Trimmer.

But it was not the room nor the rations that caught Guy's chief notice. It was a group of strange second lieutenants who occupied one of the tables and now looked up, staring and munching. Those evidently were the Depot Batch about whom they had so often heard.

Half a dozen familiar figures from the Barrack Batch sat at the other table.

'You'd better settle there for the time being,' said Captain McKinney. 'There's some of your chaps still adrift. Sorting out will have to wait till morning.' Then he raised his voice and addressed the room at large.

'I'm pushing off now to my billet,' he said. 'I hope you've got everything you want. If you haven't, you'll just have to do without. Your quarters are upstairs. They aren't allotted. Arrange all that between yourselves. Lights out downstairs at twelve. Reveille at seven. Parade tomorrow at eight-fifteen. You're free to come and go up to twelve. There are six orderlies about the place but they've been at work all day scrubbing out, so I'd be glad if you'd let them stand-easy for a bit. It won't kill you to hump your own gear for once. We haven't been able to start a bar yet. The nearest pub is on the front about half a mile down the road. It's called the Grand and it's in bounds to officers. The pub nearer is for Other Ranks only. Well, good night.'

'Do I remember a lecture on "Man-management" not long ago?' said Trimmer. '"When you make camp or move into new billets, remember that the men under your command come first, second and third. You come nowhere. A Halberdier officer never eats until he has seen the last dinner served. A Halberdier officer never sleeps until he has seen the last man bedded down." Didn't it go something like that?' He took one of the forks and moodily bent it till it broke. 'I'm off to the Grand to see if there's anything edible there.'

He was the first to go. Soon after him the Depot Batch rose from their table. One or two of them hesitated, wondering whether they ought not to speak to the newcomers, but by now all heads at the Barrack Batch table were bent over their plates. The moment passed before it was recognized.

'Matey bastards, aren't they?' said Sarum-Smith.

The meal did not last long. Soon they were in the hall with the luggage.

'Let me take yours up, Uncle,' said Leonard and Guy gratefully surrendered his kitbag and limped upstairs behind him.

The doors round the stairhead were locked. A notice scrawled in chalk on the wall-paper pointed to '*Officers Quarters*' through a baize door. A step down, bare light bulbs, a strip of linoleum with open doors on either side. The first-comers had already established themselves but it could not be said that they had gained by their priority. The rooms were uniform. Each contained six service bedsteads and a pile of blankets and palliasses.

'Let's keep away from Trimmer and Sarum-Smith,' said Leonard. 'How about this, Uncle? Take your pick.'

Guy chose a corner bed and Leonard swung his kitbag on it.

'Shan't be a jiffy with the rest,' he said. 'Hold the fort.'

Other second lieutenants looked in. 'Any room, Uncle?'

'Room for three. I'm keeping a place for Apthorpe.'

'There's four of us. We'll try farther down.'

He heard their voices next door: 'To hell with unpacking. If we're going to get a drink before closing time we've got to hurry.'

Leonard returned laden.

'I thought I'd better keep a place for Apthorpe.'

'Rather. Can't have our uncles separated. This is going to be very cosy. I don't know how long I'll be here though. Daisy's coming down as soon as I find rooms. There's a rumour married men can sleep out.'

Three cheerful youths brought in their luggage and appropriated the remaining beds.

'Coming to the pub, Leonard?'

'How about you, Uncle?'

'Don't worry about me. I'll be all right.'

'Sure?'

'We might be able to get a taxi.'

'No, you run along.'

'Well, we'll be seeing you.'

Soon Guy was left quite alone in the new quarters. He began to unpack. There were no cupboards or presses. He hung his greatcoat on a hook in the wall and laid his hair-brushes, washing things and books on the window-sill. He got out his sheets and made the bed and stuffed his pillow-case with a rolled blanket. Everything else was left unpacked. Then, leaning on his stick, he made a tour of the empty house.

The sleeping quarters had plainly been the boys' dormitories. Each was named after a battle in the First War. His was

Paschendael. He passed the doors of *Loos*, *Wipers* (so spelt) and *Anzac.* Then he found a small unnamed room, a master's perhaps, containing a single unappropriated bed and a chest of drawers. Here lay luxury. Guy's spirits rose. 'Any damn fool can make himself uncomfortable,' he thought. The old soldier 'made his recce', 'appreciated the situation', 'conformed his plan to the ground'. He began to drag his kit-bag down the linoleum. And then he remembered Leonard dragging it up there. He remembered how he had been given choice of beds. If he moved now he would be denying the welcome of his juniors, setting himself apart again, as he had already been too much set apart in barracks, from the full fellowship of his batch. He closed the door of the single room and dragged his bag back to Paschendael.

He continued his tour. The place had been thoroughly emptied, presumably during the summer holidays. On the first floor he found a row of baths in doorless cubicles; on the ground floor a changing-room with many pegs, wash basins, and a shower. He found a notice board which still bore a list of cricket colours. Certain locked rooms must have been the headmaster's private quarters. Here was plainly the masters' common-room – an empty set of oak bookshelves, cigarette burns all over the chimney-piece, a broken waste-paper basket. '*O.Rs*' was chalked on the door which led to the kitchen-quarters; beyond it the wireless was playing. In the hall a tabletop had been put on the mantelpiece. It was divided vertically with a chalk line. Over one half was written '*Standing Orders*', over the other '*Daily Orders*'. Standing Orders comprised printed notices about black-out and protection from gas, a typewritten alphabetical list of names, and *Routine: Reveille 0700. Breakfast 0730. Parade and Instruction 0830. Lunch 1300. Parade and Instruction 1415. Tea 1700. Dinner 1930. Unless otherwise ordered officers will be free from 1700.* There were no Daily Orders. A painting too large to move – acquired when, how and why? – hung in a gilt composition frame opposite the fire-place; it represented a wintry sea-scape empty save for a few distant fishing boats and an enormous illegible signature. He leant against a coil of antiquated iron pipes

91

and was surprised to find them hot. They seemed to lack all
power of radiation; a yard from them there was no sensible
warmth. He could imagine a row of little boys struggling to sit
on them, tight-trousered boys with adenoids and chilblains; or
perhaps it was a privilege to sit there enjoyed only by prefects
and the First Eleven. In its desolation he could see the whole
school as it had been made familiar to him in many recent real-
istic novels; an enterprise neither progressive nor prosperous.
The assistant masters changed often, he supposed, arriving with
bluff, departing with bluster; half the boys were taken at sur-
reptitiously reduced fees; none of them ever won a scholarship or passed into a reputable public school or returned for an
Old Boys' Day or ever thought of his years there with anything
but loathing and shame. The History lessons were patriotic in
design, turned to ridicule by the young masters. There was no
school song at Kut-al-Imara House. All this Guy thought he
snuffed in the air of the forsaken building.

Well, he reflected, he had not joined the army for his own
comfort. He had expected a grim initiation. Life in barracks
had been a survival from long years of peace, something rare
and protected, quite unconnected with his purpose. That was
over and done with; this was war.

And yet on this dark evening, his spirit sank. The occupation
of this husk of a house, perhaps, was a microcosm of that new
world he had enlisted to defeat. Something quite worthless, a
poor parody of civilization, had been driven out; he and his
fellows had moved in, bringing the new world with them; the
world that was taking firm shape everywhere all about him,
bounded by barbed wire and reeking of carbolic.

His knee hurt more tonight than ever before. He stumped
woefully to Paschendael, undressed, spread his clothes on the
foot of his bed, and lay down leaving the single bulb shining
in his eyes. Soon he fell asleep and soon after was awakened
by the cheery return of his companions.

6

THERE was nothing obnoxious about the batch from the Training Depot. There were no grounds on which the Barrack batch could assume superiority. The disconcerting quality about them was their resemblance at every point. They had their Trimmer, a black sheep named Hemp. They had their Sarum-Smith, a malcontent named Colenso. They even had their 'uncles', a genial, stoutish schoolmaster named 'Tubby' Blake and a rubber planter from Malaya named Roderick. It was as though in their advance the Barrack batch had turned a corner and suddenly been brought up sharp by a looking-glass in which they found themselves reflected. There was no enmity between the two groups but there was little friendship. They continued as they had begun, eating at separate tables and inhabiting separate bedrooms. To Guy it seemed that there were just twice too many young officers at Kut-al-Imara House. They were diminished and caricatured by duplication, and the whole hierarchic structure of army life was affronted by this congregation of so many men of perfectly equal rank. The regular officers charged with their training lived in billets, appeared more or less punctually for duty, sauntered from class to class during working hours and punctually departed. Often at their approach a sergeant instructor would say: 'Come on now, look alive. Officer coming,' oblivious of the rank of his squad. The orderlies and non-commissioned instructors were under the command of a quartermaster-sergeant. The second lieutenants had no responsibility for, nor authority over them.

Living conditions grew slightly more tolerable. Rudimentary furniture appeared; a mess-committee was formed consisting of the camp-commandant, Guy and 'Tubby' Blake; the food was improved, the bar stocked. A motion to hire a wireless-set was hotly debated and narrowly lost through the combination of the elderly with the thrifty. The regimental Comforts Fund lent a dart board and a ping-pong table; but in spite of these amenities the house was generally deserted in the evening. Southsand offered a dance hall, a cinema and several hotels and there was more money about. Each officer was greeted on his return from leave with a note crediting him with back-pay and a number of quite unexpected allowances. All Guy's creditors save Sarum-Smith repaid their loans. Sarum-Smith said: 'With regard to that little matter of a fiver, uncle, if it's all the same to you, I'll let it run a bit longer.'

It seemed to Guy that there was now a slight nuance in the use of 'Uncle'. What had before been, at heart, an expression of respect, of 'the deference which youth owes to age', was now perceptibly derisive. The young officers were much at their ease in Southsand; they picked up girls of the town, they drank in congenial palm-lounges and snuggeries, they felt their leisure free from observation. In barracks Guy had been a link between them and their seniors. Here he was a lame old buffer who did not shine at the work or join in the fun. He had always stood in their esteem on the very verge of absurdity. Now his stiff knee and supporting stick carried him over.

He was excused from parades and Physical Training. He hobbled alone to instruction in the gym where they marched as a squad, and hobbled back alone behind them. They had been given battle-dress and now wore it for classes. At night they changed into service-dress if they wished. There was no order about it. 'Blues' were out. The work of the course was Small Arms, morning and afternoon. The lessons followed the Manual page by page, designed for the comprehension of the dullest possible recruit.

'Just imagine, gentlemen, that you're playing football. I daresay some of you wish you were. All right? You're outside right. There's a wind blowing straight down the field. All right? You're taking a corner kick. All right? Do you aim straight at the goal? Can't anyone tell me? Mr Trimmer, do you aim straight at the goal?'

'Oh, yes, Sergeant.'

'You do, do you? What does anyone else think?'

'No, Sergeant.'

'No, Sergeant.'

'No, Sergeant.'

'Oh, you don't don't you? Well, where do you aim?'

'I'd try and pass.'

'That's not the answer I want. Suppose you *want* to shoot a goal, do you aim straight at it?'

'Yes.'

'No.'

'No, Sergeant.'

'Well, where *do* you aim? Come along, doesn't anyone here play football? You aim *up* field, don't you?'

'Yes, Sergeant.'

'Why? Can't any of you think? You aim *up* field because it's *into the wind*, isn't it? . . .'

Guy took his turn at the aiming-rest and laid off for wind. Later he lowered himself painfully to the gymnasium floor and pointed a rifle at Sarum-Smith's eye while Sarum-Smith squinnied at him through an 'aiming-disc' and declared all his shots wide.

It was generally known that Guy had once shot a lion. The non-commissioned officers took up the theme: 'Dreaming of big game, Mr Crouchback?' they asked when Guy's attention wandered, and they gave their fire order: 'Ahead a bushy-top tree. Right, four o'clock, ten degrees, corner of yellow field. In that corner a lion. At that lion, two rounds fire.'

Guy's position on the mess-committee was far from being a hollow dignity, indeed, it lacked dignity of any kind for it exposed him to rather sharp complaints: 'Uncle, why can't we have better pickles?' 'Uncle, why isn't whisky cheaper here than at the Grand Hotel?' 'Why do we take in *The Times*? No one reads it except you.' Throughout all the smooth revolutions of barracks life there had been accumulating tiny grits of envy which were now generating heat.

All that week Guy was increasingly lonely and dispirited. The news on the eighth day that Apthorpe was rejoining them cheered him throughout a tedious session of 'Judging Distance'.

'. . . Why do we judge distance? To estimate the range of the target correctly. All right? Correct range makes fire effective and avoids waste of ammunition. All right? At two hundred yards all parts of the body are distinctly seen. At three hundred yards the outline of the face is blurred. At four hundred yards no face. At six hundred yards the head is a dot and the body tapers. Any questions? . . .'

As he limped back from the gym to the house he repeated to himself: 'Six hundred yards the head is a dot; four hundred yards, no face,' not to fix it in his mind, but as a meaningless jingle. Before he reached the house he was saying: 'Four hundred yards, the head is a face; six hundred yards, no dot.' It was the worst afternoon since he joined the army.

Then he found Apthorpe sitting in the hall.

'I'm delighted to see you back,' said Guy, with sincerity. 'Are you all right again?'

'No, no, far from it. But I've been passed fit for light duties.'

'Bechuana tummy again?'

'It's no joking matter, old man. I met with rather a nasty accident. In the bathroom when I hadn't a stitch on.'

'Do tell me.'

'I was going to, only you seem to find it so funny. I was staying with my aunt at Peterborough. There wasn't a great deal to do and I didn't want to get out of condition, so I decided to run through some of the P.T. tables. Somehow the very first morning I slipped and came the most awful cropper. I can tell you it hurt like the devil.'

'Whereabouts, Apthorpe?'

'In my knee. It was literally agony. I quite thought I'd broken it. I had quite a business finding an M.O. My aunt wanted me to see her doctor but I insisted on going through service channels. When I did, he took it very seriously. Packed me off to hospital. As a matter of fact that was interesting. I don't think you've ever been in a military hospital, Crouchback?'

'Not yet.'

'It's well worth while. One should get to know all arms of the service. I had a sapper in the next bed to mine – with ulcers.'

'Apthorpe, there's one thing I must ask you – '

'I was there over Christmas. The VADs sang carols – '

'Apthorpe, are you lame?'

'Well, what d'you expect, old man? A thing like this doesn't clear up in a day even with the best treatment.'

'I'm lame too.'

'Very sorry to hear it. But I was telling you about Christmas in the ward. The SMO made punch – '

'Don't you realize what awful fools we're going to look, the two of us, I mean, both going lame?'

'No.'

'Like a pair of twins.'

'Frankly, old man, I think that's a bit far-fetched.'

But when he and Apthorpe appeared at the dining-room door, each leaning on his stick, there was a general turning of heads, then laughter, then a round of clapping from both tables.

'I say, Crouchback, has this been pre-arranged?'

'No. It seems quite spontaneous.'

'Well, I consider it's in pretty poor taste.'

They filled their mugs at the urn and sat down.

'Not the first tea I've had in this room!' said Apthorpe.

'How is that?'

'We used to play Kut-al-Imara when I was at Staplehurst. I was never quite first-class at cricket but I played goal for the First Eleven my last two seasons.'

Guy had come to rejoice in facts about Apthorpe's private life. They were rather rare. The aunt at Peterborough was a new character; now there was Staplehurst.

'Was that your prep school?'

'Yes. It's that rather prominent building I expect you've noticed the other side of the town. I should have thought you'd have heard of it. It's very well known. My aunt was rather High Church,' he added with the air of thus somehow confirming the school's reputation.

'Your aunt at Peterborough?'

'No, no, of course not,' said Apthorpe crossly. 'My aunt at Tunbridge Wells. My aunt at Peterborough doesn't go in for that sort of thing at all.'

'Was it a good school?'

'Staplehurst? One of the best. Quite outstanding. At least it was in my day.'

'I meant Kut-al-Imara.'

'We thought them awful little ticks. They usually beat us, of course, but then they made a fetish of games. We just took them in our stride at Staplehurst.'

Leonard joined them.

'We've kept a bed for you in our room, Uncle,' he said.

'Jolly decent of you, but to tell you the truth I've got rather a lot of gear. I had a look round before you chaps dismissed and found an empty room, so I'm moving in there alone. I shall have to read a bit at night, I expect, to catch up with you. The sapper I met in hospital lent me some very interesting books, pretty confidential ones. The sort of thing you aren't allowed to take into the front line trenches in case it fell into the hands of the enemy.'

'Sounds like an ATM.'

'This *is* an ATM.'

'We've all been issued with those.'

'Well, it can't be at all the same thing. I got it from this sapper major. He had an internal ulcer so he passed it on to me.'

'Is this the thing?' asked Leonard, taking from the pocket of his battle-dress trousers a copy of the January Army Training Memorandum that was issued to all officers.

'I couldn't say offhand,' said Apthorpe. 'Anyway I don't think I ought to talk about it.'

So Apthorpe's gear, that vast accumulation of ant-proof boxes, water-proof bundles, strangely shaped, heavily initialled tin trunks and leather cases all bound about with straps and brass buckles, was shut away from all eyes but his.

Guy had seen them often enough in barracks, incuriously. He could have asked about them then, in the days of confidence before the Captain-Commandant's luncheon party, and learned their secrets. All he knew now, from an early chance reference, was that somewhere among these possessions lay something rare and mysterious which Apthorpe spoke of as his 'Bush Thunder-box'.

That night for the first time Guy went out into the town. He and Apthorpe hired a car for the evening and drove from hotel to hotel, finding Halberdiers everywhere, drinking and moving on in search of greater privacy.

'It seems to me you've let the young gentlemen become rather uppish in my absence,' said Apthorpe.

In particular they sought an hotel called the Royal Court where Apthorpe's aunts had stayed when they came to visit him at school.

'Not one of the showy places, but everything just right. Only a few people know of it.'

No one knew of it that evening. At length when all bars were shut Guy said: 'Couldn't we visit Staplehurst?'

'There wouldn't be anyone there, old man. Holidays. And anyway it's a bit late.'

'I mean, couldn't we just go and look at it?'

'Sound scheme. Driver, go to Staplehurst.'

'Staplehurst Grove or Staplehurst Drive?'

'Staplehurst House.'

'Well, I know the Grove and the Drive. I'll try there, shall I? Is it a Private?'

'I don't follow you, driver.'

'A private hotel?'

'It is a Private School.'

There was a moon and a high wind off-shore. They followed the Parade and mounted to the outskirts of the town.

'It all seems rather changed,' said Apthorpe. 'I don't remember any of this.'

'We're in the Grove now, sir. The Drive is round on the left.'

'It stood just about here,' said Apthorpe. 'Something must have happened to it.'

They got out into the moonlight and the bitter North wind. All round them lay little shuttered villas. Here, under their feet and beyond the neat hedges, lay the fields where muddy Apthorpe had kept goal. Somewhere among these gardens and garages bits of brickwork, perhaps, survived from the sanctuary where clean Apthorpe in lace cotta had lighted the tapers.

'Vandals,' said Apthorpe bitterly.

Then the two lame men climbed into the car and drove back to Kut-al-Imara in alcoholic gloom.

7

NEXT day Apthorpe had a touch of Bechuana tummy but he rose none the less. Guy was first down, driven from bed by thirst. It was a grey and bitter morning, heavy with coming snow. He found one of the regular officers in the hall engaged at the notice board with a large sheet headed in red chalk: 'READ THIS. IT CONCERNS YOU.'

'Great bit of luck,' he said. 'We've got Mudshore for today. Embus at eight-thirty. Draw haversack rations. You'd better pass the word to your chaps.'

Guy climbed the stairs and put his head into each dormitory in turn saying: 'We've got Mudshore for today. Bus leaves in twenty minutes.'

'Who's Mudshore?'

'I've no idea.'

Then he returned to the notice board and learned that Mudshore was a rifle-range some ten miles distant.

Thus began the saddest day of the new dispensation.

Mudshore range was a stretch of sea-marsh transected at regular intervals by banks and ending in a colourless natural escarpment. It was surrounded by wire and cautionary notices; there was a tin hut by the nearest bank, the firing point. When they arrived they found a soldier in his shirt-sleeves shaving at the door; another was crouching by a Soyer stove; a third appeared buttoning his tunic, unshaved.

The major in charge of the expedition went forward to investigate. They heard his tones, ferocious at first, grow gradually softer and end with: 'Very well, Sergeant. It's clearly not your fault. Carry on. I'll try and get through to Area.'

He returned to his party.

'There seems to have been some sort of misunderstanding. The last order the range-keeper got from Area was that firing was cancelled for today. They're expecting snow. I'll see what can be done. Meanwhile since we're here, it's a good opportunity to run through Range Discipline.'

For an hour, while the light broadened into a leaden glare, they learned and practised the elaborate code of precautions which, at this stage of the Second World War, surrounded the firing of live ammunition. Then the major returned to them from the hut where he had been engaged on the telephone. 'All right. They don't expect snow for an hour or two. We can carry on. Our walking wounded can make themselves useful in the butts.'

Guy and Apthorpe set off across the five hundred yards of sedge and took their places in the brick-lined trench below the targets. A corporal and two details from the Ordnance Corps joined. After much telephoning red flags were hoisted and eventually firing began. Guy looked at his watch before marking the first shot. It was now ten minutes to eleven. At half past twelve fourteen targets had been shot and the message came to stand easy. Two of the Depot Branch arrived to relieve Guy and Apthorpe.

'They're getting pretty fed up at the firing point,' one of them said. 'They say you're marking too slow. And I'd like to see my target. I'm certain my third was on it. It must have gone through the same hole as the second. I was dead on aim.'

'It's patched out, anyway.'

Guy stumped away and emerged from the side of the trench to be greeted with distant yells and arm waving. He hobbled on, disregarding, until he was within talking distance. Then he heard from the major: 'For Christ's sake, man, d'you want to be killed? Can't you see the red flag's up?'

Guy looked and saw that it was. No one was at the firing point. All were crowded in the lee of the hut eating sandwiches. He continued his walk among the hummocks.

'Get down, for Christ's sake. Now, look for the flag.'

He lay, looked and presently saw the flag lowered. 'All right, come on now.'

When he came up with the major he said: 'I'm sorry, sir. Those other people had just come up and we'd been told to stand easy.'

'Exactly. That's how fatal accidents happen. The flag and only the flag is the signal to go by. Pay attention, everyone. You've just seen a typical example of bad range discipline. Remember it.'

Apthorpe meanwhile had just started out and was making heavy going. When he arrived, Guy said: 'Did *you* see the bloody flag?'

'Of course. One always looks out for it. It's the first rule. Besides the corporal up there tipped me off. They often play that trick the first day on the range, running up the red flag when everyone knows it ought to be down. It's simply done to impress the need of range discipline.'

'Well, you might have passed the tip on to me.'

'Hardly the thing, old man. It would defeat the whole object of the exercise. There'd be no lessons learned if everyone tipped everyone else off, if you see what I mean.'

They ate their sandwiches. The cold was intense. 'Couldn't we carry on firing, sir? Everyone's ready.'

'I daresay, but we've got to think of the men. They expect their stand-easy.'

At last firing began again.

'We shan't get through on time,' said the major. 'Cut down to five rounds a man.'

But it was not the firing which took the time; it was the falling in of details, the drill on the firing point, the inspection of arms. Light was failing when it came to Guy's turn. He and Apthorpe joined the last detail, hobbling up independently. As he lay and sighted his rifle before loading, Guy made the disconcerting discovery that the target entirely disappeared when he covered it. He lowered his rifle and looked with two eyes. There was a discernible white square. He closed one eye; the square became dimmed, flickered. He raised the rifle and at once there was a total black at the end of his foresight.

He loaded and quickly fired his five observed shots. After the first, the disc rose and covered the bull.

'Nice work, Crouchback, keep it up.'

After the second, the flag signalled a miss. After the third, the flag again.

'Hullo, Crouchback, what's gone wrong?'

The fourth was a high outer. After the fifth, the flag.

Then a telephone message: 'Correction on target two. The first shot was wrongly marked a bull. A patch had blown off. The first shot on target two was a miss.'

Apthorpe, next to him, had done very nicely.

The major led Guy aside and said gravely: 'That was a very poor show, Crouchback. What on earth went wrong?'

'I don't know, sir. The visibility was rather poor.'

'It was the same for everyone. You'll have to work hard at elementary aiming. You put up a very poor show today.'

Then began the ritual of counting the ammunition and collecting shell cases. 'Pull through now. Boil out as soon as you're dismissed.'

Then the snow began. It was dark before they took their seats in the bus and began slowly nosing a way home.

'I reckon that lion was unlucky, Uncle,' said Trimmer. But no one in his numbed audience laughed.

Even Kut-al-Imara House seemed warm and welcoming. Guy pressed himself to the hot pipes in the hall while the rush on the stairs cleared. A mess waiter passed and Guy ordered a glass of rum. Slowly he began to feel the blood move and irrigate his hands and feet.

'Hullo, Crouchback, boiled out already?'

It was the major.

'Not yet, sir. I was just waiting till the crowd had finished.'

'Well, you've no business to wait. What were the orders? Boil out *immediately* you dismiss. Nothing was said about waiting till you'd had a couple of drinks.'

The major was cold too; he, also, had had a beastly day. Moreover he had nearly a mile to walk through the snow to his billet and when he got there, he remembered now, the cook would be out and he had promised to take his wife to dinner at one of the hotels.

'Not one of your better days, Crouchback. You may not be much of a marksman but might at least keep your rifle clean for someone who is,' he said; he went off into the snow and entirely forgot the matter before he had gone a hundred yards.

Trimmer was on the stairs during this conversation.

'Hullo, Uncle, did I hear you getting a rocket?'

'You did.'

'Quite a change for our blue-eyed boy.'

A spark was struck in Guy's darkened mind; a fuse took fire.
'Go to hell,' he said.

'Tut, tut, Uncle. Aren't we a little crusty this evening?'

Bang.

'You bloody, half-baked pipsqueak, pipe down,' he said.
'One more piece of impudence out of you and I'll hit you.'

The words were not well chosen; lame or sound, Guy was
not built to inspire great physical fear, but sudden wrath is
always alarming, recalling as it does the awful unpredictable
dooms of childhood; moreover Guy was armed with a strong
stick which he now involuntarily raised a little. A court martial
might or might not have construed this gesture as a serious
threat against the life of brother officer. Trimmer did.

'Here, I say, steady on. No offence meant.'

Anger carries its own propulsive mechanism and soars far
from the point of ignition. It carried Guy now into a red incandescent stratum where he was a stranger.

'God rot your revolting little soul, I told you to pipe down,
didn't I?'

He gave the stick a definite, deliberate flourish and advanced
a halting step. Trimmer fled. Two swift *chassés* and he was
round the corner, muttering inaudibly about '. . . taking a joke
without flying off the handle . . .'

Quite slowly Guy's rage subsided and touched ground; self-
satisfaction sank with it, rather more slowly but at last that too
was on the common level.

Just such a drama, he reflected, must have been enacted
term by term at Kut-al-Imara House, when worms turned and
suddenly revealed themselves as pythons; when nasty, teasing
little boys were put to flight. But the champions of the upper
fourth needed no rum to embolden them.

Was it for this that the bugles sounded across the barrack
square and the strings sang over the hushed dinner table of the
Copper Heels? Was this the triumph for which Roger de Way-

broke took the cross; that he should exult in putting down
Trimmer?

In shame and sorrow Guy stood last in the queue for boiling
water, leaning on his fouled weapon.

8

THE week that followed brought consolation.

Health returned to Guy's knee. It had grown stronger every
day while he was acquiring a habitual limp; the pain, lately,
had come from the elastic bandage. Now, haunted by Apthorpe in the role of *doppel-gänger,* he abandoned stick and
strapping and found he could move normally, and he fell in
with his squad as proudly as on his second day in barracks.

At the same time the moustache which he had let grow for
some weeks suddenly took shape, as suddenly as a child learns
to swim; one morning it was a straggle of hair, the next a firm
and formal growth. He took it to a barber in the town who
trimmed it and brushed it and curled it with a hot iron. He rose
from the chair transmogrified. As he left the shop he noticed
an optician's over the street in whose window lay a single enormous china eyeball and a notice proclaiming: FREE TESTS.
EYE-GLASSES OF ALL KINDS FITTED WHILE YOU WAIT.
The solitary organ, the idiosyncratic choice of word 'eye-
glasses' in preference to 'spectacles', the memory of the strange
face which had just looked at him over the barber's basin, the
memory of countless German Uhlans in countless American
films, drew him across.

'I was thinking of a monocle,' he said quite accurately.

'Yes, sir. Merely the plain lens for smart appearance, or do
you suffer from faulty vision?'

'It's for shooting. I can't see the target.'

'Dear, dear, *that* won't do, will it, sir?'

'Can you cure it?'

'We *must,* mustn't we sir?'

Quarter of an hour later Guy emerged, having purchased for
fifteen shillings a strong lens in a 'rolled-gold' double rim. He

removed it from its false-leather purse, stopped before a window and stuck the glass in his right eye. It stayed there. Slowly he relaxed the muscles of his face; he stopped squinting. The monocle remained firmly in place. The man reflected to him had a cynical leer; he was every inch a junker. Guy returned to the optician. 'I think I'd better have two or three more of these, in case I break one.'

'I'm afraid that's the only one I have in stock of that particular strength.'

'Never mind. Give me the nearest you have.'

'Really, sir, the eye is a most delicate instrument. You shouldn't play ducks and drakes with it. *That* is the lens for which you have been tested. It is the only one I can recommend professionally.'

'Never mind.'

'Well, sir, I have made my protest. The man of science demurs. The man of business submits.'

The monocle combined with the moustaches, set him up with his young companions, none of whom could have transformed himself so quickly. It also improved his shooting.

A few days after he bought it, they went to Mudshore to fire the Bren. Through his eye-glass Guy saw, distinct from the patchy snow, a plain white blob and hit it every time, not with notable marksmanship but as accurately as anyone else in his detail.

He did not attempt to keep the monocle permanently in his eye but he used it rather often and regained much of his lost prestige by discomforting the sergeant-instructor with it.

His prestige rose also with the renewed incidence of poverty. Palm lounges and dance halls cost dear and the first flood-tide of ready cash ebbed fast. Young officers began counting the days until the end of the month and speculating whether, now that their existence had once been recognized by the pay-office, they could depend on regular funds. One by one all Guy's former clients returned to him; one or two others diffidently joined; and all, save Sarum-Smith, he helped (Sarum-Smith got a cold stare through the monocle), and although you could not say that the Halberdiers sold 'the deference which youth owed to age' for three or four pounds down, it was a fact that his debtors were more polite to him and often remarked to one another in extenuation of their small acts of civility: 'Old Uncle Crouchback is an awfully generous good-natured fellow really.'

His life was further mitigated by his discovery of two agreeable retreats. The first was a small restaurant on the front called 'the Garibaldi' where Guy found Genoese cooking and a warm welcome. The proprietor was a part-time spy. This Giuseppe Pelecci, fat and philoprogenitive, welcomed Guy on his first visit as a possible source of variety in the rather monotonous and meagre lists of shipping which hitherto had been his sole contribution to his country's knowledge, but when he found Guy spoke Italian, patriotism gave place to simple home-sickness. He had been born not far from Santa Dulcina and knew the Castello Crouchback. The two became more than *patron* and patron, more than agent and dupe. For the first time in his life Guy felt himself *simpatico* and he took to dining at the Garibaldi most evenings.

The second was the Southsand and Mudshore Yacht Squadron.

Guy found this particularly congenial resort in a way which was itself a joy, for it added some hard facts to the incomplete history of Apthorpe's youth.

It would be a travesty to say that Guy suspected Apthorpe of lying. His claims to distinction – porpoise-skin boots, a High Church aunt in Tunbridge Wells, a friend who was on good terms with gorillas – were not what an impostor would invent in order to impress. Yet there was about Apthorpe a sort of fundamental implausibility. Unlike the typical figure of the J.D. lesson, Apthorpe tended to become faceless and tapering the closer he approached. Guy treasured every nugget of Apthorpe but under assay he found them liable to fade like faery gold. Only so far as Apthorpe was himself true, could his enchantment work its spell. Any firm passage between Apthorpe's seemingly dreamlike universe and the world of common experience was a thing to cherish, and just such a way Guy found on the Sunday following his fiasco on Mudshore range; the start of the week which ended triumphantly with his curled moustaches and his single eye-glass.

Guy went alone to mass. There were no Halberdiers to march there and the only other Catholic officer was Hemp, the Trimmer of the Depot. Hemp was not over scrupulous in his religious duties, from which (he claimed to have read somewhere) all servicemen were categorically dispensed.

The church was as old as most buildings in Southsand and sombrely embellished by the legacies of many widows. In the porch, as he left, Guy was accosted by the neat old man who had earlier carried the collection plate.

'I think I saw you here last week, didn't I? My name is Goodall, Ambrose Goodall. I didn't speak to you last Sunday as I didn't know if you were here for long. Now I hear you are at Kut-al-Imara for some time, so may I welcome you to St Augustine's?'

'My name is Crouchback.'

'A great name, if I may say so. One of the Crouchbacks of Broome perhaps?'

'My father left Broome some years ago.'

'Of course, yes, I know. Very sad. I make a study, in a modest way, of English Catholicism in penal times so of course Broome means a lot to me. I'm a convert myself. Still I daresay I've been a Catholic nearly as long as you have. I usually take a little turn along the front after mass. If you are walking back may I accompany you a short way?'

'I'm afraid I ordered a taxi.'

'Oh dear. I couldn't induce you to stop at the Yacht Club? It's on your way.'

'I don't think I can stop, but let me drop you there.'

'That's very kind. It *is* rather sharp this morning.'

As they drove away, Mr Goodall continued. 'I'd like to do anything I can for you while you are here. I'd like to talk about Broome. I went there last summer. The sisters keep it very well all things considered.

'I might be able to show you round Southsand. There are

some very interesting old bits. I know it very well. I was a master at Staplehurst House once, you see, and I stayed on all my life.'

'You were at Staplehurst House?'

'Not for very long. You see when I became a Catholic I had to leave. It wouldn't have mattered at any other school but Staplehurst was so very High Church that of course they minded particularly.'

'I *long* to hear about Staplehurst.'

'Do you, Mr Crouchback? Do you? There's not very much to tell. It came to an end nearly ten years ago. There were said to be abuses of the Confessional. I never believed it myself. You must be descended from the Grylls, too, I think. I have always had a particular veneration for the Blessed John Gryll. And, of course, for the Blessed Gervase Crouchback. Sooner or later they'll be canonized, I'm quite sure of it.'

'Do you by any chance remember a boy at Staplehurst called Apthorpe?'

'Apthorpe? Oh dear, here we are at the Club. Are you sure I can't induce you to come in?'

'May I, after all? It's earlier than I thought.'

The Southsand and Mudshore Yacht Squadron occupied a solid villa on the front. A flag and burgee flew from a pole on the front lawn. Two brass cannon stood on the steps. Mr Goodall led Guy to a chair in the plate-glass windows and rang the bell.

'Some sherry, please, steward.'

'It must be more than twenty years since Apthorpe left.'

'That would be just the time I was there. The name seems familiar. I could look him up if you're really interested. I keep all the old Mags.'

'He's with us at Kut-al-Imara.'

'Then I will certainly look him up. He's not a Catholic?'

'No, but he has a High Church aunt.'

'Yes, I suppose so. Most of our boys did, but quite a number came into the church later. I try to keep touch with them but parish affairs take up so much time, particularly now that Canon Geoghan can't get about as he did. And then I have my work. I had rather a hard time of it at first but I get along. Private tutoring, lectures at convents. You may have seen some of my reviews in the *Tablet*. They generally send me anything connected with heraldry.'

'I'm sure Apthorpe would like to meet you again.'

'Do you think he would? After all this time? But I must look him up first. Why don't you bring him here to tea? My rooms aren't very suitable for entertaining, but I'd be very pleased to see him here. You also stem from Wrottman of Speke, do you not?'

'I've some cousins of that name.'

'But not of Speke, surely? The Wrottman's of Speke are extinct in the male line. Don't you mean Wrottman of Garesby?'

'Perhaps I do. They live in London.'

'Oh yes, Garesby was demolished under the usurper George. One of the saddest things in all that whole unhappy century. The very stones were sold to a building contractor and dragged away by oxen.'

But when a few days later the meeting was arranged Guy and Apthorpe kept the conversation on the affairs of Staplehurst.

'I was able to find two references to your football in the Mag. I copied them out. I'm afraid neither is very laudatory. First in November 1913. "*In the absence of Brinkman ma. Apthorpe acted as understudy in goal but repeatedly found the opposing forwards too strong for him.*" The score was 8–0. Then in February 1915: "*Owing to mumps we could only put up a scratch XI against St Olaf's. Apthorpe in goal was unfortunately quite outclassed.*" Then in the summer of '16 you are in the *Vale* column. It doesn't give the name of your public school.'

'No, sir. It was still rather uncertain at the time of going to press.'

'Was he ever in your form?'

'Were you, Apthorpe?'

'Not exactly. We came to you for Church History.'

'Yes. I taught that through the school. In fact I owe my

conversion to it. Otherwise I only took the scholarship boys. You were never one of those, I think?'

'No,' said Apthorpe. 'There was a muddle about it. My aunt wanted me to go to Dartmouth. But somehow I made a hash of the Admiral's interview.'

'I always think it's too formidable an ordeal for a small boy. Plenty of good candidates fail purely on nerves.'

'Oh, it wasn't that exactly. We just couldn't seem to hit it off.'

'Where *did* you go after leaving?'

'I chopped and changed rather,' said Apthorpe.

They ate their tea in deep leather arm-chairs before a fire. Presently Mr Goodall said: 'I wonder if either of you would like to become temporary members of the club while you are here. It's a cosy little place. You don't have to have a yacht. That was the original idea but lots of our members can't run to one nowadays. I can't myself. But we keep up a general interest in yachting. There's usually a very pleasant crowd in here between six and eight and you can get dinner if you give the steward a day's notice.'

'I should like it very much,' said Guy.

'There's a lot to be said for it,' said Apthorpe.

'Then let me introduce you to our Commodore. I just saw him come in. Sir Lionel Gore, a retired Harley Street man. A very good fellow in his way.'

They were introduced. Sir Lionel spoke of the Royal Corps of Halberdiers and with his own hand filled in their entries in the Candidates Book, leaving a blank for the names of their yachts.

'You'll hear from the secretary in due course. In fact at the moment *I* am the secretary. If you'll wait a minute I'll make out your cards and post you on the board. We charge temporary members ten bob a month. I don't think that's unreasonable these days.'

So Guy and Apthorpe joined the Yacht Club, and Apthorpe said: 'Thanks, Commodore' when he was handed his ticket of membership.

It was dark and freezing hard when they left. Apthorpe had not yet recovered the full use of his leg and insisted on travelling by taxi.

As they drove back he said: 'I reckon we are on a good thing there, Crouchback. I suggest we keep it to ourselves. I've been thinking lately, it won't hurt to be a bit aloof with our young friends. Living cheek by jowl breeds familiarity. It may prove a bit awkward later when one's commanding a company and they're one's platoon commanders.'

'I shan't ever get a company. I've been doing badly all round lately.'

'Well, awkward for me, at any rate. Of course, old man, I don't mind being familiar with you because I know you'd never try to take advantage of it. Can't say the same for all the batch. Besides, you never know, you might get made second-in-command and that's a captain's appointment.'

Later, he said: 'Funny old Goodall taking such a fancy to you,' and later still, when they had reached Kut-al-Imara and were sitting in the hall with their gin and vermouth, he broke a long silence with: 'I never claimed to be anything much at football.'

'No. You said you didn't make a fetish of it.'

'Exactly. To tell you the truth I never made much mark at Staplehurst. It's strange, looking back on it now, but in those days I might just have passed for one of the crowd. Some men develop late.'

'Like Winston Churchill.'

'*Exactly*. We might go back to the Club after dinner.'

'D'you think tonight?'

'Well, I'm going and it's cheaper sharing a taxi.'

So that evening and most subsequent evenings Guy and Apthorpe went to the Yacht Club. Apthorpe was welcome as a fourth in the card-room and Guy read happily before the fire surrounded by charts, burgees, binnacles, model ships and other nautical decorations.

9

ALL that January was intensely cold. In the first week an exodus began from the dormitories of Kut-al-Imara, first of the
married men who were given permission to sleep in lodgings;
then, since many of the controlling staff were themselves unmarried yet comfortably quartered, the order was stretched to
include all who could afford or contrive it. Guy moved to the
Grand Hotel, which was conveniently placed between Kut-al-
Imara and the Club. It was a large hotel built for summer
visitors, almost empty now in war-time winter. He engaged
good rooms very cheaply. Apthorpe was taken in by Sir Lionel
Gore. By the end of the month less than half the original draft
remained in quarters. They spoke of 'boarders and dayboys'.
The local bus service did not fit the times of parade nor did it
strictly conform to its timetable. Many 'dayboys' had lodgings far from the school and the bus route. The weather showed
no sign of breaking. Even the march to and from the bus stop
was now laborious on the icebound road. There were many
cases of officers late on parade with plausible excuses. The gym
was unheated and long hours there became increasingly irksome. For all these reasons working hours were cut. They began
at nine and ended at four. There was no bugler at Kut-al-
Imara and Sarum-Smith one day facetiously rang the school
bell five minutes before parade. Major McKinney thought this
a helpful innovation and gave orders to continue it. The curric-
ulum followed the text-books, lesson by lesson, exercise by
exercise, and the preparatory school way of life was completely
recreated. They were to stay there until Easter – a whole
term.

The first week of February filled no dykes that year. Everything was hard and numb. Sometimes about midday there was
a bleak glitter of sun; more often the skies were near and
drab, darker than the snowbound downland inshore, leaden
and lightless on the seaward horizon. The laurels round Kut-al-

Imara were sheathed in ice, the drive rutted in crisp snow.

On the morning of Ash Wednesday Guy rose early and went to mass.

With the ash still on his forehead he breakfasted and tramped up the hill to Kut-al-Imara, where he found the place full of boyish excitement.

'I say, Uncle, have you heard? The Brigadier's arrived.'

'He was here last night. I came into the hall and there he was, covered in red, glaring at the notice board.'

'I'd made a resolution to dine in every night till the end of the month, but I slipped out by the side door. So did everyone else.'

'Something tells me he's up to no good.'

The school bell rang. Apthorpe was now restored to general duties and fell in with the squad.

'The Brigadier has come.'

'So I hear.'

'High time, too, if you ask me. There are quite a number of things here need putting in order, starting with the staff.'

They marched to the gymnasium and broke up into the usual four classes. All were being initiated in the same hard way into the mysteries of Fixed Lines.

'Stores,' said the colour sergeant instructor. 'Gun, spare barrel, dummies, magazines, carrier's wallet, tripod, aiming peg and night firing lamp. All right?'

'Right, Sergeant.'

'Right, eh? Any gentleman see anything not right? Where's the peg ; where's the lamp? Not available. So this here piece of chalk will substitute for peg and lamp. All right?'

Every half-hour they stood easy for ten minutes. During the second of these periods of glacial rest there was a warning: 'Pipes out. Officers coming. Party, shun.'

'Carry on, Sergeants,' said a voice unfamiliar to most. 'Never hold up instruction. Don't look at me, gentlemen. All eyes on the guns.'

Ritchie-Hook was among them, clothed as a brigadier, attended by the officer commanding the course and his second-in-command. He went from class to class. Parts of what was said reached the corner where Guy's squad worked. Most of it sounded cross. At last he reached Guy's squad.

'First detail; prepare for action.'

Two young officers flung themselves on the floorboards and reported: 'Magazines and spare barrel correct.'

'Action.'

The Brigadier watched. Presently he said: 'Get up, you two. Stand easy, everyone. Now tell me what a fixed line is for.'

Apthorpe said: 'To deny an area to the enemy by means of interlocking beaten zones.'

'Sounds as though you'd stopped giving him sweets. I'd like to hear less about denying things to the enemy and more about biffing him. Remember that, gentlemen. All fire-plans are just biffing. Now, you, number one at the gun. You've just been laying an aim on that chalk mark on the floor, haven't you? D'you think you'd hit it?'

'Yes, sir.'

'Look again.'

Sarum-Smith lay down and carefully checked his aim.

'Yes, sir.'

'With the sights at 1800?'

'That's the range we were given, sir.'

'But God damn it, man, what's the use of aiming at a chalk mark ten yards away with the sights at 1800?'

'That's the fixed line, sir.'

'Fixed on what?'

'The chalk mark, sir.'

'Anyone care to help him?'

'There is no aiming peg or night firing lamp available, sir,' said Apthorpe.

'What the hell's that got to do with it?'

'That's why we're using a chalk mark, sir.'

'You young officers have been doing small arms for six weeks. Can none of you tell me what a fixed line is for?'

'For biffing, sir,' suggested Trimmer.

'For biffing what?'

'The aiming peg or night firing lamp if available, sir. Otherwise the chalk mark.'

'I see,' said the Brigadier, baffled. He strode out of the gym followed by the staff.

'Now you've been and let me down,' said the sergeant-instructor.

In a few minutes a message arrived that the Brigadier would see all officers in the mess at twelve o'clock.

'Rockets all round,' said Sarum-Smith. 'I shouldn't wonder if the staff aren't having rather a sticky morning, too.'

So it seemed from their glum looks as they sat facing their juniors assembled in the school dining-hall. Places were already laid for luncheon and there was a smell of brussels sprouts boiling not far away. They sat silent as in a monastery refectory. The Brigadier rose, *Cesare armato con un occhio grifano*, as though to say Grace. He said: 'Gentlemen, you may not smoke.'

It had not occurred to anyone to do so.

'But you need not sit at attention,' he added, for everyone was instinctively stiff and motionless. They tried to arrange themselves less formally but there was no ease in that audience. Trimmer rested an elbow on the table and rattled the cutlery.

'It is not yet time to eat,' said the Brigadier.

Guy remembered the anecdote about 'six of the best'. It would really not have surprised him greatly if the Brigadier had produced a cane and called Trimmer up for correction. No charge had been preferred, no specific rebuke (except to Trimmer) uttered but under that solitary ferocious eye all were held in universal guilt.

The spirits of countless scared schoolboys still haunted and dominated the hall. How often must the word have been passed under those rafters of painted and grained plaster, in this same stench of brussels sprouts: 'the Head's in a frightful wax.' 'Who is it this time?' 'Why me?'

The words of that day's liturgy echoed dreadfully in Guy's mind: *Memento, homo, quia pulvis es, et in pulverem reverteris.*

Then the Brigadier began his speech: 'Gentlemen, it seems to me that you could all do with a week's leave,' and his smile, more alarming than any scowl, convulsed the grey face. 'In fact some of you needn't bother to come back at all. They'll be notified later through what are laughingly called the "correct channels".'

It was a masterly opening. The Brigadier was no scold and he was barely one part bully. What he liked was to surprise people. In gratifying this simple taste he had often to resort to violence, sometimes to heavy injury, but there was no pleasure for him in these concomitants. Surprise was everything. He must have known, glaring at his audience, that morning, that he had scored a triumph. He continued:

'I can only say that I am sorry I have not been to visit you before. There is more work than you can possibly know in forming a new brigade. I have been looking after that side of your affairs. I heard reports that when you arrived the accommodation was not perfect but Halberdier officers must learn to look after themselves. I came here last night on a friendly visit expecting to find you all happily settled in. I arrived at seven o'clock. There was not one officer in camp. Of course there is no military rule that you must dine in on any particular night. I supposed you were all out on some celebration. I asked the civilian caterer and learned that yesterday was not an exceptional occasion. He did not know the name of a single member of the mess committee. This does not strike me as being what the blue-jobs call a "happy ship".

'I looked at your work this morning. It was pretty moderate – and in case any young officer doesn't know what that means, it means damned awful. I do not say that it is entirely your fault. No military offence that I know of has been committed. But an officer's worth does not consist in avoiding military offences.

'What's more, gentlemen, you aren't officers. There are advantages in your present equivocal position. Advantages for you and for me. You none of you hold His Majesty's Commission. You are on probation. I can send the lot of you packing tomorrow without giving any explanation.

'As you know, the normal channel to a commission nowadays in the rest of the army is through the ranks and then to an OCTU. Halberdiers have been specially privileged to collect and train our new officers by direct entry. It won't occur again. We were given this single opportunity to train one batch of young officers because the War Office have faith in the traditions of the Corps. They know we wouldn't take a dud. Your replacements, when you're "expended"' – a cyclopean flash – 'will have gone through the modern mill of the ranks and an OCTU. You are the last men to be accepted and trained in the old way. And I'd sooner report total failure than let in one man I can't trust.

'Don't think you've done something clever in getting a commission easily by the backstairs. You'll go down those stairs arse over tip with my foot behind you, if you don't pull yourselves together.

'The rule of attack is "Never reinforce failure". In plain English that means: if you see some silly asses getting into a mess, don't get mixed up with 'em. The best help you can give is to go straight on biffing the enemy where it hurts him most.

'This course has been a failure. I'm not going to reinforce it. We'll start again this time next week. I shall be in charge.'

The Brigadier did not stay for luncheon. He mounted his motor-cycle and drove away noisily among the icy ruts. Major McKinney and the directing staff packed into their cosy private cars. The probationary officers remained. Strangely enough the atmosphere was one of exhilaration, not at the prospect of leave (that created many problems), but because all, or nearly all, had been unhappy during the past weeks. They were all, or nearly all, brave, unromantic, conscientious young men who joined the army expecting to work rather harder than they had done in peace time. Regimental pride had taken them unawares and quite afflated them. At Kut the Bitter they had been betrayed; deserted among dance halls and slot machines.

'Rather strong worded, I thought,' said Apthorpe. 'He might have made it clearer that there were certain exceptions.'

'You don't think he meant you when he said some of us need not come back?'

'Hardly, old man,' Apthorpe said, and added: 'I think in the circumstances I shall dine in mess tonight.'

Guy went alone to the Garibaldi where he found it difficult to explain to Mr Pelecci, a deeply superstitious Catholic but in the manner of his townsmen not given to ascetic practices, that he did not want meat that evening. Ash Wednesday was for Mrs Pelecci. Mr Pelecci feasted for St Joseph and fasted for no one.

But that evening Guy felt full of meat, gorged like a lion on Ritchie-Hook's kill.

10

PERHAPS the Brigadier believed that besides clearing space for his own work, he was softening the force of his reprimand by sending the course on leave. The 'boarders' left cheerfully but the 'dayboys' were committed to various arrangements in the town. Many had overspent themselves in establishing their wives. For them there was the prospect of five days loafing in lodgings. Guy was not rich. He was spending rather more than usual. There was no great attraction in changing an hotel bedroom in Southsand for a more expensive one in London. He decided to remain.

On the second evening Mr Goodall was due to dine with him at the Garibaldi. Afterwards they went to the Yacht Club, and sat alone among the trophies in the shuttered morning-room. Both were elated by that evening's news, the boarding of the *Altmark*, but soon Mr Goodall was back on his favourite topic. He was very slightly flown with wine and looser than usual in his conversation.

He spoke of the extinction (in the male line), some fifty years back, of an historic Catholic family.

'... They were a connexion of yours through the Wrottmans of Garesby. It was a most curious case. The last heir took his wife from a family (which shall be nameless) which has an unfortunate record of instability in recent generations. They had two daughters and then the wretched girl eloped with a neighbour. It made a terrible ado at the time. It was before divorce was common. Anyway they *were* divorced and this woman married this man. If you'll forgive me I won't tell you his name.

Then ten years later your kinsman met this woman alone, abroad. A kind of rapprochment occurred but she went back to her so-called husband and in due time bore a son. It was in fact your kinsman's. It was by law the so-called husband's, who recognized it as his. That boy is alive today and in the eyes of God the rightful heir to all his father's quarterings.'

Guy was less interested in the quarterings than in the morality.

'You mean to say that theologically the original husband committed no sin in resuming sexual relations with his former wife?'

'Certainly not. The wretched girl of course was guilty in every other way and is no doubt paying for it now. But the husband was entirely blameless. And so under another and quite uninteresting name a great family has been preserved. What is more the son married a Catholic so that *his* son is being brought up in the Church. Explain it how you will, I see the workings of Providence there.'

'Mr Goodall,' Guy could not resist asking, 'do you seriously believe that God's Providence concerns itself with the perpetuation of the English Catholic aristocracy?'

'But, of course. And with sparrows, too, we are taught. But I am afraid that genealogy is a hobby-horse I ride too hard when I get the chance. So much of my life is spent with people who aren't interested and might even think it snobbish or something – one evening a week for the Vincent de Paul Society, one evening at the boys' club; then I go to the Canon one evening to help him with his correspondence. And I have to keep some time for my sister who lives with me. She's not really interested in genealogy. Not that it matters. We are both unmarried and the last of our family, such as it was. Oh dear, I think your hospitality has made my tongue run away with me.'

'Not at all, dear Mr Goodall. Not at all. Some port?'

'No more, thank you.' Mr Goodall looked crestfallen. 'I must be on my way.'

'You're quite sure about that point you raised. About the husband committing no sin with his former wife?'

'Quite sure, of course. Think it out for yourself. What possible sin could he have committed?'

. Guy did think long and late about that blameless and auspicious pseudo-adultery. The thought was still with him when he woke next day. He went to London by a morning train.

The name of Crouchback, so lustrous to Mr Goodall, cut no ice at Claridge's: Guy was politely informed that there was no room available for him. He asked for Mrs Troy and learned that she had left instructions not to be disturbed. He went crossly to Bellamy's and explained his predicament at the bar, which, at half past eleven, was beginning to fill.

Tommy Blackhouse said: 'Who did you ask?'

'Just the chap at the desk.'

'That's no good. When in difficulties always take the matter to a higher level. It never fails. I'm staying there myself at the moment. In fact I'm going round there now. Would you like me to fix it for you?'

Half an hour later the hotel telephoned to say that there was a room awaiting him. He returned and was welcomed at the desk. 'We are so grateful to Major Blackhouse for telling us where to find you. There was a cancellation just as you left the hotel and we had no address for you.' The receptionist took a key from his rack and led Guy to the lift. 'We are fortunate in being able to offer you a very nice little suite.'

'I was thinking of a bedroom only.'

'This has a very nice little sitting-room that goes with it. I'm sure you will find it more quiet.'

They reached the floor; doors were thrown open on rooms which in all points proclaimed costliness. Guy remembered why he had come and the laws of propriety which govern hotels; a sitting-room constituted a chaperon.

'Yes,' he said, 'I think these will do very nicely.'

When he was left alone, he asked on the telephone for Mrs Troy.

'Guy? *Guy*. Where are you?'

'Here in the hotel.'

'Darling, how *beastly* of you not to let me know.'

'But I am letting you know now. I've only this minute arrived.'

'I mean let me know in advance. Are you here for a lovely long time?'

'Two days.'

'How *beastly*.'

'When am I going to see you?'

'Well, it's rather difficult. You should have let me know. I've got to go out almost at once. Come now. Number 650.'

It was on his floor, not a dozen rooms away, round two corners. The doors all stood ajar.

'Come in, I'm just finishing my face.'

He passed through the sitting-room – also a chaperon? he wondered. The bedroom door was open; the bed unmade; clothes and towels and newspapers all over the place. Virginia sat at a dressing-table covered with powder and wads of cotton wool and crumpled paper napkins. She was staring intently in the glass doing something to her eye. Tommy Blackhouse came unconcernedly from the bathroom.

'Hullo, Guy,' he said. 'Didn't know you were in London.'

'Make a drink for us all,' Virginia told him. 'I'll be with you in a second.'

Guy and Tommy went into the sitting-room where Tommy began cutting up a lemon and shovelling ice into a cocktail-shaker.

'They fixed you up all right?'

'Yes. I'm most grateful to you.'

'No trouble at all. By the way, better not say anything to Virginia' – Guy noticed that he had shut the bedroom door behind him – 'about our having met at Bellamy's. I told her I came straight from a conference, but as you know I stopped on the way. She's never jealous of other women, but she does hate Bellamy's. Once, while we were married, she said: "Bellamy's. I'd like to burn the place down." Meant it, too, bless her. Here for long?'

'Two nights.'

'I go back to Aldershot tomorrow. I ran into a brigadier of yours the other day at the War Office; they're scared stiff of him there. Call him "the one-eyed monster". Is he a bit cracked?'

'No.'

'I didn't think so either. They all say he's stark crazy at the War Office.'

Soon from the disorderly slum of her bedroom Virginia emerged spruce as a Halberdier.

'I hope you haven't made them too strong, Tommy. You know how I hate strong cocktails. Guy, *your moustache.*'

'Don't you like it?'

'It's perfectly awful.'

'I must say,' said Tommy, 'it took me aback rather.'

'It's greatly admired by the Halberdiers. Is this any better?' He inserted the monocle.

'I think it is,' said Virginia. 'It was just plain common before. Now it's comic.'

'I thought that, taken together, they achieved a military effect.'

'There you're wrong,' said Tommy. 'You must accept my opinion on a point of that kind.'

'Not attractive to women?'

'No,' said Virginia. 'Not to nice women.'

'Damn.'

'We ought to be going,' said Tommy. 'Drink up.'

'Oh dear,' said Virginia. 'What a short meeting. Am I going to see you again? I shall be free of this burden tomorrow. Couldn't we do something in the evening?'

'Not before?'

'How can I, darling, with this lout around? Tomorrow evening.'

They were gone.

Guy returned to Bellamy's as though to the Southsand Yacht Club. He washed and gazed in the glass over the basin as steadfastly as Virginia had done in hers. The moustache was fair, inclined to ginger, much lighter than the hair of his head. It was strictly symmetrical, sweeping up from a neat central parting, curled from the lip, cut sharp and slightly oblique from the corners of his mouth, ending in firm points. He put up his monocle. How, he asked himself, would he regard another man so decorated? He had seen such moustaches before and such monocles on the faces of clandestine homosexuals, on touts with accents to hide, on Americans trying to look European, on business-men disguised as sportsmen. True, he had also seen them in the Halberdier mess, but on faces innocent of all guile, quite beyond suspicion. After all, he reflected, his whole uniform was a disguise, his whole new calling a masquerade.

Ian Kilbannock, an arch-imposter in his Air Force dress, came up behind him and said: 'I say, are you doing anything this evening? I'm trying to get some people in for cocktails. Do come.'

'I might. Why?'

'Sucking up to my air marshal. He likes to meet people.'

'Well, I'm not much of a catch.'

'He won't know that. He just likes meeting people. I'd be awfully grateful if you could bear it.'

'I've certainly nothing else to do.'

'Well, come then. Some of the other people won't be quite as awful as the marshal.'

Later, upstairs in the coffee-room, Guy watched Kilbannock going round the tables, collecting his party.

'What's the point of all this, Ian?'

'Well, I told you. I've put the marshal up for this club.'

'But they aren't letting him in?'

'I hope not.'

'But I thought it was all fixed.'

'It's not quite as easy as that, Guy. The marshal is rather fly in his way. He's not giving anything away except for value received. He insists on meeting some members and getting their support. If he only knew, his best chance of getting in is to meet no one. So it's all in a good cause really.'

That afternoon Guy had his moustache shaven. The barber expressed professional admiration for the growth and did his work with reluctance, like the gardeners who all over the country had that autumn ploughed up their finest turf and transformed herbaceous borders into vegetable plots. When it was done, Guy studied himself once more in the glass and recognized an old acquaintance he could never cut, to whom he could never hope to give the slip for long, the uncongenial fellow traveller who would accompany him through life. But his naked lip felt strangely exposed.

Later he went to Ian Kilbannock's party. Virginia was there with Tommy. Neither noticed the change until he called attention to it.

'I knew it wasn't real,' said Virginia.

The air marshal was the centre of the party, in the sense that everyone was introduced to him and almost immediately withdrew. He stood like the entrance to a bee-hive, a point of vacuity with a constant buzzing movement to and from it. He was a stout man, just too short to pass for a Metropolitan policeman, with a cheerful manner and shifty little eyes.

There was a polar-bear rug before the fire.

'That reminds me of a clever rhyme I once heard,' he said.

> 'Would you like to sin
> With Eleanor Glyn
> On a tiger skin?
> Or would you prefer
> With her
> To err
> On some other fur?'

All in his immediate ambience looked at the rug in sad embarrassment.

'Who's Eleanor Glyn?' asked Virginia.

'Oh, just a name, you know. Put in to make it rhyme, I expect. Neat, isn't it?'

When he came to go, Guy found himself at the door with Ian and the marshal.

'My car's here. Can I give you a lift?'

It was snowing again and dark as the grave.

'That's very good of you, sir. I was going to St James's Street.'

'Hop in.'

'I'll come too, sir, if I may,' said Ian, surprisingly for there were still guests lingering upstairs.

When they reached Bellamy's, Ian said: 'Won't you come in for a final one, sir?'

'A sound idea.'

The three of them went to the bar.

'By the way, Guy,' said Ian, 'Air Marshal Beech is thinking of joining us here. Parsons, got the Candidates Book with you?'

The book was brought and the marshal's virgin page presented to view. Ian Kilbannock's fountain-pen was gently put into Guy's hand. He signed.

'I'm sure you'll find it amusing here, sir,' said Ian.

'I've no doubt I shall,' said the air marshal. 'I often thought of joining in the piping days of peace, but I wasn't in London often enough for it to be worth while. Now I need a little place like this where I can slip away and relax.'

It was St Valentine's Day.

Februato Juno, dispossessed, has taken a shrewish revenge on that steadfast clergyman, bludgeoned and beheaded seventeen centuries back, and set him in the ignominious role of patron to killers and facetious lovers. Guy honoured him for the mischance and whenever possible went to mass on his feast-day. He walked from Claridge's to Farm Street, from Farm Street to Bellamy's and settled down to a bleak day of waiting.

The newspapers were still full of the *Altmark*, now dubbed 'the Hell Ship'. There were long accounts of the indignities and discomforts of the prisoners, officially designed to rouse indignation among a public quite indifferent to those trains of locked vans still rolling East and West from Poland and the Baltic, that were to roll on year after year bearing their innocent loads to ghastly unknown destinations. And Guy, oblivious also, thought all that winter's day of his coming meeting with his wife. In the late afternoon when all was black, he telephoned to her room.

'What are our plans for the evening?'

'Oh good, are there plans? I quite forgot. Tommy's just left and I was thinking of a lonely early night, dinner in bed with the cross-word. I'd *much* rather have plans. Shall I come along to you? Everything looks rather squalid here.' So she came to the six-guinea chaperon sitting-room and Guy ordered cocktails.

'Not as cosy as mine,' she said, looking round the rich little room.

Guy sat beside her on the sofa. He put his arm on the back, edged towards her, put his hand on her shoulder.

'What's going on?' she asked in unaffected surprise.

'I just wanted to kiss you.'

'What an odd way to go about it. You'll make me spill my drink. Here.' She put her glass carefully on the table at her side, took hold of him by the ears and gave him a full firm kiss on either cheek.

'Is that what you want?'

'Rather like a French general presenting medals.' He kissed her on the lips. 'That's what I want.'

'Guy, are you tight?'

'No.'

'You've been spending the day at that revolting Bellamy's. Admit.'

'Yes.'

'Then of course you're tight.'

'No. It's just that I want you. D'you mind?'

'Oh, nobody ever minds about being wanted. But it's rather unexpected.'

The telephone bell rang.

'Damn,' said Guy.

The telephone was on the writing-table. Guy rose from the sofa and lifted the receiver. Familiar tones greeted him.

'Hullo, old man, Apthorpe here. I thought I'd just give you a ring. Hullo, hullo. That is Crouchback, isn't it?'

'What d'you want?'

'Nothing special. I thought I could do with a change from Southsand so I ran up to town for the day. I got your address out of the Leave Book. Are you doing anything this evening?'

'Yes.'

'You mean, you have an engagement?'

'Yes.'

'I couldn't join you anywhere?'

'No.'

'Very well, Crouchback. I'm sorry I disturbed you.' Huffily: 'I can tell when I'm not wanted.'

'It's a rare gift.'

'I don't quite get you, old man.'

'Never mind. See you tomorrow.'

'Things seem a bit flat in town.'

'I should go and have a drink.'

'I daresay I shall. Forgive me if I ring off now.'

'Who was that?' asked Virginia. 'Why were you so beastly to him?'

'He's just a chap from my regiment. I didn't want him butting in.'

'Some horrible member at Bellamy's?'

'Not at all like that.'

'Mightn't he have been rather fun?'

'No.'

Virginia had now moved to an arm-chair.

'What were we talking about?' she asked.

'I was making love to you.'

'Yes. Let's think of something different for a change.'

'It *is* a change. For me, anyway.'

'Darling, I haven't had time to get my breath from Tommy. Two husbands in a day is rather much.'

Guy sat down and stared at her.

'Virginia, did you ever love me at all?'

'But of course, darling. Don't you remember? Don't look so gloomy. We had lovely times together, didn't we? Never a cross word. *Quite* different to Mr Troy.'

They talked of old times together. First of Kenya. The group of bungalows that constituted their home, timber-built, round stone chimneys and open English hearths, furnished with wedding presents and good old pieces of furniture from the lumber-rooms at Broome; the estate, so huge by European standards, so modest in East Africa, the ruddy earth roads, the Ford van and the horses; the white-gowned servants and their naked children always tumbling in the dust and sunshine round the kitchen quarters; the families always on the march to and from the native reserves, stopping to beg for medicine; the old lion Guy shot among the mealies. Evening bathes in the lake, dinner parties in pyjamas with their neighbours. Race Week in Nairobi, all the flagrant, forgotten scandals of the Muthaiga Club, fights, adulteries, arson, bankruptcies, card-sharping, insanity, suicides, even duels – the whole Restoration scene reenacted by farmers, eight thousand feet above the steaming seaboard.

'Goodness it was fun,' said Virginia. 'I don't think anything has been quite such fun since. How things just do happen to one!'

In February 1940 coal still burned in the grates of six-guinea hotel sitting-rooms. Virginia and Guy sat in the fire-light and their talk turned to gentle matters, their earliest meeting, their courtship, Virginia's first visit to Broome, their wedding at the Oratory, their honeymoon at Santa Dulcina. Virginia sat on the floor with her head on the sofa, touching Guy's leg. Presently Guy slid down beside her. Her eyes were wide and amorous.

'Silly of me to say you are drunk,' she said.

It was all going as Guy had planned, and, as though hearing his unspoken boast, she added: 'It's no good planning anything,' and she said again: 'Things just happen to one.'

What happened then was a strident summons from the telephone.

'Let it ring,' she said.

It rang six times. Then Guy said: 'Damn. I must answer it.' Once again he heard the voice of Apthorpe.

'I'm doing what you advised, old man; I've had a drink. Rather more than one as it happens.'

'Good. *Continuez, mon cher*. But for Christ's sake don't bother me.'

'I've met some very interesting chaps. I thought perhaps you'd like to join us.'

'No.'

'Still engaged?'

'Very much so.'

'Pity. I'm sure you'd like these chaps. They're in Ack-Ack.'

'Well, have a good time with them. Count me out.'

'Shall I ring up later to see if you can give your chaps the slip?'

'No.'

'We might all join forces.'

'No.'

'Well, you're missing a very interesting palaver.'

'Good night.'

'Good night, old man.'

'I'm sorry about that,' said Guy, turning from the telephone.

'While you're there you might order some more to drink,' said Virginia.

She rose to her feet and arranged herself suitably for the waiter's arrival. 'Better put on the lights,' she said.

They sat opposite one another on either side of the fire, estranged and restless. The cocktails were a long time in coming. Virginia said: 'How about some dinner?'

'Now?'

'It's half past eight.'

'Here?'

'If you like.'

He sent for the menu and they ordered. There was half an hour in which waiters came and went, wheeling a table carrying an ice bucket, a hot-plate, eventually food. The sitting-room suddenly seemed more public than the restaurant below. All the fire-side intimacy was dissipated. Virginia said: 'What are we going to do afterwards?'

'I can think of something.'

'Can you indeed?'

Her eyes were sharp and humorous, all the glowing expectation and acceptance of an hour ago quite extinguished. Finally the waiter removed all his apparatus; the chairs on which they had sat at dinner were back against the wall; the room looked just as it had when it was first thrown open to him, costly and uninhabited. Even the fire, newly banked up with coal and smoking darkly, had the air of being newly lit. Virgin-

ia leaned on the chimney piece with a cigarette training a line
of smoke between her fingers. Guy came to stand by her and
she moved very slightly away.

'Can't a girl have time to digest?' she said.

Virginia had a weak head for wine. She had drunk rather
freely at dinner and there was a hint of tipsiness in her manner,
which, he knew from of old, might at any minute turn to truc-
ulence. In a minute it did.

'As long as you like,' said Guy.

'I should just think so. You take too much for granted.'

'That's an absolutely awful expression,' said Guy. 'Only
tarts use it.'

'Isn't that rather what you think I am?'

'Isn't it rather what you are?'

They were both aghast at what had happened and stared at
one another, wordless. Then Guy said: 'Virginia, you know I
didn't mean that. I'm sorry. I must have gone out of my mind.
Please forgive me. Please forget it.'

'Go and sit down,' said Virginia. 'Now tell me just what you
did mean.'

'I didn't mean anything at all.'

'You had a free evening and you thought I was a nice easy
pick-up. That's what you meant, isn't it?'

'No. As a matter of fact I've been thinking about you ever
since we met after Christmas. That's why I came here. Please
believe me, Virginia.'

'And anyway what do you know about picking up tarts? If
I remember our honeymoon correctly, you weren't so experienced then. Not a particularly expert performance as I remember it.'

The moral balance swung sharply up and tipped. Now
Virginia had gone too far, put herself in the wrong. There was
another silence until she said: 'I was wrong in thinking the
army had changed you for the better. Whatever your faults in
the old days you weren't a cad. You're worse than Augustus
now.'

'You forget I don't know Augustus.'

'Well, take it from me he was a monumental cad.'

A tiny light gleamed in their darkness, a pin-point in each easy tear which swelled in her eyes and fell.

'Admit I'm not as bad as Augustus.'

'Very little to choose. But he was fatter. I'll admit that.'

'Virginia, for God's sake don't let's quarrel. It's my last chance of seeing you for I don't know how long.'

'There you go again. The warrior back from the wars. "I take my fun where I find it."'

'You know I didn't mean that.'

'Perhaps you didn't.'

Guy was beside her again with his hands on her. 'Don't let's be beastly?'

She looked at him, not loving yet, but without any anger; sharp and humorous again.

'Go back and sit down,' she said, giving him one friendly kiss. 'I haven't finished with you yet. Perhaps I do look like an easy pick-up. Lots of people seem to think so, anyway. I suppose I shouldn't complain. But I can't understand you, Guy, not at all. You were never one for casual affairs. I can't somehow believe you are now.'

'I'm not. This isn't.'

'You used to be so strict and pious. I rather liked it in you. What's happened to all that?'

'It's still there. More than ever. I told you so when we first met again.'

'Well, what would your priests say about your goings-on tonight; picking up a notorious divorcee in an hotel?'

'They wouldn't mind. You're my wife.'

'Oh, rot.'

'Well, you asked what the priests would say. They'd say: "Go ahead."'

The light that had shone and waxed in their blackness suddenly snapped out as though at the order of an air-raid warden.

'But this is horrible,' said Virginia.

Guy was taken by surprise this time.

'What's horrible?' he said.

'It's absolutely disgusting. It's worse than anything Augustus or Mr Troy could ever dream of. Can't you see, you pig, you?'

'No,' said Guy in deep, innocent sincerity. 'No, I don't see.'

'I'd far rather be taken for a tart. I'd rather have been off-ered five pounds to do something ridiculous in high heels or drive you round the room in toy harness or any of the things they write about in books.' Tears of rage and humiliation were flowing unresisted. 'I thought you'd taken a fancy to me again and wanted a bit of fun for the sake of old times. I thought you'd chosen me specially, and by God you had. Be-cause I was the only woman in the whole world your priests would let you go to bed with. That was my attraction. You wet, smug, obscene, pompous, sexless, lunatic pig.'

Even in this discomfiture Guy was reminded of his brawl with Trimmer.

She turned to leave him. Guy sat frozen. On the silence left by her strident voice there broke a sound more strident still. While her hand was on the door-knob, she instinctively paused at the summons. For the third time that evening the telephone bell sang out between them.

'I say, Crouchback, old man, I'm in something of a quan-dary. I've just put a man under close arrest.'

'That's a rash thing to do.'

'He's a civilian.'

'Then you can't.'

'That, Crouchback, is what the prisoner maintains. I hope you aren't going to take his part.'

'Virginia, don't go.'

'What's that? I don't get you, old man. Apthorpe here. Did you say it was "No go"?'

Virginia went. Apthorpe continued.

'Did you speak or was it just someone on the line? Look here, this is a serious matter. I don't happen to have my King's Regulations with me. That's why I'm asking for your help. Ought I to go out and try and collect an NCO and some men for prisoner's escort in the street? Not so easy in the black-out, old man. Or can I just hand the fellow over to the civilian police? ... I say, Crouchback, are you listening? I don't think you quite appreciate that this is an official communication. I am calling on you as an officer of His Majesty's Forces ...'

Guy hung up the receiver and from the telephone in his bedroom gave instructions that he was taking no more calls that night, unless by any chance he was rung up from Number 650 in the hotel.

He went to bed and lay restless, half awake, for half the night. But the telephone did not disturb him again.

Next day when he met Apthorpe at the train he said: 'You got out of your trouble last night?'

'Trouble, old man?'

'You telephoned to me, do you remember?'

'Did I? Oh, yes, about some point of military law. I thought you might be able to help.'

'Did you solve the problem?'

'It blew over, old man. It just blew over.'

Presently he said: 'Not wishing to be personal, may I ask what's happened to your moustache?'

'It's gone.'

'Exactly. Just what I mean.'

'I had it shaved off.'

'Did you? What a pity. It suited you, Crouchback. Suited you very well.'

BOOK TWO

Apthorpe Furibundus

1

ORDERS were to report back at Kut-al-Imara by 1800 hours on 15 February.

Guy travelled through the familiar drab landscape. The frost was over and the countryside sodden and dripping. He drove through the darkling streets of Southsand where blinds were going down in the lightless windows. This was no home-coming. He was a stray cat, slinking back mauled from the rooftops, to a dark corner among the dustbins where he could lick his wounds.

Southsand was a place of solace. Hotel and Yacht Club would shelter him, he thought. Giuseppe Pelecci would feed him and flatter him; Mr Goodall raise him. Mist from the sea and the melting snow would hide him. The spell of Apthorpe would bind him, and gently bear him away to the far gardens of fantasy.

In his melancholy Guy had taken no account of the Ritchie-Hook Seven Day Plan.

Later in his military experience, when Guy had caught sight of that vast uniformed and bemedalled bureaucracy by whose power alone a man might stick his bayonet into another, and had felt something of its measureless obstructive strength, Guy came to appreciate the scope and speed of the Brigadier's achievement. Now he innocently supposed that someone of the Brigadier's eminence merely said what he wanted, gave his orders and the thing was done; but even so he marvelled, for in seven days Kut-al-Imara had been transformed, body and soul.

Gone were Major McKinney and the former directing staff and the civilian caterers. Gone, too, was Trimmer. A notice on the board, headed *Strength, Decrease of*, stated that his temporary commission had been terminated. With him went

Helm and a third delinquent, a young man from the Depot whose name was unfamiliar to Guy for the sufficient reason that he had been absent without leave for the whole of the course at Southsand. In their stead were a group of regular officers, Major Tickeridge among them, many of whom Guy recognized from the barracks. They sat at the back of the mess behind the Brigadier when at six o'clock on the first evening he rose to introduce them.

He held his audience for a moment with his single eye. Then he said: 'Gentlemen, these are the officers who will command you in battle.'

At those words Guy's shame left him and pride flowed back. He ceased for the time being to be the lonely and ineffective man – the man he so often thought he saw in himself, past his first youth, cuckold, wastrel, prig – who had washed and shaved and dressed at Claridge's, lunched at Bellamy's and caught the afternoon train; he was one with his regiment, with all their historic feats of arms behind him, with great opportunities to come. He felt from head to foot a physical tingling and bristling as though charged with galvanic current.

The rest of his speech was an explanation of the new organization and régime. The brigade had already taken embryonic form. The temporary officers were divided into three battalion groups of a dozen each under the regular major and captain who would eventually become respectively their commanding officer and adjutant. All would live in. Permission to sleep out would be given to married men for Saturday and Sunday nights only. All would dine in mess at least four nights a week.

'That is all, gentlemen. We will meet again at dinner.'

When they left the mess, they found that the table top over the fireplace in the hall had been covered in their brief absence with type-written sheets. Gradually spelling his way through the official abbreviations Guy learned that he was in the Second Battalion under Major Tickeridge and the Captain Sanders with whom Apthorpe had once so notably played golf. With him were Apthorpe, Sarum-Smith, de Souza, Leonard and seven others all from the barracks. Sleeping quarters had been reallocated. They lived by battalions, six to a room. He was back in Paschendael; as was Apthorpe.

Then and later he learned of other changes. The closed rooms of the house were now thrown open. One was labelled '*Bde. HQ*' and held a brigade major and two clerks. The head-master's study housed three Battalion Orderly Rooms. There were also a regular quartermaster, with an office and a clerk, three regimental sergeant majors, Halberdier cooks, new, younger Halberdier servants, three lorries, a Humber Snipe, three motor-bicycles, drivers, a bugler. The day's routine was a continuous succession of parades, exercises and lectures from eight in the morning till six. 'Discussions' would be held after dinner on Mondays and Fridays. 'Night Operations', also, were two a week.

'I don't know how Daisy will take this,' said Leonard.

She took it, Guy learned later, very badly, and returned heavy and cross to her parents.

Guy welcomed the new arrangements. After the expenses of London he had been uneasy about his hotel bill at the Grand. But most of the young officers were worried. Apthorpe, who had mentioned in the train that he was suffering from 'a touch of tummy', looked more worried than anyone.

'It's the question of my gear,' he said.

'Why not leave it at your digs?'

'At the Commodore's? Pretty awkward, old man, in the case of a sudden move. I think I'd better have a palaver with the Q.M. about it.'

And later: 'D'you know, the Q.M. wasn't a bit helpful. Said he was busy. Seemed to think I was talking about superfluous clothing. He even suggested I might have to scrap half of it when we move under canvas. He's just one of those box-wallahs. No experience of campaigning. I told him so and he said he'd served in the ranks in Hongkong. Hongkong – I ask you! About the cushiest spot in the whole empire. I told him that too.'

'Why is it all so important to you, Apthorpe?'

'My dear fellow, it's taken me years to collect.'

'Yes, but what's in it?'

'That, old man, is not an easy question to answer in one word.'

Everyone dined in the mess that first evening. There were three tables now, one for each battalion. The Brigadier, who from now on sat wherever his fancy took him, said Grace, banging the table with the handle of his fork and saying simply and loudly: 'Thank God.'

He was in high good humour and gave evidence of it first by providing a collapsible spoon for the brigade major which spilt soup over his chest, and secondly by announcing after dinner: 'When the tables have been cleared there will be a game of Housey-housey, here. For the benefit of the young officers I should explain that it is what civilians, I believe, call Bingo. As you are no doubt aware, it is the only game which may be played for money by His Majesty's Forces. Ten per cent of each bank goes to the Regimental Comforts Fund and Old Comrades' Association. The price of each card will be three pence.'

'Housey-housey?'

'Bingo?'

The junior officers looked at one another in wild surmise. 'Tubby' Blake alone, the veteran of the Depot Batch, claimed he had played the game on board ship crossing the Atlantic to Canada.

'It's quite simple. You just cross out the numbers as they're called.'

'What numbers?'

'The ones they call.'

Mystified, Guy returned to the mess. The brigade major sat at the corner of a table with a tin cash box and a heap of cards printed with squares and numbers. Each bought a card as he came in. The Brigadier, smiling ferociously, stood at the brigade major's side with a pillow-case in his hand. When they were all seated the Brigadier said: 'One object of this exercise is to see how many of you carry pencils.'

About half did. Sarum-Smith, surprisingly, had three or four, including a metal one with different coloured leads.

Someone asked: 'Will a fountain-pen do, sir?'

'Every officer should always carry a pencil.'

It was back to prep. school again, but a better school than McKinney's.

At last after much borrowing and searching of pockets the game began suddenly with the command: 'Eyes down for a house.'

Guy stared blankly at the Brigadier, who now plunged his hand in the pillow-case and produced a little square card.

'Clickety-click,' said the Brigadier disconcertingly. Then: 'Sixty-six.' Then in rapid succession, in a loud sing-song tone: 'Marine's breakfast number ten add two twelve all the fives fifty-five never been kissed sweet sixteen key of the door twenty-one add six twenty-seven legs eleven Kelly's eye number one and we'll . . .'

He paused. The regular officers and 'Tubby' Blake gave tongue: 'Shake the bag.'

Slowly the terms of this noisy sport became clearer to Guy and he began making crosses on his card until there was a cry of 'House' from Captain Sanders, who then read his numbers aloud.

'House correct,' said the brigade major, and Sanders collected about nine shillings, and the other players crowded round the brigade major to buy new cards.

They played for two hours. The Brigadier's eye teeth flashed like a questing tiger's. As the players began to grasp what was going on, an element of enjoyment just perceptible warmed them here and there. The Brigadier became more jolly. 'Who wants one number?'

'Sir.'

'Sir.'

'Sir.'

'What do you want?'

'Eight.'

'Fifteen.'

'Seventy-one.'

'Well it's . . . .' Pause. The Brigadier made a pantomime of being unable to read it; fixed the card with his monocle. 'Did

someone say they *wanted* seventy-one. Well it is seventy . . .'
pause 'seven. All the sevens and we'll . . .'

'Shake the bag.'

At half past ten the Brigadier said: 'Well, gentlemen, Bed-
fordshire for you. I've got work. You haven't got a training
programme yet.'

He led his staff away into the room marked '*Bde. HQ*'. It
was two o'clock when Guy heard them disperse.

The Training Programme followed no text-book. Tactics as
interpreted by Brigadier Ritchie-Hook consisted of the art of
biffing. Defence was studied cursorily and only as the period of
reorganization between two bloody assaults. The Withdrawal
was never mentioned. The Attack and the Element of Surprise
were all. Long raw misty days were passed in the surrounding
country with maps and binoculars. Sometimes they stood on
the beach and biffed imaginary defenders into the hills; sometimes they biffed imaginary invaders from the hills into the sea.
They invested downland hamlets and savagely biffed imaginary
hostile inhabitants. Sometimes they merely collided with imaginary rivals for the use of the main road and biffed them out
of the way.

Guy found that he had an aptitude for this sort of warfare.
He read his map easily and had a good eye for country. When
townsmen like Sarum-Smith gazed blankly about them Guy
could always recognize 'dead ground' and 'covered lines of
approach'. Sometimes they worked singly, sometimes in 'syn-
dicates'; Guy's answers usually turned out to be the 'staff solution'. At night when they were dropped about the downs, with
compass bearings to guide them to a meeting-place, Guy was
usually home one of the first. There were great advantages
in a rural upbringing. In the 'discussion', too, he did well. These
were debates on the various more recondite aspects of biffing.
The subjects were announced beforehand with the implication
that the matter should be given thought and research. When
the evening came most were drowsy and Apthorpe's fine show
of technical vocabulary fell flat. Guy spoke up clearly and con-

cisely. He realized that he was once more attracting favourable notice.

The thaw gave place to clear, cold weather. They returned to Mudshore range but with the Brigadier in charge. This was a period before the invention of 'Battle Schools'. The firing of a live round, as Guy well knew, was attended with all the solemnity of a salute at a funeral, always and everywhere, except when Brigadier Ritchie-Hook was about. The sound of flying bullets exhilarated him to heights of levity.

He went to the butts to organize snap-shooting. Markers raised figure-targets at unpredictable points drawing bursts of Bren fire. The Brigadier soon tired of this, put his hat on his stick and ran up and down the trench, raising, lowering, waving it, promising down the telephone a sovereign to the man who hit it. All missed. Enraged he popped his head over the parapet shouting: 'Come on, you young blighters, shoot me.' He did this for some time, running, laughing, ducking, jumping, until he was exhausted though unwounded.

It was a period when ammunition was short. Five rounds a man was the normal training allowance. Brigadier Ritchie-Hook had all the Brens firing at once, continuously, their barrels overheated, changed, plunged sizzling into buckets of water, while he led his young officers on all fours in front of the targets a few inches below the rain of bullets.

2

THE newspapers, hastily scanned, were full of Finnish triumphs. Ghostly ski-troops, Guy read, swept through the sunless Arctic forests harassing the mechanized divisions of the Soviet who had advanced with massed bands and portraits of Stalin expecting a welcome, whose prisoners were ill-equipped, underfed, quite ignorant of whom they were fighting and why. English forces, delayed only by a few diplomatic complications, were on their way to help. Russian might had proved to be an illusion. Mannerheim held the place in English hearts won in

1914 by King Albert of the Belgians. Then quite suddenly it appeared that the Finns were beaten.

No one at Kut-al-Imara House seemed much put out by the disaster. For Guy the news quickened the sickening suspicion he had tried to ignore, had succeeded in ignoring more often than not in his service in the Halberdiers; that he was engaged in a war in which courage and a just cause were quite irrelevant to the issue.

That day Apthorpe said: 'After all, it's only what one expected.'

'Did you, Apthorpe? You never told me.'

'Stuck out a mile, old man, to anyone who troubled to weigh the pros and cons. It was simply the case of Poland over again. But there was no point in talking about it. It would only have spread alarm and despondency among the weaker brethren. Personally I can see quite a few advantages in the situation.'

'What, for instance?'

'Simplifies the whole strategy, if you know what I mean.'

'Am I to take this as part of your campaign to prevent alarm and despondency?'

'Take it how you like, old man. I've other things to worry about.'

And Guy at once knew that there must have been a new development in the tense personal drama which all that Lent was being played against the background of the Brigadier's training methods; which, indeed, drew all its poignancy from them and itself formed their culminating illustration.

This adventure had begun on the first Sunday of the new régime.

The schoolrooms were almost deserted that afternoon; everyone was either upstairs asleep or else in the town. Guy was reading his weekly papers in the hall when he saw through the plate-glass window a taxi drive up and Apthorpe emerge carrying, with the help of the driver, a large square object, which they placed in the porch. Guy went out to offer his help.

'That's all right, thank you,' said Apthorpe rather stiffly. 'I'm just shifting some of my gear.'

'Where d'you want to put it?'

142

'I don't quite know yet. I shall manage quite well, thank you.'

Guy returned to the hall and stood in the window gazing idly out. It was getting too dark to read comfortably and the man had not yet appeared to put up the black-out screens. Presently he saw Apthorpe emerge from the front door into the twilight and begin furtively burrowing about in the shrubbery. He watched fascinated until some ten minutes later he saw him return. The front porch opened directly into the hall. Apthorpe entered backwards dragging his piece of gear.

'Are you sure I can't help?'

'Quite sure, thank you.'

There was a large cupboard under the stairs. Into this Apthorpe with difficulty shoved his burden. He removed his gloves and coat and cap and came with an air of unconcern to the fire saying: 'The Commodore sent you his compliments. Says he misses us at the Club.'

'Have you been there?'

'Not exactly. I just dropped in on the old man to fetch something.'

'That piece of gear?'

'Well, yes, as a matter of fact.'

'Is it something very private, Apthorpe?'

'Something of no general interest, old man. None at all.'

At that moment the duty servant came in to fix the black-out. Apthorpe said: 'Smethers.'

'Sir.'

'Your name is Smethers, isn't it?'

'No, sir. Crock.'

'Well, never mind. What I wanted to ask you was about the offices, the back-parts of the house.'

'Sir?'

'I need some sort of little shed or store-house, a gardener's hut would do, a wash-house, dairy, anything of that kind. Is there such a place?'

'Was you wanting it just for the moment, sir?'

'No, no, no. For as long as we're here.'

'Couldn't say, I'm sure, sir. That's for the Q.M.'

'Yes. I was only wondering,' and when the man had gone: 'Stupid fellow that. I always thought he was called Smethers.'

Guy turned back to his weekly papers. Apthorpe sat opposite him gazing at his boots. Once he got up, walked to the cupboard, peered in, shut it and returned to his chair.

'I can *keep* it there, I suppose, but I can't possibly *use* it there, can I?'

'Can't you?'

'Well, how *can* I?'

There was a pause during which Guy read an article about the inviolability of the Mikkeli Marshes. (These were the brave days before the fall of Finland.) Then Apthorpe said:

'I thought I could find a place for it in the shrubbery but it's all much more open than I realized.'

Guy said nothing and turned a page of the *Tablet*. It was clear that Apthorpe was longing to divulge his secret and would shortly do so.

'It is no good going to the Q.M. *He* wouldn't understand. It's not exactly an easy thing to explain to anyone.'

Then, after another pause, he said: 'Well, if you *must* know, it's my thunder-box.'

This was far above Guy's hopes; his mind had been running on food, medicine, fire-arms; at the very best he had hoped for something exotic in footwear.

'May I see it?' he asked reverently.

'I don't see why not,' said Apthorpe. 'As a matter of fact I think it will interest you; it's pretty neat, a type they don't make any more. Too expensive, I suppose.'

He went to the cupboard and dragged out the treasure, a brass-bound, oak cube.

'It's a beautiful piece of work really.'

He opened it, showing a mechanism of heavy cast-brass and patterned earthenware of solid Edwardian workmanship. On the inside of the lid was a plaque bearing the embossed title of *Connelly's Chemical Closet*.

'What do you think of it?' said Apthorpe.

Guy was not sure of the proper terms in which to praise such an exhibit.

'It's clearly been very well looked after,' said Guy.

It seemed Guy had said the right thing.

'I got it from a High Court Judge, the year they put drains into the Government buildings at Karonga. Gave him five pounds for it. I doubt if you could find one for twenty today. There's not the craftsmanship any more.'

'You must be very proud of it.'

'I am.'

'But I don't quite see why you need it here.'

'Don't you, old man? Don't you?' A curiously solemn and fatuous expression replaced the innocent light of ownership that had until now beamed from Apthorpe. 'Have you ever heard of a rather unpleasant complaint called "clap", Crouch-back?'

Guy was dumbfounded.

'I say, what a beastly thing. I am sorry. I had no idea. I suppose you picked it up the other night in London when you were tight. But are you having it properly seen to? Oughtn't you to go sick?'

'No, no, no, no. *I* haven't got it.'

'Then who has?'

'Sarum-Smith for one.'

'How do you know?'

'I don't *know*. I simply chose Sarum-Smith as an example. He's just the sort of young idiot who would. Any of them might. And I don't intend to take any risks.'

He shut his box and pushed it away under the stairs. The effort seemed to rile him.

'What's more, old man,' he said, 'I don't much like the way you spoke to me just now, accusing me of having clap. It's a pretty serious thing, you know.'

'I'm sorry. It was rather a natural mistake in the circumstances.'

'Not natural to me, old man, and I don't quite know what you mean by "circumstances". I *never* get tight. I should have thought you would have noticed that. Merry, perhaps, on occasions, but never *tight*. It's a thing I keep clear of. I've seen far too much of it.'

Apthorpe was up at first light next day exploring the out-buildings and before breakfast had discovered an empty shed where the school perhaps had kept bats and pads. There with the help of Halberdier Crock he installed his chemical closet and thither for several tranquil days he resorted for his com-fort. It was two days after the fall of Finland that his troubles began.

Back from biffing about the downs and, after a late luncheon inclined for half an hour's rest, Guy was disturbed by Ap-thorpe. He wore a face of doom.

'Crouchback, a word with you.'

'Well.'

'In private if you don't mind.'

'I do mind. What is it?'

Apthorpe looked round the ante-room. Everyone seemed occupied.

'You've been using my thunder-box.'

'No, I haven't.'

'Someone has.'

'Well, it isn't me.'

'No one else knows of it.'

'How about Halberdier Crock?'

'He wouldn't dare.'

'Nor would I, my dear fellow.'

'Is that your last word?'

'Yes.'

'Very well. But in future I shall keep a look-out.'

'Yes, I should.'

'It's a serious matter, you know. It almost amounts to pil-fering. The chemical is far from cheap.'

'How much a go?'

'It isn't the money. It's the principle.'

'And the risk of infection?'

'Exactly.'

For two days Apthorpe posted himself in the bushes near his shed and spent every available minute on watch. On the third day he drew Guy aside and said: 'Crouchback, I owe you an apology. It isn't you who has been using my thunder-box.'

'I knew that.'

'Yes, but you must admit the circumstances were very suspicious. Anyway I've found out who it is, and it's most disturbing.'

'Not Sarum-Smith?'

'No. Much more disturbing than that. *It's the Brigadier.*'

'Do you think *he's* got clap?'

'No. Most unlikely. Far too much a man of the world. But the question arises, what action ought I to take?'

'None.'

'It's a matter of principle. As my superior officer he has no more right to use my thunder-box than to wear my boots.

'Well, I'd lend him my boots if he wanted them.'

'Perhaps; but then, if you'll forgive my saying so, you're not very particular about your boots, are you, old man? Anyway you think it my duty to submit without protest.'

'I think you'll make a tremendous ass of yourself if you don't.'

'I shall have to think about it. Do you think I ought to consult the B.M.?'

'No.'

'You may be right.'

Next day Apthorpe reported: 'Things are looking worse.'

It showed how much the thunder-box had occupied Guy's thoughts that he at once knew what Apthorpe meant.

'More intruders?'

'No, not that. But this morning as I was coming out I met the Brigadier going in. He gave me a very odd look – you may have noticed he has rather a disagreeable stare on occasions. His look seemed to suggest that *I* had no business there.'

'He's a man of action,' said Guy. 'You won't have to wait long to know what he thinks about it.'

All day Apthorpe was distracted. He answered haphazard when asked an opinion on tactics. His solutions of the problems set them were wild. It was a particularly cold day. At every pause in the routine he kept vigil by the hut. He missed tea and did not return until ten minutes before the evening lecture. He was red-nosed and blue-cheeked.

'You'll make yourself ill, if this goes on,' said Guy.

'It can't go on. The worst has happened already.'

'What?'

'Come and see. I wouldn't have believed it, if I hadn't seen it with my own eyes.'

They went out into the gloom.

'Just five minutes ago. I'd been on watch since tea and was getting infernally cold, so I started walking about. And the Brigadier came right past me. I saluted. He said nothing. Then he did this thing right under my very eyes. Then he came past me again and I saluted and he positively grinned. I tell you, Crouchback, it was *devilish*.'

They had reached the hut. Guy could just see something large and white hanging on the door. Apthorpe turned his torch on it and Guy saw a neatly inscribed notice: *Out of Bounds to all ranks below Brigadier.*

'He must have had it specially made by one of the clerks,' said Apthorpe awfully.

'It's put you in rather a fix, hasn't it?' said Guy.

'I shall send in my papers.'

'I don't believe you can in war-time.'

'I can ask for a transfer to another regiment.'

'I should miss you, Apthorpe, more than you can possibly believe. Anyway there's a lecture in two minutes. Let's go in.'

The Brigadier himself lectured. Booby traps, it appeared, were proving an important feature of patrol-work on the Western front. The Brigadier spoke of trip-wires, detonators, anti-personnel mines. He described in detail an explosive goat which he had once contrived and driven into a Bedouin encampment. Seldom had he been more exuberant.

This was one of the evenings when there was no discussion or night exercise and it was generally accepted that those who wished might dine out.

'Let's go to the Garibaldi,' said Apthorpe. 'I won't sit at the same table with that man. You must dine with me as my guest.'

There, in the steam of *minestrone,* Apthorpe's face became

a healthier colour and strengthened by Barolo his despair gave place to defiance. Pelecci leant very near while Apthorpe rehearsed his wrongs. The conversation was abstruse. 'Thunderbox', an invention of this capable officer's, unjustly misappropriated by a superior, was clearly a new weapon of value.

'I don't think,' said Apthorpe, 'it would be any good appealing to the Army Council, do you?'

'No.'

'You could not expect them to meet a case like this with purely open minds. I don't suggest positive prejudice but, after all, it's in their interest to support authority if they possibly can. If they found a loophole . . .'

'You think there are loopholes in your case?'

'Quite frankly, old man, I do. In a court of honour, of course, the thing would be different, but in its purely legal aspect one has to admit that the Brigadier is within his rights in putting any part of the brigade premises out of bounds. It is also true that I installed my thunder-box without permission. That's just the sort of point the Army Council would jump on.'

'Of course,' said Guy, 'it's arguable that since the thunderbox has not risen to the rank of brigadier, it is itself at the moment out of bounds.'

'You've got it, Crouchback. You've hit the nail right on the head.' He goggled across the table with frank admiration. 'There's such a thing, you know, as being too near to a problem. Here I've been turning this thing over and over in my mind till I felt quite ill with worry. I knew I needed an outside opinion ; anybody's, just someone who wasn't personally implicated. I've no doubt I'd have come to the same solution myself sooner or later, but I might have worried half the night. I owe you a real debt of gratitude, old man.'

More food arrived and more wine. Giuseppe Pelecci was out of his depth. 'Thunder-box', it now appeared, was the code-name of some politician of importance but no military rank, held concealed in the district. He would pass the information on for what it was worth ; keener brains than his should make what they could of it. He had no ambition to rise in his profession. He was doing nicely out of the restaurant. He had worked up the good-will of the place himself. Politics bored him and battles frightened him. It was only in order to escape military service that he had come here in the first place.

'And afterwards a special *zabaglione*, gentlemen?'

'Yes,' said Apthorpe. 'Yes, rather. Let's have all you've got.' And to Guy: 'You must understand that this is *my* dinner.'

So Guy had understood from the first; this reminder, Guy thought, was perhaps a clumsy expression of gratitude. It was in fact a sly appeal for further services.

'I think we've cleared up the whole legal aspect very neatly,' Apthorpe continued. 'But there's now the question of action. How are we going to get the thunder-box out?'

'The way you got it in, I suppose.'

'Not so easy, old man. There's wheels within wheels. Halberdier Crock and I carried it there. How can we carry it away without going out of bounds? One can't order a man to perform an unlawful action. You must remember that. Besides I shouldn't really care to *ask* him. He was distinctly uncooperative about the whole undertaking.'

'Couldn't you lasso it from the door?'

'Pretty ticklish, old man. Besides, my lariat is with the rest of my gear at the Commodore's.'

'Couldn't you draw it out with a magnet?'

'I say, are you trying to be funny, Crouchback?'

'It was just a suggestion.'

'*Not* a very practical one, if you don't mind my saying so. No. Someone must go in and get it.'

'Out of bounds?'

'Someone who doesn't know, or at least who the Brigadier doesn't know knows, that the hut is out of bounds. If he was caught he could always plead that he didn't see the notice in the dark.'

'You mean me?'

'Well, you're more or less the obvious person, aren't you, old man?'

'All right,' said Guy, 'I don't mind.'

'Good for you,' said Apthorpe, greatly relieved.

They finished their dinner. Apthorpe grumbled about the bill but he paid it. They returned to Kut-al-Imara. There was no one about. Apthorpe kept *cave* and Guy, without much difficulty, dragged the object into the open.

'Where to now?'

'That's the question. Where do you think will be the best place?'

'The latrines.'

'Really, old man, this is scarcely the time or place for humour.'

'I was only thinking of Chesterton's observation, "Where is the best place to hide a leaf? In a tree." '

'I don't get you, old man. It would be jolly awkward up a tree, from *every* point of view.'

'Well, let's not take it far. It's bloody heavy.'

'There's a potting shed I found when I was making my recce.'

They took it there, fifty yards away. It was less commodious than the hut, but Apthorpe said it would do. As they were returning from their adventure he paused in the path and said with unusual warmth: 'I shan't forget this evening's work, Crouchback. Thank you very much.'

'And thank you for the dinner.'

'That wop did pile it on, didn't he?'

After a few more steps Apthorpe said: 'Look here, old man, if you'd care to use the thunder-box, too, it's all right with me.'

It was a moment of heightened emotion; an historic moment, had Guy recognized it, when in their complicated relationship Apthorpe came nearest to love and trust. It passed, as such moments do between Englishmen.

'It's very good of you but I'm quite content as I am.'

'Sure?'

'Yes.'

'That's all right then,' said Apthorpe, greatly relieved.

Thus Guy stood high in Apthorpe's favour and became with him joint custodian of the thunder-box.

IN full retrospect all the last weeks of March resolved themselves into the saga of the chemical closet. Apthorpe soon forgot his original motive for installing it.

He was no longer driven by fear of infection. His right of property was at stake. Waiting to fall in, on the morning after the first translation, Apthorpe drew Guy aside. Their new comradeship was on a different plane from frank geniality; they were fellow conspirators now. 'It's still there.'

'Good.'

'Untouched.'

'Fine.'

'I think, old man, that in the circumstances we had better not be seen talking together too much.'

Later, as they went into the mess for luncheon Guy had the odd impression that someone in the crowd was attempting to hold his hand. He looked about him and saw Apthorpe near, with averted face, talking with great emphasis to Captain Sanders. Then he realized that a note was being passed to him.

Apthorpe made for a place at table as far as possible from his. Guy opened the screw of paper and read: '*The notice has been taken down from the hut. Unconditional surrender?*'

Not until tea-time did Apthorpe consider it safe to speak.

'I don't think we've any more to worry about. The Brig. has given us best.'

'It doesn't sound like him.'

'Oh, he's unscrupulous enough for anything. I know that. But he has his dignity to consider.'

Guy did not wish to upset Apthorpe's new, gleeful mood, but he doubted whether these adversaries had an identical sense of dignity. Next day it was apparent that they had not.

Apthorpe arrived for parade (under the new régime there was half an hour's drill and physical training every morning) with a face of horror. He fell in next to Guy. Again there was an odd inter-fumbling of fingers and Guy found himself holding a message. He read it at the first stand-easy while Apthorpe turned ostentatiously away. '*Must speak to you alone first opportunity. Gravest developments.*'

An opportunity came half-way through the morning.

'The man's mad. A dangerous, certifiable maniac. I don't know what I ought to do about it.'

'What's he done now?'

'He came within an inch of killing me, that's all. If I hadn't been wearing my steel helmet I shouldn't be here to tell you. He caught me with a bloody great flower-pot, full of earth and a dead geranium, square on the top of my head. That's what he did this morning.'

'He threw it at you?'

'It was on top of the potting-shed door.'

'Why were you wearing your tin-hat?'

'Instinct, old man. Self-preservation.'

'But you said last night you thought the whole thing was over. Apthorpe, do you always wear your tin-hat on the thunder-box?'

'All this is irrelevant. The point is that this man simply isn't responsible. It's a very serious matter for someone in his position – and ours. A time may come when he holds our lives in his hands. What ought I to do?'

'Move the box again.'

'And not report the matter?'

'Well, there's your dignity to consider.'

'You mean there are people who might think it funny?'

'Awfully funny.'

'Damn,' said Apthorpe. 'I hadn't considered that side of the question.'

'I wish you'd tell me the truth about the tin-hat.'

'Well, if you must know, I *have* been wearing it lately. I suppose it really boils down to home-sickness, old man. The helmet has rather the feel of a solar topee, if you see what I mean. It makes the thunder-box more homely.'

'You don't start out wearing it?'

'No, under my arm.'

'And when do you put it on, before or after lowering the costume? I must know.'

'On the threshold, as it happens. Very luckily for me this morning. But, you know, really, old man, I don't quite get you. Why all the interest?'

'I must visualize the scene, Apthorpe. When we are old men, memories of things like this will be our chief comfort.'

'Crouchback, there are times when you talk almost as though you found it funny.'

'Please don't think that, Apthorpe. I beg you, think anything but that.'

Already after so brief a reconciliation Apthorpe was getting suspicious. He would have liked to be huffy but did not dare. He was pitted against a ruthless and resourceful enemy and must hold fast to Guy or go down.

'Well, what is our next move?' he asked.

That night they crept out to the potting-shed and Apthorpe in silence showed with his torch the broken shards, the scattered mould and the dead geranium of that morning's great fright. In silence he and Guy lifted the box and bore it as they had planned, back to its original home in the games-hut.

Next day, the Brigadier appeared at first parade.

'ATM 24, as no doubt you all know, recommends the use of of games for training in observation and field-craft. This morning, gentlemen, you will play such a game. Somewhere about these grounds has been concealed an antiquated field latrine, no doubt left here as valueless by the former occupants of the camp. It looks like a plain square box. Work singly. The first officer to find it will report to me. Fall out.'

'His effrontery staggers me,' said Apthorpe. 'Crouchback, guard the shed. I will draw off the hunt.'

New strength had come to Apthorpe. He was master of the moment. He strode off purposefully towards the area of coal bunkers and petrol dump and, sure enough, the Brigadier was soon seen to follow behind him. Guy made deviously for the games-hut and sauntered near it. Twice other seekers approached and Guy said: 'I've just looked in there. Nothing to see.'

Presently the bugle recalled them. The Brigadier received the 'nil report', mounted his motor-cycle and drove away scowling ominously but without a word; he did not reappear at all that day.

'A bad loser, old man,' said Apthorpe.

But next day the *Out of Bounds* notice was back on the shed.

As Guy foresaw, those mad March days and nights of hide-and-seek drained into a deep well of refreshment in his mind, but in retrospect the detail of alternate ruse and counter-ruse faded and grew legendary. He never again smelled wet laurel, or trod among pine needles, without reliving those encumbered night prowls with Apthorpe, those mornings of triumph or disappointment. But the precise succession of episodes, indeed their very number, faded and were lost among later, less childlike memories.

The climax came in Holy Week at the very end of the course. The Brigadier had been in London for three days on the business of their next move. The thunder-box stood in a corner of the playing field, unhoused but well hidden between an elm tree and a huge roller. There for the three days Apthorpe enjoyed undisputed rights of property.

The Brigadier returned in alarmingly high spirits. He had bought some trick glasses at a toy-shop which, when raised, spilled their contents down the drinker's chin, and these he secretly distributed round the table before dinner. After dinner there was a long session of Housey-housey. When he had called the last house he said: 'Gentlemen, everyone except the B.M. and I goes on leave tomorrow. We meet under canvas in the lowlands of Scotland where you will have ample space to put into practice the lessons you have learned here. Details of the move will be posted as soon as the B.M. has sweated them out. You will particularly notice that officers' baggage and equipment is defined by a scale laid down at the War House. Those limits will be strictly observed. I think that's all, isn't it, B.M.? Oh, no, one other thing. You are all improperly dressed.

You've been promoted as from this morning. Get those second pips up before leaving camp.'

That night there was singing in the dormitories:

> 'This time tomorrow I shall be
> Far from this Academee.'

Leonard improvised

> 'No more TEWTS and no more drill,
> No night ops to cause a chill.'

'I say,' said Guy to Apthorpe. 'That scale of equipment won't allow for your gear.'

'I know, old man. It's very worrying.'

'And the thunder-box.'

'I shall find a place for it. Somewhere quite safe, a crypt, a vault, somewhere like that where I shall know it's waiting for me until the end of the war.'

> 'No more swamps through which to creep,
> No more lectures to make me sleep.'

The cheerful voices reached the room marked '*Bde. HQ*' where the Brigadier was at work with his brigade major.

'That reminds me,' he said, 'I've some unfinished business to attend to outside.'

Next morning as soon as the sun touched the unshaded window of Paschendael, Apthorpe was up, jabbing his shoulder straps with a pair of nail scissors. Then he tricked himself out as a lieutenant. He nothing common did or mean on their morning of departure. His last act before leaving the dormitory was a friendly one; he offered to lend Guy a pair of stars from a neat leather stud-box which he now revealed to be full of such adornments and of crowns also. Then before Guy had finished shaving, Apthorpe, correctly dressed and bearing his steel helmet under his arm, set out for his corner of the playing field.

The spot was not a furlong away. In less than five minutes an explosion rattled the windows of the schoolhouse. Various jolly end-of-term voices rose from the dormitories: 'Air raid'; 'Take cover'; 'Gas'.

Guy buckled his belt and hurried out to what he knew must be the scene of the disaster. Wisps of smoke were visible. He crossed the playing field. At first there was no sign of Apthorpe. Then he came upon him, standing, leaning against the elm, wearing his steel helmet, fumbling with his trouser buttons and gazing with dazed horror on the wreckage which lay all round the roller.

'I say, are you hurt?'

'Who is that? Crouchback? I don't know. I simply don't know, old man.'

Of the thunder-box there remained only a heap of smoking wood, brass valves, pinkish chemical powder scattered many yards, and great jags of patterned china.

'What happened?'

'I don't know, old man. I just sat down. There was a frightful bang and the next thing I knew I was on all fours on the grass, right over there.'

'Are you hurt?' Guy asked again.

'Shock,' said Apthorpe. 'I don't feel at all the thing.'

Guy looked more closely at the wreckage. It was plain enough from his memories of the last lecture what had happened.

Apthorpe removed his steel helmet, recovered his cap, straightened his uniform, put up a hand to assure himself that his new stars were still in place. He looked once more on all that remained of his thunder-box; the *mot juste,* thought Guy.

He seemed too dazed for grief.

Guy was at a loss for words of condolence.

'Better come back to breakfast.'

They turned silently towards the house.

Apthorpe walked unsteadily across the wet, patchy field with his eyes fixed before him.

On the steps he paused once and looked back.

There was more of high tragedy than of bitterness in the epitaph he spoke.

'*Biffed.*'

4

GUY had considered going to Downside for Holy Week but decided instead on Matchet. The Marine Hotel was still crowded but there was now no sense of bustle. Management and servants had settled down to the simple policy of doing less than they had done before, for rather more money. A notice board hung in the hall. Except that they began: '*Guests are respectfully reminded* ...', '*Guests are respectfully requested* ...', '*Guests are regretfully informed* ...', the announcements were curiously like military orders and each proclaimed some small curtailment of amenity.

'Seems to me this place is going off rather,' said Tickeridge, who now wore the badges of lieutenant-colonel.

'I'm sure they're doing their best,' said Mr Crouchback.

'I notice they've put up the prices too.'

'I believe they're finding everything rather difficult.'

All his life Mr Crouchback abstained from wine and tobacco during Lent, but his table still bore its decanter of port and the Tickeridges joined them every evening.

As they stood at the windy front door that Maundy Thursday night, while Felix gambolled off into the darkness, Mr Crouchback said:

'I'm so glad you're in Tickeridge's battalion. He's such a pleasant fellow. His wife and little girl miss him dreadfully. ...'

'He tells me you're probably being given a company.'

'Hardly that. I think I may get made second-in-command.'

'He said you'd get your own company. He thinks the world of you. I'm so glad. You're wearing that medal?'

'Yes, indeed.'

'I really am delighted you're doing so well. Not that I'm at all surprised. By the way I shall be taking my turn at the Altar of Repose. I don't suppose you care to come too?'

'What time?'

'Well, they seem to find it hardest to get people for the early

158

morning watches. It's all the same for me so I said I'd be there from five to seven.'

'That's a bit long for me. I might look in for half an hour.'

'Do. They've got it looking very pretty this year.'

Dawn was breaking that Good Friday when Guy arrived at the little church, but inside it was as still as night. The air was heavy with the smell of flowers and candles. His father was alone, kneeling stiff and upright at a prie-dieu before the improvised altar, gazing straight before him into the golden lights of the altar. He turned to smile at Guy and then resumed his prayer.

Guy knelt not far from him and prayed too.

Presently a sacristan came in and drew the black curtains from the east windows; brilliant sunlight blinded their eyes, momentarily, to candles and chalice.

At that moment in London – for in this most secret headquarters it was thought more secret to work at unconventional hours – Guy was being talked about.

'There's some more stuff come in about the Southsand affair, sir.'

'Is that the Welsh professor who's taken against the RAF?'

'No, sir. You remember the short-wave message from L18 we intercepted. It's here. *Two Halberdier officers state that important politician Box visited Southsand in secret and conferred with high military commander.*'

'I've never thought there was much in that. We've no suspect called Box as far as I know and there's no high military commander anywhere near Southsand. Might be a code name, of course.'

'Well, sir, we got to work on it as you told us and we've learned that there's a Member of Parliament named Box-Bender who has a brother-in-law named Crouchback in the Halberdiers. Now Box-Bender was born plain Box. His father added to the name in 1897.'

'Well, that seems to dispose of it, eh? No reason why this fellow shouldn't visit his own brother-in-law.'

'In secret, sir?'

'Have we anything on this Box? Nothing very suspicious about a hyphenated name, I hope?'

'We've nothing very significant, sir,' said the junior officer whose name was Grace-Groundling-Marchpole, each junction of which represented a provident marriage in the age of landed property. 'He went to Salzburg twice, ostensibly for some kind of musical festival. But Crouchback's quite another fish. Until September of last year he lived in Italy and is known to have been on good terms with the Fascist authorities. Don't you think I'd better open a file for him?'

'Yes, perhaps it would be as well.'

'For both, sir?'

'Yes. Pop 'em all in.'

They, too, took down the black-out screens and admitted the dawn.

Thus two new items were added to the Most Secret index, which later was micro-filmed and multiplied and dispersed into a dozen indexes in all the Counter-Espionage Headquarters of the Free World and became a permanent part of the Most Secret archives of the Second World War.

5

THE great promised event, 'When the brigade forms', had glowed in Guy's mind, as in the minds of nearly all his companions, for more than five months; a numinous idea. None knew what to expect.

Once Guy saw a film of the Rising of 45. Prince Charles and his intimates stood on a mound of heather, making a sad little group, dressed as though for the Caledonian Ball, looking, indeed, precisely as though they were a party of despairing revellers mustered in the outer suburbs to meet a friend with a motor-car who had not turned up.

An awful moment came when the sun touched the horizon behind them. The Prince bowed his head, sheathed his claymore and said in rich Milwaukee accents: 'I guess it's all off,

Mackingtosh.' (Mackingtosh from the first had counselled immediate withdrawal.)

At that moment, suddenly, a faint skirl of pipes rose and swelled to an unendurable volume, while from all the converging glens files of kilted extras came winding into view. ''Tis Invercauld comes younder.' 'Aye and Lochiel', 'And stout Montrose', 'The Laird of Cockpen', 'The bonnets of bonnie Dundee', 'The Campbells are coming. Hurrah, Hurrah ...' until across the crimson panorama the little bands swept together into one mighty army. Unconquerable they seemed to anyone ignorant of history, as they marched into the setting sun ; straight, as anyone knowledgeable in Highland geography could have told them, into the chilly waters of Loch Moidart.

Guy had come to expect something almost like that ; something at any rate totally different from what did happen.

They reassembled from Easter leave at Penkirk, a lowland valley some twenty miles from Edinburgh, covered in farm land and small homesteads. At its head stood a solid little mid-Victorian Castle. It was there they met and there they messed and slept for the first two days. Their numbers were swollen by many unfamiliar regulars of all ranks, a Medical Officer, an Undenominational Chaplain and a cantankerous, much beribboned veteran who commanded the Pioneers. Still there were only officers. The drafts of men had been postponed until there was accommodation for them.

The pioneers, it was supposed, had prepared a camp, but on the appointed day nothing was visible above ground. They had been there all the winter cosily established in the Castle stables. Some of them had grown fond of the place, particularly the reservists who made friends in the neighbourhood, sheltered at their hearths during working hours and paid for their hospitality with tools and provisions from the company stores. These veterans were designed to be the stiffening of a force otherwise composed of anti-fascist 'cellists and dealers in abstract painting from the Danubian Basin.

'If they'd given me one section of *fascists,*' said their commander, 'I'd have had the place finished in a week.'

But he did not repine. He had billeted himself in very fair

comfort at the Station Hotel three miles distant. He was versed in all the arcana of the Pay Office and drew a multitude of peculiar special allowances. If he liked the new commander he was quite ready to prolong his task until the end of the summer.

Five minutes with Brigadier Ritchie-Hook decided him to make an end and be gone. The veterans were caught and put to bully the anti-fascists. Construction began in earnest but not earnestly enough for Ritchie-Hook. A second Ruskin, on the first morning at Penkirk, he ordered his young officers to dig and carry. Unfortunately he had had them all inoculated the evening before with every virus in the medical store. Noting a lack of enthusiasm he tried to stir up competition between Halberdiers and Pioneers. The musicians responded with temperamental fire; the art-dealers less zealously, but seriously and well; the Halberdiers not at all, for they could barely move.

They dug drains and carried tent-boards (the most awkward burden ever devised by man for man); they unloaded lorryloads of Soyer stoves and zinc water pipes; they ached and staggered and in a few cases fainted. Not until the work was nearly done, did the poisons lose their strength.

For the first two nights they spread their blankets and messed higgledy-piggledy in the Castle. It was Major McKinney's Kut-al-Imara all over again. Then on the third day officers' lines were complete in each battalion area, with a mess tent, a water tap and a field kitchen. They moved out and in. The adjutant procured a case of spirits. The quartermaster improvised a dinner. Colonel Tickeridge stood round after round of drinks and later gave his obscene performance of 'The One-Armed Flautist'. The Second Battalion had found a home and established its identity.

Guy groped his way among the ropes and tent pegs that first evening under canvas, fuddled with gin, fatigue, and germs, to the tent he was sharing with Apthorpe.

Apthorpe, the old campaigner, had defied orders (as, it soon appeared, had done all the regulars) and brought with him a substantial part of his 'gear'. He had left the mess before Guy. He lay now, on a high collapsible bed, in a nest of white muslin illuminated from inside by a patent, incandescent oil lamp, like a great baby in a bassinette, smoking his pipe and reading his Manual of Military Law. A table, a chair, a bath, a wash-hand-stand all collapsible; chests and trunks, very solid, surrounded his roost; also a curious structure like a gallows from which hung his uniforms. Guy gazed, fascinated by this smoky, luminous cocoon.

'I trust I've left you enough room,' said Apthorpe.

'Yes, rather.'

Guy had only a rubber mattress, a storm lantern and a three-legged canvas wash-basin.

'You may think it odd that I prefer to sleep under a net.'

'I expect it's wise to take every precaution.'

'No, no, no. This isn't a *precaution*. It's just that I sleep better.'

Guy undressed, throwing his clothes on his suitcase, and lay down on the floor, between blankets, on his strip of rubber. It was intensely cold. He felt in his bag for a pair of woollen socks and the balaclava helmet knitted for him by one of the ladies at the Marine Hotel, Matchet. He added his great-coat to his mattress.

'Chilly?' asked Apthorpe.

'Yes.'

'It's not really a cold night,' said Apthorpe. 'Far from it. Of course we're some way north of Southsand.'

'Yes.'

'If you'd care to have a rub down with liniment, I can lend you some.'

'Thanks awfully. I shall be all right.'

'You ought to, you know. It makes a lot of difference.'

Guy did not answer.

'Of course this is only a temporary arrangement,' said Apthorpe, 'until the lists are out. Company commanders have tents to themselves. I'd double in with Leonard if I were you. He's about the best of the subalterns. His wife had a baby last week. I should have thought it the kind of thing that would rather spoil one's leave, but he seems quite cheerful about it.'

'Yes. He told me.'

'What you want to avoid in a room-mate is someone who's always trying to borrow one's gear.'

'Yes.'

'Well, I'm turning in now. If you to get up in the night you'll take care where you walk, won't you? I've got some pretty valuable stuff lying around I haven't found a place for yet.'

He laid his pipe on his table and extinguished his light. Soon, invisible in his netting, embraced in cloud, soothed and wooed and gently overborne like Hera in the arms of Zeus, he was asleep.

Guy turned down his lantern and lay long awake, cold and aching but not discontented.

He was thinking of this strange faculty of the army of putting itself into order. Shake up a colony of ants and for some minutes all seems chaos. The creatures scramble aimlessly, frantically about; then instinct reasserts itself. They find their proper places and proper functions. As ants, so soldiers.

In the years to come he was to see the process at work again and again, sometimes in grim circumstances, sometimes in pleasant domesticity. Men unnaturally removed from wives and family began at once to build substitute homes, to paint and furnish, to make flower-beds and edge them with whitewashed pebbles, to stitch cushion-covers on lonely gun-sites.

He thought, too, about Apthorpe.

Apthorpe had been in his proper element during the building operations.

When his turn had come to be inoculated that first evening he had insisted on waiting until last and had then given the Medical Officer such an impressive account of the diseases from which he had, from time to time, suffered, of the various inoculations he had undergone and their precise effects, of the warnings he had been given by eminent specialists about the dangers of future inoculations, of idiosyncratic allergies and the like, that the Medical Officer readily agreed to perform a purely ceremonial injection of quite non-injurious matter.

He was thus in full vigour of mind and was usually to be found in consultation with the Pioneer officer giving sage advice about the siting of camp kitchens in relation to the prevailing wind, or pointing out defects in the guy-ropes.

He had taken advantage of the two days mucking-in with the brigade staff to make himself well known to them all. He had discovered an old friendship with a cousin of the brigade major's. He had done very well indeed.

And yet, Guy thought, and yet there was something rum about him; not 'off colour'; far from it; gloriously over-Technicolored like Bonnie Prince Charlie in the film. It was not anything that could be defined. Just a look in the eye; not even that – an aura. But it was distinctly rum.

So fitfully sleeping and thinking he passed the hours until reveille.

6

ON the fourth afternoon the last tent went up. Across and down the valley, from the Castle to the main road, lay the battalion lines, the kitchens, stores, mess-tents, latrines. Much was missing, much had been scamped, but it was ready for occupation. On the morrow the men were due to arrive. That evening the officers assembled in the Castle, which for now was the Brigade Headquarters, and the Brigadier addressed them:

'Gentlemen,' he began, 'tomorrow you meet the men you will lead in battle.'

It was the old, potent spell, big magic. Those two phrases, 'the officers who will command you ...', 'the men you will lead...', set the junior officers precisely in their place, in the heart of the battle. For Guy they set swinging all the chimes of his boyhood's reading ...

'... "I've chosen your squadron for the task, Truslove." "Thank you, sir. What are our chances of getting through?" "It can be done, Truslove, or I shouldn't be sending you. If anyone can do it, you can. And I can tell you this, my boy, I'd give all my seniority and all these bits of ribbon on my chest to be with you. But my duty lies here with the Regiment. Good luck to you, my boy. You'll need it" ...'

The words came back to him from a summer Sunday evening at his preparatory school, in the headmaster's drawing-room, the three top forms sitting about on the floor, some in a dream of home, others – Guy among them – spell-bound.

That was during the first World War but the story came from an earlier chapter of military history. Pathans were Captain Truslove's business. Troy, Agincourt and Zululand were more real to Guy in those days than the world of mud and wire and gas where Gervase fell. Pathans for Truslove; paynims for Sir Robert de Waybroke; for Gervase, Bernard Partridge's flamboyant, guilty Emperor, top-booted, eagle-crowned. For Guy at the age of twelve there were few enemies. They, in their hordes, came later.

The Brigadier continued. It was the first of April, a day which might have provoked him to fun, but he was serious and for once Guy listened with only half his mind. This crowd of officers, many quite strange to him, seemed no longer his proper habitat. In less than forty-eight hours he had made his new, more hallowed home with the Second Battalion and his thoughts were with the men who were coming next day.

The assembly was dismissed and from that moment the Brigadier, who until then had been the dominant personality in their lives, became for the time remote. He lived in his castle with his staff. He came and went, to London, to Edinburgh, to the Training Depot, and no one knew why or when. He became the source of annoying, impersonal orders. 'Brigade says we have to dig slit trenches' ... 'Brigade says only a third of the battalion can be absent from camp at any given time' ...

'More bumf from Brigade' ... That was Ritchie-Hook with his wounds and his escapades; a stupendous warrior shrunk to a mean abstraction – 'Brigade'.

Each battalion went to its lines. There were four oil-stoves in the mess-tent now but the evening chill entered the Second Battalion as they sat on the benches to hear Colonel Tickeridge's list of appointments.

He read slowly: first the headquarters; himself, the second-in-command, the adjutant, all regulars; intelligence-gas-welfare-transport-assistant-adjutant and 'general dogsbody',

Sarum-Smith; Headquarter Company; commander, Apthorpe; second-in-command, one of the very young regulars.

This caused a stir of interest. There had been rumours among the temporary officers that one or two of them might be promoted; no one except Apthorpe supposed he might get his own company at this early stage; not even Apthorpe imagined he would be put in command of a regular, however juvenile.

It was a shock, too, to the regulars, who looked at one another askance.

A Company had a regular commander and second-in-command, three temporary officers as platoon commanders. B Company followed the same plan. In C Company Leonard was second-in-command. There were now left Guy, two other temporary officers and one of the cockiest young regulars, named Hayter.

'D Company,' said Colonel Tickeridge. 'Commander Major Erskine, who apparently can't be spared at the moment. He ought to be with us in the next few days. Meanwhile the second-in-command, Hayter, will be in command single-handed. Platoon commanders, de Souza, Crouchback and Jervis.'

It was a bitter moment. At no previous stage in his life had Guy expected success. His 'handkerchief' at Downside took him by surprise. When a group of his College suggested he should stand as secretary of the J.C.R. he had at once assumed that his leg was being inoffensively pulled. So it had been throughout his life. The very few, very small distinctions that had come to him had all come as a surprise. But in the Halberdiers he had had a sense of well-doing. There had been repeated hints. He had not expected or desired much but he had looked forward rather confidently to promotion of some kind and he had come to want it simply as a sign that he had, in fact, done well in training and that the occasional words of approbation had not been merely 'the deference due to age'. Well, now he knew. He was not as bad as Trimmer, not quite as bad as Sarum-Smith, whose appointment was contemptible; he had just scraped through without honours. He should have realized, he saw now, that Leonard was obviously the better man. Moreover he was the poorer man and newly a father; Leonard needed the extra pay that would come eventually with his captaincy. Guy felt no resentment; he was a good loser – at any rate an experienced one. He merely felt a deep sinking of spirit such as he had felt in Claridge's with Virginia, such as he had felt times beyond number through all his life. Sir Roger, maybe, had felt thus when he drew his dedicated sword in a local brawl, not forseeing that one day he would acquire the odd title of 'il Santo Inglese'.

Colonel Tickeridge continued: 'Of course all these appointments are just a try-out. We may have a reshuffle later. But they're the best we can think of at the moment.'

The meeting broke up. The orderly behind the bar busily served pink gins.

'Congratulations, Apthorpe,' said Guy.

'Thanks, old man. I confess I never expected the Headquarter Company. It's twice the size of any other, you know.'

'I'm sure you'll manage it very well.'

'Yes. I may have to sit on my 2IC a bit.'

'On your what, Apthorpe? Is that a new sort of thunderbox?'

'No, no, no. Second-in-command, of course. You really ought to get the correct terms, you know. It's the kind of thing they notice higher up. By the way I think it's bad luck you didn't do better. I heard a buzz that one of our batch was going to be a 2IC. I quite thought that meant you.'

'Leonard's very efficient.'

'Yes. *They* know best, of course. Still I'm sorry it wasn't you. If it's a bore to move your gear immediately, you can use my tent for tonight.'

'Thanks. I will.'

'But get it clear first thing tomorrow, won't you, old man.'

It was so cold in the mess-tent that they dined in great-coats. In accordance with regimental custom, Apthorpe and Leonard stood drinks to all.

Several of the temporary officers said: 'Bad luck, Uncle.' Guy's reverse seemed to have made him more *simpatico*.

Hayter said: 'You're Crouchback, aren't you? Have a drink.

Time I got to know my little flock. You won't find me a hard chap to work with, when you're used to my ways. What did you do in the piping days of peace?'

'Nothing.'

'Oh.'

'What's Major Erskine like?'

'Brainy. He's spent a lot of his service in rather special jobs. But you'll get on all right with him if you do what you're told. He won't expect anything much of you new chaps at first.'

'What time do the men arrive tomorrow?'

'The Brig. was shooting rather a line about that. It's only the old sweats who come tomorrow. The National Service chaps won't be here for some days.'

They drank pink gin together and eyed one another without confidence.

'Which are de Souza and Jervis? I ought to have a word with them, too, I suppose.'

That evening when Guy went in for the last time to Apthorpe's tent, he found his host awake and illuminated.

'Crouchback,' he said, 'there's something I have to say to you. I never want to hear another word about that happening at Southsand. Never. Do you understand? Otherwise I shall have to take action.'

'What sort of action, Apthorpe?'

'*Drastic* action.'

Rum. Very rum indeed.

7

NEARLY three weeks later there appeared *Army Training Memorandum No. 31 War. April 1940*. A canvas letter rack with a stitched section for every officer was one of the pieces of furniture which, with hired arm-chairs, a wireless set and other amenities, had lately appeared in the mess of the Second Battalion. Returning from an afternoon of 'company schemes', each of them found a copy of the tract protruding from his pouch. General Ironside commended it with the words: '*I direct all commanding officers to ensure that every junior officer is thoroughly examined in the questions set in Part 1 of this Memorandum and not to rest content until the answers are satisfactory.'*

Colonel Tickeridge said: 'You chaps had better take a dekko at the ATM this month. It seems to be important for some reason or other.'

There were one hundred and forty-three questions in the tract.

April 21st; the nine o'clock news announced that General Paget was at Lillehammer and that all was going well in Norway. When the news was over, music began. Guy found an arm-chair as far from the wireless as possible and in an atmosphere in which the scents of trodden grass, gin and roast beef were subdued by paraffin and hot iron, he began to study the *'life and death responsibilities of a sub. unit commander'*.

Many of the questions related either to the regular routine, of which no Halberdier officer could conceivably be negligent, or to abstruse technicalities quite outside his ken.

'I say, have *you* acquired – out of your grant – an old motor-car chassis and engine parts to assist M.T. training?'

'No. How many men in *your* platoon have you earmarked for signallers?'

'None.'

It was like a game of 'Happy Families'.

'Can you tell me why camouflage done late is more dangerous than no camouflage at all?'

'I suppose you might get stuck on the wet paint.'

'Are your men's arrangements for drying their clothes as good as yours?'

'They couldn't possibly be worse.'

'I say, Uncle, have you tested whether your platoon can cook in their mess-tins?'

'Yes. We did it last week.'

'What are the advantages during training of beginning night operations an hour before dawn?'

'They can only last an hour, I suppose.'

'No, seriously.'

'It seems a great advantage to me.'

The camp seemed to whisper and chatter with the questionnaire like Apthorpe's home-jungle at sundown.

Guy dreamily turned the pages. It was all rather like the advertisement of a correspondence course in Business Efficiency. 'How to catch the boss's eye in five lessons.' 'Why didn't *I* get promoted?' . . . But a question here and there set him thinking about the last three weeks.

Are you trying to make yourself competent to take over the job of the next senior man to you?

Guy had no respect for Hayter. He was confident he could now do his job much better than Hayter. Moreover, he had lately learned that when he did take over another job, it would not be Hayter's.

Major Erskine had arrived on the same day as the National Service men. His 'braininess' was not oppressive. The imputation derived chiefly from the facts that he read Mr J. B. Priestley's novels, and was strangely dishevelled in appearance. His uniform was correct and clean but it never seemed to fit him, not through any fault of the tailor's, but rather because the major seemed to change shape from time to time during the day. One moment his tunic seemed too long, the next, too short. His pockets were too full. His anklets got twisted. He was more like a Sapper than a Halberdier. But he and Guy got on well together. Major Erskine did not talk much, but when he did it was with great simplicity and frankness.

One evening when Hayter had been more cocky than usual, Major Erskine and Guy walked back together from the company lines to the mess.

'That little tick wants his bottom kicked,' said Major Erskine. 'I think I *shall* kick it. Good for him and pleasant for me.'

'Yes. I can see that.'

Major Erskine then said: 'I shouldn't talk to you like that about your superior officer. Did anyone ever tell you why you're only commanding a platoon, Uncle?'

'No. I didn't think any explanation necessary.'

'They ought to have. You see, you were down for a company. Then the Brig. said he wouldn't have anyone commanding a *fighting* company who hadn't had a platoon first. I see his point. Headquarters is different. Old Uncle Apthorpe will stay there until he becomes GSO2(Q) or something wet like that. None of the temporary officers who've started high will ever get a rifle company. You will, before we go into action, unless you blot your copy-book in a pretty sensational way. I thought I'd tell you, in case you felt depressed about it.'

'I did rather.'

'Yes, I thought as much.'

Who runs the platoon – you or your platoon sergeant?

Guy's platoon sergeant was named Soames. Neither found the other *simpatico*. The normal relationship in the Halberdiers between platoon commander and sergeant was that of child and nannie. The sergeant should keep his officer out of mischief. The officer's job was to sign things, to take the blame and quite simply to walk ahead and get shot first. And, as an officer, he should have a certain intangibility belonging, as in old-fashioned households, to the further side of the baize-doors. All this was disordered in the relationship of Guy and Sergeant Soames. Soames reverenced officers in a more modern way, as men who had been sharp and got ahead; moreover he distinguished between regulars and temporaries. He regarded Guy as a nannie might some child, not of 'the family' but of inferior and suspicious origin, suddenly, by a whim of the mistress of the house, dumped, as a guest of indefinite duration, in her nursery. Moreover he was far too young, and Guy far too old, for him to be a nannie at all. Soames had signed on for long service in 1937. He had been a corporal for three months when the declaration of war and the formation of the brigade had precociously exalted him. He often bluffed and was exposed. Guy ran the platoon, but not in easy cooperation. Sergeant Soames wore his moustache in a gangster's cut. There was a great deal in him that reminded Guy of Trimmer.

How many men have you earmarked in your mind as possible candidates for a commission?

One. Sergeant Soames. Guy had done more than earmark him in his mind. He had presented a slip of paper bearing Sergeant Soames's name, number and history, to Major Erskine at the Company Office some days ago.

Major Erskine had said: 'Yes. I can't blame you. I have this morning sent in Hayter's name as an officer suitable for special training in Air Liaison, whatever Air Liaison may be. I expect it means he will be a full colonel in a year. Now you want to make Soames an officer just because *he's* a nasty bit of work. Jolly sort of army we're going to have in two years time when all the shits have got to the top.'

'But Soames won't come back to the Corps if he's commissioned.'

'That's exactly why I'm sending his name up. The same with Hayter, if he gets through his course on whatever it is.'

How many of your men do you know by name and what do you know of their characters?

Guy knew every name. The difficulty was to identify them. Each had three faces: an inhuman and rather hostile mask when he stood at attention; a vivacious and variable expression, mostly clownish, sometimes furious, sometimes heartsore, as he saw the men amongst themselves off duty or at stand-easies, going to the N.A.A.F.I. or arguing in the company lines; and thirdly a guarded but on the whole amiable grin when he spoke to them personally at these times or at stand-easies. Most English gentlemen at this time believed that they had a particular aptitude for endearing themselves to the lower classes. Guy was not troubled by this illusion, but he believed he was rather liked by these particular thirty men. He did not greatly care. He liked them. He wished them well. He did well by them so far as his limited knowledge of 'the ropes' allowed. He was perfectly ready, should need arise, to sacrifice himself for them – throw himself on a grenade, give away the last drop of water – anything like that. But he did not distinguish between them as human beings, any more or less than he did between his brother officers; he preferred Major Erskine to the young man, Jervis, with whom he shared a tent; he nursed a respect and slight suspicion for de Souza. For his platoon and company and battalion and for all Halberdiers everywhere he had a warmer sentiment than for anyone out-side his family. It was not much but it was something to thank God for.

And at the very opening of this heterogeneous catechism stood the question that was quintessential to his very presence among those unchosen companions.

What are we fighting for?

The Training Memorandum mentioned with shame that many private soldiers had been found to entertain hazy ideas on the subject. Could Box-Bender have given a clear answer? Guy wondered. Could Ritchie-Hook? Had he any idea what all this biffing was for? Had General Ironside himself?

Guy believed he knew something of this matter that was hidden from the mighty.

England had declared war to defend the independence of Poland. Now that country had quite disappeared and the two strongest states in the world guaranteed her extinction. Now General Paget was at Lillehammer and it was announced that all was going well. Guy knew things were going badly. They had no well-informed friends, here in Penkirk, they had access to no intelligence files, but the smell of failure had been borne to them from Norway on the east wind.

But Guy's spirit was as high as on the day he had bade fare-well to St Roger.

He was a good loser, but he did not believe his country would lose this war; each apparent defeat seemed strangely to sustain it. There was in romance great virtue in unequal odds. There were in morals two requisites for a lawful war, a just cause and the chance of victory. The cause was now, past all question, just. The enemy was exorbitant. His actions in Austria and Bohemia had been defensible. There was even a shadow of plausibility in his quarrel with Poland. But now, however victorious, he was an outlaw. And the more victorious he was the more he drew to himself the enmity of the world and the punishment of God.

Guy thought of this as he lay in his tent that night. He clasped Gervase's medal as he said his night prayers. And, just before sleep, came a personal comforting thought. However inconvenient it was for the Scandinavians to have Germans there, it was very nice for the Halberdiers. They had been assigned their special role of Hazardous Offensive Operations, but until last month there seemed little opportunity for playing it. Now a whole new coastline was open for biffing.

8

ON the day that Mr Churchill became Prime Minister, Apthorpe was promoted Captain.

He had been forewarned by the adjutant and his servant was standing by in the Headquarter Company's office. As the first note of Battalion orders sounded from the orderly-room – before the cyclostyled sheets announcing the appointment had been collected, much less distributed – Apthorpe's pips were up. The rest of the forenoon passed in solemn ecstasy. He sauntered round the transport lines, called on the medical officer, ostensibly to inquire about a tonic he thought he needed, he flushed the quartermaster drinking tea in his store, but no one seemed to notice the new constellation. He was content to bide.

At midday the companies could be heard marching into camp from their training areas and dismissing. Apthorpe was waiting serenely in the mess-tent to welcome his brother officers.

'Ah, Crouchback, what can I offer you to drink?'

Guy was surprised, for Apthorpe had almost ceased to speak to him in the last few weeks.

'Oh, that's very nice of you. I've marched miles this morning. Can I have a glass of beer?'

'And you Jervis? de Souza?'

This was more surprising still, since Apthorpe had never at any stage of incubation spoken to de Souza or Jervis.

'Hayter, old man, what's yours?'

Hayter said: 'What's this? A birthday?'

'I understand it's usual in the Halberdiers to stand drinks on these occasions.'

'What occasions?'

It was unfortunate that he had chosen Hayter. Hayter thought nothing of temporary officers and was himself still a lieutenant.

'Good God,' said Hayter. 'You don't mean to say they've made you a captain?'

'With effect from April 1st,' said Apthorpe with dignity.

'Quite a suitable date. Still I don't mind taking a pink gin off you.'

There were moments, as in the gym barracks, when Apthorpe rose above the ridiculous. This was one of them.

'Give these young officers what they require, Crock,' he said and royally turned to new arrivals at the bar: 'Draw up, Adj. Drinks are on me. Colonel, I hope you'll join us.'

The mess-tent was filled for luncheon. Apthorpe dispensed hospitality. No one but Hayter much grudged him his elevation.

There was less interest in the change of Prime Ministers. Politics were considered an unsoldierly topic among the Halberdiers. There had been some rejoicing and dispute at Mr Hore-Belisha's fall in the winter. Since then Guy had not heard a politician's name mentioned. Some of Mr Churchill's broadcasts had been played on the mess wireless-set. Guy had found them painfully boastful and they had, most of them, been immediately followed by the news of some disaster, as though in retribution from the God of Kipling's *Recessional*.

Guy knew of Mr Churchill only as a professional politician, a master of sham-Augustan prose, a Zionist, an advocate of the Popular Front in Europe, an associate of the press-lords and of Lloyd George. He was asked:

'Uncle, what sort of fellow is this Winston Churchill?'

'Like Hore-Belisha except that for some reason his hats are thought to be funny.'

'Well, I suppose they had to make someone carry the can after the balls-up in Norway.'

'Yes.'

'He can't be much worse than the other fellow?'

'Better, if anything.'

Here Major Erskine leant across the table.

'Churchill is about the only man who may save us from losing this war,' he said.

It was the first time that Guy had heard a Halberdier suggest that any result, other than complete victory, was possible. They had had a lecture, it is true, from an officer lately returned from Norway, who had spoken frankly about the incompetent loading of ships, the disconcerting effect of dive-bombing, the activities of organized traitors and such matters. He had even hinted at the inferior fighting qualities of British troops. But he had made little impression. Halberdiers always assumed that 'the Staff' and 'the Q side' were useless, that all other regiments were scarcely worthy of the name of soldier, that foreigners let one down. Naturally things were going badly in the absence of the Halberdiers. No one thought of losing the war.

Apthorpe's promotion was a matter of more immediate interest.

Brigadier Ritchie-Hook could disappear behind his Victorian battlements, and lose his personality. Not so Apthorpe. That afternoon, the day of his promotion, Guy happened to pass him on the battalion parade ground and with one of those pathetic spasms of fourth-form fun that came easily in military life, Guy solemnly saluted him. Apthorpe as solemnly returned the attention. He was a little unsteady on his pins after the morning's celebrations, his face was oddly grave, but the incident passed off cheerfully.

Later that evening, just before dark, they met again. Apthorpe had evidently stuck close to the bottle, and was now in the state he called 'merry' – a state recognizable by his air of preternatural solemnity. As he approached, Guy with amazement saw him go through all the motions they used to practise in barracks before passing a senior officer. He put his stick under his left arm, he swung his right with exaggerated zest and he fixed his glassy eyes straight before him. Guy walked on with a genial 'Evening, Captain' and too late noticed that Apthorpe's hand was shoulder high, in the rudimentary stage of a salute. The hand fell, the eyes fixed themselves far ahead on the other side of the valley and Apthorpe passed, stumbling over a night bucket.

Somehow the memory of Guy's first, jocular salute had fixed itself indelibly in Apthorpe's mind; it survived his evening's merriment. Next day he was out of the clouds, slightly disturbed internally, but with a new *idée fixe*.

Before the first parade he said to Guy: 'I say, old man, I'd greatly appreciate it if you'd salute me when we pass one another in the camp area.'

'What on earth for?'

'Well, I salute Major Trench.'

'Of course you do.'

'The difference between him and me is only the same as between you and me if you see what I mean.'

'My dear fellow, it was all explained to us when we first joined, whom we saluted and when.'

'Yes, but don't you see that I am an exceptional case. There is no precedent for *me* in regimental customs. We all started equal not so long ago. I happen to have forged ahead a bit so naturally I have to do more to assert my authority than if I had years of seniority. Please, Crouchback, salute me. I am asking you as a friend.'

'I'm sorry, Apthorpe, I simply can't. I should feel such an ass.'

'Well, anyway, you might tell the other chaps.'

'You really mean that? You've thought the matter out?'

'I've thought of nothing else.'

'All right, Apthorpe, I'll tell them.'

'I can't order them, of course. Just say it is my wish.'

Apthorpe's 'wish' became quickly known and for some days he suffered a concerted persecution. He could always be seen approaching yards off, tensely self-conscious preparing for he knew not what. Sometimes his junior officers would salute him with unsmiling correctness; sometimes they would stroll past ignoring him; sometimes they would give a little flick of the cap and say: 'Hello, Uncle.'

The cruellest technique was devised by de Souza. On sighting Apthorpe he would put his stick under his left arm and march at attention gazing straight into Apthorpe's eyes with an expression of awe. Then two paces away he would suddenly relax, switch negligently at a weed, or on one occasion, drop suddenly on one knee and, still fixing the captain with his worshipping stare, fiddle with a bootlace.

'You know you'll drive that unhappy man stark mad,' said Guy to him.

'I think I shall, Uncle; I honestly think I shall.'

The fun came to an end one evening when Colonel Tickeridge summoned Guy to the orderly room.

'Sit down, Guy. I want to speak to you unofficially. I'm getting worried about Apthorpe. Frankly, is he quite right in the head?'

'He has his peculiarities, Colonel. I don't think he's likely to do anything dangerous.'

'I hope you're right. I'm getting the most extraordinary report of him from all sides.'

'He had a rather nasty accident the morning we left Southsand.'

'Yes, I heard about it. Surely that could not have affected his *head*? Let me tell you his latest. He's just formed up and asked me to put it in orders that the junior officers should salute him. That's not quite normal you'll admit.'

'No, Colonel.'

'Either that, he says, or will I put it in orders that you're *not* to salute him. That's not normal either. What exactly has been going on?'

'Well, I think he's been ragged a bit.'

'I'm bloody sure he has and it's gone far enough. Just pass it round that it's got to stop. You may find yourself in his shoes before long. Then you'll find you have plenty on your hands without being ragged by a lot of young asses.'

This happened, though the news did not reach Penkirk for some time, on the day when the Germans crossed the Meuse.

9

GUY passed the colonel's order round the mess and the affair, which de Souza preciously dubbed 'The Matter of the

Captain's Salutation', came to an abrupt end. But in other ways, too, Apthorpe had been showing marked abnormality.

There was the question of the Castle. From the first day of his appointment, while still a lieutenant, Apthorpe took to dropping in there two or three times a week without ostensible cause, at the eleven-o'clock break, when tea was drunk in various ante-rooms and dens. Apthorpe would join the staff-captain and his peers and they, supposing he was on an errand from his battalion, entertained him. In this way he heard much 'shop' and was often able to surprise the adjutant with prior information on matters of minor policy. When tea was over and the staff went back to their rooms Apthorpe would saunter into the chief clerk's room and say: 'Anything special today about the Second Battalion, Staff?' After the third of these visits the sergeant clerk reported to the brigade major and asked whether these inquiries were authorized. The result was an order reminding all officers that they must not approach Brigade Headquarters except through the proper channels.

When this was posted Apthorpe said to the adjutant: 'I take this to mean that they come to me for permission?'

'For Christ's sake, why to *you*?'

'Well, after all I *am* the Headquarters commander here, am I not?'

'Apthorpe, are you tight?'

'Certainly not.'

'Well, come and see the C.O. about this. He can explain it better than I.'

'Yes, I suppose it *is* rather a nice point.'

It was not often that Colonel Tickeridge 'went off the handle'. That morning the whole camp heard the roars in his orderly room. But Apthorpe emerged as bland as ever.

'My God, Uncle, that was a rocket. We could hear it on the parade ground. What was it about?'

'Just a bit of red tape, old man.'

Since the loss of his thunder-box Apthorpe was impervious to shock.

The army was not then troubled, as it was later, by psychiatrists. Had it been, Apthorpe would no doubt have been lost to the Halberdiers. He remained – to the great comfort of his fellows.

Apthorpe's wildest aberration was his one-man war with the Royal Corps of Signals. This campaign was his predominant obsession during all his difficult days at Penkirk and from it he emerged with the honours of war.

It began by a simple misunderstanding.

Studying his duties by the light of his incandescent lamp, Apthorpe learned that the regimental signallers of his battalion came under his command for administrative purposes.

From the first this statement bulked over-large in Apthorpe's imagination. It was plain to him that this was where he joined, indeed controlled, the battle. There were ten of these signallers on the fateful 1st of April, volunteers for what they had supposed was a light duty, little trained, equipped with nothing but flags. Apthorpe was a man of certain odd accomplishments, among them a mastery of Morse. Accordingly for several days he made these men his special care and spent many chilly hours wagging a flag at them.

Then brigade signals arrived under their own officer, laden with radio telegraphy sets. These were men of the Royal Corps of Signals. By chance they were alloted lines next to the Second Battalion. Their officer was invited to mess with the battalion, rather than at the Castle a mile distant; their quartermaster was instructed to draw rations from the Second Battalion quartermaster. They thus became accidentally, but quite closely, associated with the battalion.

The situation was clear enough to all except Apthorpe, who conceived that they were under his personal command. He was still a lieutenant at this time. The Signals Officer was also a lieutenant, much younger than Apthorpe and younger than his age in looks. His name was Dunn. On his first appearance in the mess Apthorpe took him in charge, introducing him with courtly patronage as 'my latest subaltern'. Dunn did not quite know what to make of this, but since it involved many free drinks and since he was by nature shy to the point of gaucherie, he submitted cheerfully.

Next morning Apthorpe sent an orderly to the brigade signallers' lines.

'Mr Apthorpe's compliments and will Mr Dunn kindly report when his lines are ready for inspection.'

'What inspection? Is the Brigadier coming round? No one told me.'

'No, sir, Mr Apthorpe's inspection.'.

Dunn was a shy man but this was too much for him.

'Tell Mr Apthorpe that when I have finished inspecting my own lines I shall be quite ready to come and inspect Mr Apthorpe's head.'

The Halberdier, a regular, showed no emotion. 'Could I have that message in writing, please, sir?'

'No. On second thoughts I'll see his adjutant.'

This first skirmish was treated lightly and unofficially.

'Don't be an ass, Uncle.'

'But, Adj. it's in my establishment. *Signallers*.'

'Battalion signals, Uncle. Not brigade signals.' Then, speaking as he supposed Apthorpe spoke to his men in Africa: 'No savvy? These boys, Royal Corp of Signals boys. Your boys, Halberdier boys. Damn it, d'you want me to draw you the badges?'

But the adjutant, in his haste, had made things too simple, for in fact the battalion signallers, though Halberdiers for all purposes except signalling, came under the Brigade Signals Officer for training. This fact, Apthorpe could not or would not, and certainly never did, grasp. Whenever Dunn ordered a training exercise, Apthorpe devised camp duties for all his signal section. He did more. He paraded his Halberdiers and told them they were never to accept orders from anyone but himself. The matter was moving up to an official level.

Apthorpe's case, though untenable, was strengthened by the fact that no one liked Dunn. When he formed up at the Second Battalion Orderly Room, the adjutant told him coldly that he was merely a guest in their mess and that for all official purposes he was at the Castle. Any complaints against his hosts should be addressed to the brigade major. Dunn tramped to the Castle and was told by the brigade major to settle the thing sensibly with Colonel Tickeridge. Colonel Tickeridge duly told Apthorpe that his men must work with brigade signals. Apthorpe immediately sent them all away on urgent compassionate leave. Back to the Castle went Dunn, all shyness shed. The Brigadier was then absent on one of his trips to London. The brigade major was the busiest man in Scotland. He said he would raise the matter at the next Battalion Commanders' Conference.

Apthorpe, meanwhile, withdrew his friendship from Dunn, and refused to speak to him. This quarrel in high places quickly spread to the men. There were hard words in the N.A.A.F.I. and between lines. Dunn put six Halberdiers on a charge of prejudicial conduct. In the orderly room they drew on the limitless pool of fellow Halberdiers who were always ready to give false witness in defence of the Corps, and Colonel Tickeridge dismissed the case.

So far it had been a feud of a normal military kind, differing from others only in the fact that Apthorpe had no case at all. In the middle of it he got his captaincy. In Apthorpe's story that event corresponds to Alexander's visit to Siwa. It was an illumination that changed all the colours and shapes about him. Fiends like de Souza lurked in black shadow, but a shining path led upward to the conquest of Dunn.

On the afternoon following the day of his promotion he proceeded to inspect the signallers' lines. Dunn found him there and stood momentarily confounded by what he saw.

It was Apthorpe's old interest, boots. He had found one that was in need of repair, and there he stood in the centre of a curious circle of signalmen, carefully dismembering it with a clasp knife.

'Apart from the quality of the leather,' he was saying, 'this boot is a disgrace to the Service. Look at the stitching. Look how the tongue has been fitted. Look at the construction of the eyeholes. Now in a well-made boot' . . . and he raised his foot placing it where all might admire it, on the nearby gas-detector.

'What the devil are you doing?' asked Dunn.

'Mr Dunn, I think you forget you are addressing a superior officer.'

'What are you doing in my lines?'

'I am verifying my suspicion that your boots are in need of attention.'

Dunn realized that for the moment he was beaten. Nothing short of physical violence would suit the occasion and that way lay endless disasters.

'We can discuss that later. At the moment they ought to be on parade.'

'You mustn't blame your sergeant. He reminded me of that fact more than once. It was I detained them.'

The two officers separated, Dunn to the Castle to lay his case before the brigade major, Apthorpe with a much stranger purpose. He sat down in his company office and penned a challenge to Dunn to meet him, armed with a heliograph, before their men, for a Trial by Combat in proficiency in Morse.

The Brigadier was at the Castle. He had just returned from London on the night train, hag-ridden by the news from France.

The brigade major said: 'I am afraid I've a serious disciplinary problem for you, sir. It will probably involve an Officer's Court Martial.'

'Yes,' said the Brigadier, 'yes.' He was gazing out of the window. His mind was far away, still trying to comprehend the unspeakable truths he had learned in London.

'An officer of the Second Battalion,' continued the brigade major, in rather louder tones, 'has been accused of entering Brigade Headquarters' lines and deliberately destroying the men's boots.'

'Yes,' said the Brigadier. 'Drunk?'

'Sober, sir.'

'Any excuse?'

'He considered the workmanship defective, sir.'

'Yes.'

The Brigadier stared out of the window. The brigade major gave a lucid account of the Dunn-Apthorpe campaign. Presently the Brigadier said:

'Were the boots good enough to run away in?'

'I haven't asked about that yet. It will no doubt come out when the Summary of Evidence is taken.'

'If they're good enough to run away in, they're good enough for our army. Damn it, if they lost their boots, they might have to meet the enemy. It's, as you say, a very serious matter.'

'Then shall I carry on with the preliminaries of a court martial, sir?'

'No. We've no time for that. Do you realize that the whole of our army and the French are on the run leaving everything behind them, half of them without firing à shot? Make these young idiots work together. Lay on a Brigade Exercise for the signallers. Let's see if they can work their instruments with or without boots. That's all that matters.'

So two days later, after feverish work at the Castle and in the orderly rooms, the Halberdier Brigade marched out into the dripping Midlothian countryside.

That day was memorable for Guy as the most futile he had yet spent in the army. His platoon lay on a rain-swept hill-side doing absolutely nothing. They were quite near one of the brigade signalling posts and from it there rose from dawn to noon a monotonous, liturgical incantation: ... 'Hullo Nan, Hullo Nan. Report my signals. Over Hullo Nan, Hullo Nan. Are you hearing me. Over. Hullo King, Hullo King. Are you hearing me. Over. Hullo Nan. Hullo King. Nothing heard. Out. Hullo Able. Hullo Able. Am hearing you strength one, interference five. Out. Hullo all stations. Able. Baker. Charlie. Dog. Easy. Fox. Are you hearing me. Over ...' Throughout the chill forenoon the prayer rose to the disdainful gods.

The men rolled themselves in their anti-gas capes and ate their sodden rations. At length, walking very slowly, a signal-man appeared out of the haze. He was greeted derisively by the platoon. He approached the signal station and from the depths of his clothing produced a damp piece of paper. The corporal brought it to Guy. '*Able Dog Yoke*,' it read. '*Close down RT stop signals will be by runner stop ack.*'

Another two hours passed. Then a 'runner' stumbled up the hill with a message for Guy. '*From OC D Coy to OC 2 pl.*

Exercise terminated. Rally forthwith road junction 643202.'
Guy saw no reason to inform the signallers. He fell in the platoon and marched off, leaving them quite alone where they
had been lying.

'Well,' said Colonel Tickeridge in the mess, 'I've written my
report on today's nonsense. I have recommended that brigade
signals go away and get trained.'

It was generally recognized as being a personal success for
Apthorpe. There had been a general attempt to be pleasant to
him in the last two days since ragging had ceased. That evening he was the centre of hospitality. Next morning two com-
mandeered civilian buses arrived near the Second Battalion
lines. The signallers piled in and drove away.

'Brigade really showed some pace for once,' said de Souza.

The Halberdiers congratulated themselves on a triumph.

But the departure of the signalmen had been ordered the day
before, far away in London, while at Penkirk they were first
erecting their aerials into the rain, and for a reason quite unconnected with the failure of their apparatus.

Had they known it, the Halberdiers would have been even
more jubilant. This was, for them, the start of the war.

10

THIS was Friday; pay day. Every Friday after Pay Parade
Major Erskine lectured his company on the progress of the war.
Lately there had been much detail of 'dents' and 'bulges' in the
Allied line, of 'armour breaking through and fanning out', of
'pincers' and 'pockets'. The exposition was lucid and grave but
most men's thoughts were on the week-end leave which began
when he ceased speaking.

This Friday was different. An hour after the signalmen left
an order was issued cancelling all leave and Major Erskine had
an attentive and resentful audience. He said:

'I am sorry that your leave has been cancelled. This is not
an order that applies only to us. All leave has been stopped
throughout the Home Forces. You may form your own conclu-

sion that there is a state of unusual danger. This morning, as you know, the brigade signallers were withdrawn. Some of you may think this was a consequence of yesterday's unsuccessful exercise. It was not. This afternoon we shall lose all our transport and carriers. The reason is this. We are not, as you know, fully equipped or trained. All specialists and all equipment is needed at once in France. That may give you some further idea of the seriousness of the situation there.'

He continued with his customary explanation of dents and bulges and of armour breaking through and fanning out. For the first time these things seemed to his hearers to have become a force in their own lives.

That evening a report, emanating from the clerks, filled the camp that the brigade was going immediately to the Orkneys. The Brigadier was known to be back in London and the Castle to be surrounded by cars from the Scottish Command.

Next day Guy's servant called him with the words: 'Sounds like I shan't be doing this many more days, sir.'

Halberdier Glass was a regular soldier. Most of the conscripts had been shy of volunteering as batmen, holding that 'that wasn't what they'd joined the bloody army for'. Old soldiers knew that menial duties brought numerous comforts and privileges, and competed for the job. Halberdier Glass was a surly man who liked to call his master with bad news. 'Two of our platoon overstayed their leave this morning'; 'Major Trench made a visit to the lines last night. Went on something awful about the bread in the swill tubs'; 'Corporal Hill shot himself just down by the bridge. They're bringing the body in now'; some small titbit of gossip of the kind calculated to make Guy start the day in low spirits. But this announcement was more serious.

'What d'you mean, Glass?'

'Well, that's the buzz, sir. Jackson got it in the sergeants' mess last night.'

'What's happening?'

'All regulars standing by to move, sir. Nothing said about the National Service men.'

When Guy reached the mess-tent everyone was talking about

this rumour. Guy asked Major Erskine: 'Is there anything in it, sir?'

Major Erskine answered: 'You'll hear soon enough. The C.O. wants all officers in here at eight-thirty.'

The men were set to Physical Training and fatigue duties under their non-commissioned officers and the officers duly assembled. In every Halberdier battalion at that moment the Commanding Officers were breaking bad news, each in his way. Colonel Tickeridge said:

'What I have to say is most unpleasant for most of you. In an hour's time I shall be telling the men. It is all the harder for me to tell you because, for myself, I cannot help being glad. I had hoped we should have gone into action together. That is what we have all been working for. I think we should have given a good account of ourselves. But you know as well as I do that we aren't ready. Things are pretty sticky in France, stickier than most of you realize. Fully trained reinforcements are needed at once to make a decisive counter-attack. It has therefore been decided to send a regular battalion of Halberdiers to France *now*. I expect you can guess who will lead us. The Brigadier has been in London two days and has persuaded them to let him go down a step and command a battalion. I am very proud to say he's picked me to go down a step too and join him as second-in-command. We are taking most of the regular officers and other ranks now in camp. Those of you who are being left behind will naturally want to know what is to become of you. That, I am afraid, I can't answer. You realize, of course, that you will be enormously weakened, particularly in senior NCOs. You also realize that for the moment at any rate the brigade ceases to exist as a separate formation with a special role. It's just one of those things you have to accept in army life. You may be sure that the Captain-Commandant will do all he can to see that you keep your identity as Halberdiers and don't get pushed about too much. But at a time of national danger even regimental tradition has to go by the board. If I knew what was going to happen to you, I'd tell you. I hope we all join up together one day. Don't count on it or feel a grievance if you find yourselves attached elsewhere. Just show the Halberdier spirit wherever you are. Your duty now, as always, is to your men. Don't let their *morale* drop. Get some football going. Organize concerts and housey-housey. All ranks are confined to camp until further notice.'

The temporary officers left the tent, went out into the brilliant sunshine, in deep gloom.

Apthorpe's comment was: 'Wheels within wheels, old man. It's all the work of these signallers.'

Later the battalion paraded. Colonel (now Major) Tickeridge made much the same speech as he had made to the officers, but that simple man contrived to give a slightly different impression. They would all join up together again soon, he seemed to say; the Expeditionary Battalion was merely an advance party. They would all be united for the final biff.

In these conditions Guy at last got command of a company. Chaos prevailed. The order was always to stand by for orders. The regulars who were leaving attended the medical officers for final examination. Venerable figures emerged from their places of concealment, were pronounced unfit, and sent back to store. The conscripts played football and under the chaplain's aegis sang *'We'll hang out the washing on the Siegfried Line'*.

In order, it was supposed, to avoid confusion, the remaining battalions were named X and Y. Guy sat in a tent in X Battalion lines attended by a sergeant major with fallen arches. All through the afternoon he received requests for week-end leave on urgent compassionate grounds from men whom neither he nor his decrepit assistant had ever seen before. 'My wife's expecting, sir', 'My brother's on embarkation leave, sir', 'Trouble at home, sir', 'My mother's been evacuated, sir'.

'We know nothing about them, sir,' said the sergeant major. 'If you give in to one you'll only have trouble.'

Guy miserably refused them all.

It was his first experience of that common military situation, 'a general flap'.

Not until 'Retreat' had been sounded, did a move-order arrive for the Expeditionary Battalion.

At reveille that Sunday morning X and Y Battalions turned

out to see the battalion off. The call for breakfast sounded and they dispersed. At length a fleet of buses appeared up the valley. The battalion embussed. The remnants of the brigade cheered as they left and then turned back to the part-deserted camp and an empty day.

Chaos remained, without animation. Guy's commander in X Battalion was a major whom he did not know. At this season of prodigies Apthorpe emerged as second-in-command of Y Battalion with Sarum-Smith as his adjutant.

The week-end yawned before them.

On Sunday mornings at Penkirk a priest came out from the town and said mass at the Castle. He came that Sunday too, untroubled by the 'flap', and for three-quarters of an hour all was peace.

When Guy returned he was asked: 'You didn't by any chance pick up any orders at the Castle?'

'Not a word. Everything seemed dead quiet.'

'I expect everyone has forgotten about us. The best thing would be to send everyone on long leave.'

The company office, all company offices, were besieged with applications for leave. The remnant who were, for want of another name, still called 'Brigade Headquarters' were standing by for orders.

Rumours spread everywhere that they were to return to the Barracks and the Depot; that they were to be broken up and sent to Infantry Training Centres; that they were to be brigaded with a Highland regiment and sent to guard the docks; that they were to be transformed into Anti-Aircraft units. The men kicked footballs about and played mouth-organs. Not for the first time Guy was awed by their huge patience.

Halberdier Glass, who, despite his prognostications, had contrived to remain with Guy, reported these 'buzzes' to him at intervals throughout the day.

At last, late at night, orders were issued.

They were preposterous.

An enemy landing by parachute was imminent in the neighbourhood of Penkirk. All ranks were confined to camp. Each battalion was to keep a company, night and day, in immediate readiness to repel the attack. These would sleep in their boots, their rifles beside them with charged magazines; they would stand to at dusk, at dawn and once during the night. Guards were doubled. A platoon would ceaselessly patrol the perimeter of the camp. Other platoons would stop all traffic, day and night, on all roads within a five-mile radius and examine civilian identity cards. All officers would carry loaded revolvers, anti-gas capes, steel helmets and maps at all hours.

'I have *not* received these orders,' said the unknown major, giving his first, indeed his only, hint of character. 'I'll have them brought with my tea tomorrow morning. If Germans land tonight they will have no opposition from X Battalion. That, I think, is called the Nelson touch.'

Monday passed in the defence of Penkirk and two cowmen were arrested whose strong Scottish accents gave colour to the suspicion that they were conversing in German.

It was fine parachuting weather. The storm had quite passed and premature summer bathed the valley. On Monday night Guy's company was on emergency duty. He had an outlying patrol on the hill above the camp which he visited at midnight. Later he sat gazing into the stars, with the men bivouacked round him. The regular battalion was probably in France, by now, he reflected; perhaps in the battle. Halberdier Glass had it for certain that they were in Boulogne. Suddenly from below came the sound of bugles and whistles. The platoon doubled back and found the whole camp astir. Apthorpe had distinctly seen a parachute land a few fields distant. Patrols, pickets and duty-companies rushed to the scene. Two or three rounds were waywardly fired.

'They always bury their parachutes,' said Apthorpe. 'Look for newly dug ground.'

All night they trampled down the young wheat until at reveille they handed over the duty to their reliefs. Several bus-loads of kilted soldiers had meanwhile arrived from a neighbouring camp. These were seasoned men who were sceptical of Apthorpe's vision. An indignant farmer spent most of the morning at the Castle computing the damage done him.

On Wednesday a move-order arrived. X and Y Battalions were to stand by at two hours' notice. Late that evening buses again appeared. There was no 'unconsumed portion of the day's ration' to encumber them. Halberdier Glass reported that the whole brigade staff were moving too.

'Iceland,' he said; 'that's where we're off to. I got it straight from the Castle.'

Guy asked his Commanding Officer where they were going.

'Aldershot Area. No information about what happens when we get there. What does it sound like to you?'

'Nothing.'

'It doesn't sound like a Halberdier establishment, does it? If you want to know what I think it sounds like, it sounds like Infantry Training Centres. I don't suppose *they* sound like anything to you?'

'Not much.'

'They sound like hell on earth to me. You fellows have had a raw deal. You've been in the Halberdiers, you've lived with us and been one of us. Now you'll probably find yourself in the Beds and Herts or the Black Watch. But you've only had six months of us. Look at me. God knows when I shall get back to the Corps, and it's been my whole life. All the fellows I entered with are at Boulogne now. D'you know why I'm left behind? One bad mark, my second year as a subaltern. That's the army all over. One bad mark follows you wherever you go till you die.'

'The battalion is definitely in Boulogne, sir?' asked Guy, anxious to stem these confidences.

'Definitely. And there's the hell of a fight going on there now, from all I hear.'

They were driven to Edinburgh and put into a lightless train. Guy shared a compartment with a subaltern he hardly knew. Almost at once the fatigue of the last days overcame him. He slept long and heavily, not waking until another brilliant day was creeping through the blackout. He raised a blind. They were still in Edinburgh station.

There was no water on that train and all the doors were locked. But Halberdier Glass appeared, mysteriously provided with a jug of shaving water and a cup of tea, carried Guy's belt into the corridor and began polishing. Presently they started and very slowly jolted their way south.

At Crewe the train stopped for an hour. Base little men with bands on their arms trotted about the platform bearing lists. Then a hand-wagon from Movement Control deposited a tank of warm cocoa in each coach, some tins of bully beef and a number of cardboard packets of sliced bread.

The journey continued. Guy could hear mouth-organs and singing above the roll of the wheels. He had nothing to read. The young officer opposite him whistled when he was awake, but mostly he slept.

Another stop. Another night. Another dawn. They were travelling now through an area of red brick and carefully kept little gardens. They passed a red London omnibus.

'This is Woking,' said his companion.

Soon the train stopped.

'Brookwood,' said the knowledgeable subaltern.

There was a Railway Transport Officer on the platform with lists. The Commander of X Battalion, redolent of anonymity, came down the platform peering anxiously through the steamy windows, looking for his officers.

'Crouchback,' he said. 'Davidson. We're getting out here. Fall in by companies in the station yard. Tell off a platoon to handle stores. Call the roll and inspect the men. They can't shave, of course, but see they are respectable otherwise. We've two miles march to camp.'

Somehow the dishevelled, comatose figures transformed themselves into Halberdiers. No one seemed lost. Everyone had a rifle. The kit-bags came bouncing out.

X Battalion moved off first. Guy marched at the head of his company, following the company in front, through the suburban lanes and delicious morning air. Presently they came to a field gate and the familiar smell of Soyer stoves. He followed the company commander in front in calling his men to attention. He heard the command ahead: 'Eyes left.' His turn came. He gave the command, saluting, and saw a Halberdier guard fallen in at the guard-house.

He gave the command: 'C Company, eyes front.'

From the distance of a hundred marching men he heard a head: 'B Company, eyes right.'

What was it this time? he wondered.

'C Company, eyes right.'

He swung his head and found himself gazing straight into a single, glittering eye.

It was Ritchie-Hook.

A guide had been posted to lead the battalion to their parade ground. They formed close column of companies, ordered arms, stood easy. Brigadier Ritchie-Hook was standing beside the major.

'Glad to see you all again,' he roared. 'I expect you want breakfast. Get cleaned up first. You are all confined to camp. We're at two hours' notice to go overseas.'

The major saluted and turned to face the battalion he had so briefly dominated.

'For the time being this is our battalion area.' He said: 'I gather it won't be long. Guides will show you where to clean up. Battalion, shun. Slope arms. Fall out the officers.'

Guy marched forward, ranged himself with the other officers, saluted and marched off the parade ground. The battalion was dismissed. He heard the non-commissioned officers break out into a babble of orders. He was dazed. So was the major with the black mark against him.

'What does it mean, sir?'

'I only know what the Brigadier said as we marched in. Apparently there's a complete as-you-were. He's been fighting the War Office for days to keep the brigade in existence. As usual, he's won. That's all there is to it.'

'Does that mean things are better in France?'

'No. They're so bloody well worse that the Brigadier has got us all accepted as fully trained and ready for action.'

'D'you mean we're off to France too?'

'I shouldn't get too excited about that if I were you. The Regular Battalion got turned off their ship just as they were sailing. I rather feel in my bones that it may be some time yet before we go to France. There's been a lot happening over there while we were hunting parachutists in Scotland. It appears, among other things, that the Germans took Boulogne yesterday.'

BOOK THREE

Apthorpe Immolatus

1

NINE weeks of 'flap', of alternating chaos and order.

The Halberdiers were far from the battle, out of sight and hearing, but delicate nerves stretched to them from the front where the Allied armies were falling apart; each new shock carried its small painful agitation to the extremities. Chaos came from without in sudden, unexplained commands and cancellations; order grew from within as company, battalion and brigade each rearranged itself for the new unexpected task. They were so busy in those weeks with their own home-building, repairing, rearranging, improvising, that the great storm that was shaking the world passed overhead unnoticed until the crash of a bough set all the hidden roots again vibrating.

First, the task was Calais. No secret was made of their destination. Maps of that *terra incognita* were issued and Guy studied the street names, the approaches, the surrounding topography of the town he had crossed countless times, settling down to an aperitif in the Gare Maritime, glancing idly at the passing roofs from the windows of the restaurant-car; windy town of Mary Tudor, and Beau Brummel, and Rodin's Burghers; the most frequented, least known town in all the continent of Europe. There, perhaps, he would leave his bones.

But it was only at night that there was time for study or speculation. The days were spent in ceaseless, ant-like business. In the move from Penkirk much had been lost, objects such as anti-tank rifles and aiming stands which no man could covet or conceal; among them Hayter, who went on his course of Air Liaison and was not seen again among the Halberdiers. Various regular officers, too, had proved medically unfit and left for Barracks or the Training Depot. Guy found himself

back in the Second Battalion and still in command of a company.

It was far different from 'taking over' in normal conditions.
When Ritchie-Hook spoke of his brigade as being at two
hours' readiness to move into action, he was, indeed, 'shooting
a line'. It was two days before it could take over its routine
duties in the Area. These were arduous, for parachutists were
hourly expected at Aldershot as at Penkirk. Standing Orders
kept almost every man on duty every hour of the day. And
first the men had to be collected. None had deserted but most
were lost.

'You don't know what your battalion was?'

'First it was one and then another, sir.'

'Well, which was the first?'

'Can't say, sir.'

'Do you know who commanded it?'

'Oh yes, sir. C.S.M. Rawkes.'

Few of the conscripts knew the names of their officers.

When they joined, Rawkes had said: 'I am Company Sergeant-Major Rawkes. Take a good look so you'll know me
again. I'm here to help you if you behave yourselves right. Or
I'm here to make your life hell if you don't. It's for you to
choose.'

They remembered that. Rawkes drew up the leave roster
and detailed the fatigues. Officers, for men who had not yet
been in battle, were as indistinguishable as Chinese. Few men,
regular or conscript, had associations beyond their company.
They knew of the Earl of Essex's Honourable Company of
Free Halberdiers, they were proud to be dubbed 'Copper
Heels' and 'Applejacks', but the brigade was a complex and
remote conception. They did not know where the biffs came
from; they were one of the hindmost wagons in a shunting
train. A Kingdom was lost in Europe and somewhere in the
Home Counties a Halberdier found himself with his leave
stopped, manhandling stores for another move.

Guy in D Company was short of a second-in-command and
a platoon commander, but he had Sergeant Major Rawkes and
Quartermaster-Sergeant Yorke, both elderly, experienced and,

above all, calm assistants. Ten men were unaccounted for; one man had broken camp; the company roll had been sent to Records; G.1098 Stores were arriving.

'Carry on Sergeant Major.' 'Carry on, Colour Sergeant.' And they carried on.

Guy felt giddy but protected, as though the victim of an accident, dozing in bed, scarcely aware of how he had got there. Instead of medicine and grapes they brought him at regular intervals sheafs of paper that required his signature. A great forefinger, capped by what looked like a toe-nail, would point out the place for his name. He felt like a constitutional monarch of tender years, living in the shadow of world-respected, inherited councillors-of-state. He felt like a confidence trickster when at last, at noon the second day, he reported D Company as all present and correct.

'Good work, Uncle,' said Colonel Tickeridge. 'You're the first to report in.'

'The senior NCOs really did everything, sir.'

'Of course they did. You don't have to tell me that. But you'll have to take all the rockets when things go wrong, whether it's your fault or not. So take the occasional dewdrop in the same spirit.'

Guy was a little shy of giving orders to the two platoon commanders who had so lately been his fellows. They took them with perfect correctitude. Only when he said: 'Any questions?' de Souza's drawl would sometimes break in with: 'I don't quite understand the *purpose* of the order. What exactly are we looking for, when we stop civilian cars and ask for their identity cards?'

'Fifth columnists, I understand.'

'But, surely, they would have identity cards? They were issued compulsorily, you know, last year. I tried to refuse mine but the policeman positively pressed it on me.'

Or: 'Could you please explain why we have to have both a lying-in fire-picket *and* an anti-parachute platoon? I mean to say if I was a parachutist and I saw all the gorse on fire underneath I should take jolly good care to jump somewhere else.'

'Damn it, I didn't invent these orders. I'm just passing them on.'

'Yes, I know that. I just wondered if they make any sense to you. They don't to me.'

But whether orders made sense or not de Souza could be trusted to carry them out. Indeed he seemed to find a curious private pleasure in doing something he knew to be absurd, with minute efficiency. The other officer, Jervis, needed constant supervision.

The sun blazed down, withering the turf until it was slippery as a dance-floor and starting fires in the surrounding scrub. Routine was resumed. On the fourth evening of his command, Guy marched his company at nightfall into the training area where the place names are incongruously taken from Central Africa, the memorial to a long-departed explorer; 'the heart of the Apthorpe country' as de Souza called it. They performed an exercise of 'company in the attack', became entirely intermixed, extricated themselves and bivouacked under the stars. A warm night, smelling of dry furze. Guy made a round of the sentries and then lay awake. Dawn came quickly, bringing momentary beauty even to that sorry countryside. They fell in and marched back to camp. Rather light-headed after his sleepless night Guy marched in front beside de Souza. From behind them came the songs: 'Roll out the barrel'; 'There are rats, rats, rats as big as cats in the quartermaster's store'; 'We'll hang out the washing on the Siegfried Line'.

'That sounds a little out of date at the moment,' said Guy.

'Do you know what it always makes me think of, Uncle? A drawing of the last war, in one of the galleries, of barbed wire and a corpse hanging across it like a scarecrow. Not a very good drawing. I forget who did it. A sort of sham Goya.'

'I don't think the men really like it. They hear it at Ensa concerts and pick it up. I suppose as the war goes on, some good songs will grow out of it, as they did last time.'

'Somehow I rather doubt it,' said de Souza. 'There's probably a department of martial music in the Ministry of Information. Last-war songs were all eminently lacking in what's called morale-building qualities. "We're here because we're here, because we're here, because we're here", and "Take me back to dear old Blighty", "Nobody knows how bored we are and nobody seems to care". Not at all the kind of thing that would get official approval today. This war has begun in darkness and it will end in silence.'

'Do you say these things simply to depress me, Frank?'

'No, Uncle, simply to cheer myself up.'

When they reached camp, they found all the evidences of another 'flap'.

'Report at once to the orderly-room, sir.'

Guy found the battalion clerk and Sarum-Smith packing papers; the adjutant, telephoning, waved him into the presence of Colonel Tickeridge.

'What the devil do you mean by taking your company out at night without establishing a signal link with Headquarters? Do you realize that if it wasn't for Movement Control having made their usual balls-up, the whole brigade would have upsticked and off and you'd have found the whole camp empty and bloody well serve you right? Don't you know that any training scheme has to be sent in to the adjutant with full map references?'

Guy had done this. Sanders was out at the time and he had given it to Sarum-Smith. He said nothing.

'Nothing to say?'

'I'm sorry, sir.'

'Well, see that D Company is ready to move by twelve hundred hours.'

'Very good, sir. May we know where we're going?'

'Embarking at Pembroke Dock.'

'For Calais, sir?'

'That's about the wettest question I've ever heard asked. Don't you even follow the news?'

'Not last night or this morning, sir.'

'Well, they've chucked in at Calais. Now go back to your company and get a move on.'

'Very good, sir.'

As he returned to his lines he remembered that, when last he heard, Tony Box-Bender's regiment was at Calais.

2

FOR a fortnight the Halberdier Brigade got no mail. When Guy at length heard news of Tony it was in two letters from his father written at an interval of ten days.

> Marine Hotel, Matchet,
> 2nd June

My dear Guy,

I do not know where you are and I suppose you are not allowed to tell me, but I hope this letter will reach you wherever you are to tell you that you are always in my thoughts and prayers.

You may have heard that Tony was at Calais and that none of them came back. He is posted as missing. Angela has made up her mind he is a prisoner but I think you and I know him and his regiment too well to think of them giving themselves up.

He was always a good and happy boy and I could not ask a better death for anyone I loved. It is the *bona mors* for which we pray.

If you get this, write to Angela.

> Ever your affec. father,
> G. Crouchback.

> Marine Hotel, Matchet,
> 12th June

My dear Guy,

I know you would have written to me if you could.

Have you heard the news of Tony? He is a prisoner and Angela, naturally I suppose, is elated simply that he is alive. It is God's will for the boy but I cannot rejoice. Everything points to a long war – longer perhaps than the last. It is a terrible experience for someone of Tony's age to spend years in idleness, cut off from his own people – one full of temptation.

It was not the fault of the garrison that they surrendered. They were ordered to do so from higher up.

Well, now our country is quite alone and I feel that that is good for us. An Englishman is at his best with his back to the wall and often in the past we have had quarrels with our allies which I believe were our own fault.

And last Tuesday was Ivo's anniversary, so that he has been much in my thoughts.

I am not quite useless yet. A boys' preparatory school (Catholic) has moved here from the East Coast. I can't remember whether I told you. A charming headmaster and his wife stayed here while they moved in. They were very short of masters and to my great surprise and delight they asked me to take a form for them. The boys are very good and I even get paid! which is a help as they have had to put their prices up in the hotel. It has been interesting brushing up my rusty Greek.

Ever your affec. father,
G. Crouchback.

These letters arrived together on the day when the Germans marched into Paris. Guy and his company were then quartered in a seaside hotel in Cornwall.

Much had happened since they left Aldershot eighteen days before. For those who followed events and thought about the future, the world's foundations seemed to shake. For the Halberdiers it was one damned thing after another. An urgent order came through Area Headquarters on the morning of their departure that the men were to be fortified for bad news. It was bad news enough that they were moving to Wales. They embarked in three ancient heterogeneous merchantmen, and hung hammocks in their dusty holds. They ate hard tack. During the warm night they lay anywhere about the decks. Steam was up; all communication with the shore forbidden.

Colonel Tickeridge said: 'I have no idea where we are going. I had a talk with the E.S.O. He seemed surprised we were here at all.'

Next morning they disembarked and saw the three ships sail away empty. The brigade split up and went into billets by battalions in neighbouring market towns, in shops and warehouses that had stood empty for nine years since the slump. The units and sub-units began home-building, training, playing cricket.

Then the brigade reassembled at the docks, re-embarked in the same ships, shabbier still now, for in the meantime they had been ferrying a broken army across the Channel from Dunkirk. There was a battery of Dutch gunners, without their guns, ensconced in one of them. Somehow they had got on board at Dunkirk. No one seemed to have a place for them in England. There they remained, sad and stolid and very polite.

The ships resembled blocks of slum tenements. Guy was occupied mainly in the effort of keeping his stores and men together. They disembarked for an hour's Physical Training, a company at a time. For the rest of the day they sat on their kitbags. A staff officer arrived from far away and produced a proclamation which was to be read to all troops, contradicting reports spread by the enemy, that the Air Force had been idle at Dunkirk. If British planes had not been noticed there, it was because they were busy on the enemy's lines of communication. The Halberdiers were more interested in the rumour that a German army had landed in Limerick and that their own role was to dislodge it.

'Hadn't we better dispel that rumour, sir?'

'No,' said Colonel Tickeridge. 'It's quite true. Not that the Germans are there yet. But our little operation is to meet them there if they do land.'

'Just us?'

'Just us,' said Colonel Tickeridge. 'So far as anyone seems to know – except, of course, for our Dutch chums.'

They were at two hours' notice to sail. After two days orders were relaxed to allow troops in formed bodies ashore for training and recreation. They had to remain within sight of the mast of their ship, which would hoist a flag to summon them in case of immediate sailing orders.

Colonel Tickeridge had an officers' conference in the saloon where he explained the details of the Limerick campaign. The Germans were expected with a fully equipped mechanized corps and ample air support and probably some help from the natives. The Halberdier Brigade would hold them off as long as possible.

'As to how long that will be,' said Colonel Tickeridge, 'your guess is as good as mine.'

Provided with a map of Limerick and this depressing intelligence, Guy returned to his huddled company.

'Halberdier Shanks, sir, has put in a request for leave,' said Rawkes.

'But he must know it's no use.'

'Urgent compassionate grounds, sir.'

'What are they, Sergeant-Major?'

'Won't say, sir. Insists, as his right, on seeing the Company Commander in private, sir.'

'Very well. He's a good man, isn't he?'

'One of the best, sir. That is to say of the National Service men.'

Halberdier Shanks was marched up. Guy knew him well, a handsome, capable, willing man.

'Well, Shanks, what is the trouble?'

'Please, sir, it's the competition. I *must* be at Blackpool to-morrow night. I've promised. My girl will never forgive me if I'm not.'

'Competition for what, Shanks?'

'The slow valse, sir. We've practised together three years now. We won at Salford last year. We'll win at Blackpool, sir. I know we will. And I'll be back in the two days, honest, sir.'

'Shanks, do you realize that France has fallen? That there is every likelihood of the invasion of England? That the whole railway system of the country is disorganized for the Dunkirk men? That our brigade is on two hours' notice for active service? Do you?'

'Yes, sir.'

'Then how can you come to me with this absurd application?'

'But, sir, we've been practising three years. We got a first at Salford last year. I can't give up now, sir.'

Was it 'the spirit of Dunkirk'?

'Request dismissed, Sergeant-Major.'

In accordance with custom C.S.M. Rawkes had been waiting within view in case the applicant for a private interview attempted personal violence on his officer. He now took over.

'Request dismissed. About turn, quick march.'

And Guy remained to wonder: was this the already advertised spirit of Dunkirk? He rather thought it was.

The days 'in the hulks', as de Souza called them, were few in number but they formed a distinct period of Guy's life in the Halberdiers; real discomfort for the first time, beastly food, responsibility in its most irksome form, claustrophobia, all these oppressed him; but he was free of all sense of national disaster. The rising and falling in the tides in the harbour, the greater or smaller number of daily sick, the men up on charges, the indications more or fewer, of failing temper – these were the concerns of the day. Sarum-Smith was appointed 'Entertainments Officer' and organized a concert at which three senior non-commissioned officers performed a strange piece of mummery traditional in the Halberdiers and derived, de Souza said, from a remote folk ceremony, dressed in blankets, carrying on a ritual dialogue under the names of 'Silly Bean', 'Black Bean' and 'Awful Bean'.

He organized a debate on the question: 'Any man who marries under thirty is a fool' which soon became a series of testimonies. 'All I can say is my father married at twenty-two and I never wish to see a happier homier house or a better mother nor I've had.'

He organized boxing matches.

Apthorpe was asked to lecture on Africa. He chose, instead, an unexpected subject: 'The Jurisdiction of Lyon King of Arms compared with that of Garter King of Arms.'

'But, Uncle, do you think it will interest the men?'

'Not all of them perhaps. Those that *are* interested will be very much interested indeed.'

'I believe they would greatly prefer something about elephants or cannibals.'

'Take it or leave it, Sarum-Smith.'

Sarum-Smith left it.

Guy lectured on the Art of Wine Making and had a surprising success. The men relished information on any technical subject.

Extraneous figures came to add to the congestion. An odd, old captain like a cockatoo in the gaudy service dress of a defunct regiment of Irish cavalry. He said he was the cipher

officer and was roped in to lecture on 'Court Life at St Peters-
burg'.

Dunn and his men turned up. They had got to France and
travelled in a great arc of insecurity behind the breaking lines
from Boulogne to Bordeaux, without once leaving their railway coach. This experience of foreign travel, within sound of
the guns, under fire once when an agitated airman passed their
way, added perceptibly to Dunn's self-confidence. Sarum-
Smith tried to induce him to give a lecture on 'the lessons
learned in combat' but Dunn explained that he had spent the
journey in holding a Court of Inquiry under the authority of
the senior officer in the train, to examine the case of the carved
boot. The verdict had been one of deliberate damage but since
he had parted company with the convening officer he was not
sure where the papers should be sent. He was reading the matter up in his Manual of Military Law.

A sinister super-cargo labelled 'Chemical Warfare (Offensive)' was delivered to the quay and left there for all to see.

Guy got a second-in-command, a dull young regular named
Brent, and a third subaltern. So the days passed. Suddenly
there was a warning order and another move. They disembarked. The Dutch gunners waved them a farewell as their
train steamed away into the unknown. The maps of County
Limerick were collected. They jolted slowly for ten hours, with
many stops at sidings and many altercations with Transport
Officers. They detrained at night, a magnificent, moonlit, scented night, and bivouacked in the woods surrounding a park,
where all the paths glowed underfoot with phosphorescent
deadwood. They were put into buses and dispersed along the
sounding coast where Guy received the news of his cousin
Tony.

He had two miles of cliff to defend against invasion. When
de Souza was shown his platoon front he said: 'But, Uncle, it
doesn't make sense. The Germans are mad as hatters but not
in quite this way. They aren't going to land here.'

'They might put agents ashore. Or some of their landing
craft might drift off course.'

'I think we've been sent here because we aren't fit for the likely beaches.'

After two days an inspecting general arrived with several staff officers and Ritchie-Hook, sulking; three car-loads of them. Guy showed them his gun pits, which were sited to cover every bathers path from the shore. The general stood with his back to the sea and gazed inland.

'Not much field of fire,' he said.

'No, sir. We expect the enemy from the other direction.'

'Must have all-round defence.'

'Don't you think they're a bit thin on the ground for that?' said Ritchie-Hook. 'They're covering a battalion front.'

'Parachutes,' said the general, 'are the very devil. Well, remember. The positions are to be held to the last man and the last round.'

'Yes, sir,' said Guy.

'Do your men understand that?'

'Yes, sir.'

'And remember, you must never speak of "*If* the enemy comes" but "*When* they come". They are coming *here*, *this* month. Understand?'

'Yes, sir.'

'All right, I think we've seen everything.'

'May I say a word?' asked a neat young staff officer.

'Carry on, I.O.'

'Fifth Columnists,' said the Intelligence Officer, 'will be your special concern. You know what they did on the Continent. They'll do the same here. Suspect everyone – the vicar, the village grocer, the farmer whose family have lived here a hundred years, all the most unlikely people. Look out for signalling at night – lights, short-wave transmitters. And here's a bit of information for your ears alone. It mustn't go below platoon-commander level. We happen to know that the telegraph posts have been marked to lead the invading units to their rendezvous. Little metal numbers. I've seen them myself. Remove them and report to headquarters when you find them.'

'Very good, sir.'

The three cars drove on. Guy had been with de Souza's platoon when the final words of encouragement were spoken. Here the high road ran almost on the edge of the cliff. He and Brent walked to the next platoon position. On the way they counted a dozen telegraph poles, each marked with a metal number.

'All telegraph poles are,' said Brent, 'by the Post Office.'

'Sure?'

'Perfectly.'

Local Defence Volunteers helped patrol the area at night and reported frequent lamp-signals from fifth columnists. One story was so well told that Guy spent a night alone with Halberdier Glass, armed to the teeth, on the sands of a little cove; a boat was said to beach there often in darkness. But no one came their way that night. The only incident was a single tremendous flash which momentarily lit the whole coast. Guy remembered afterwards that in the momentary stillness he foolishly said: 'Here they come.' Then from far away came the thump and tremor of an explosion.

'Land-mine,' said Glass. 'Plymouth probably.'

In his vigils Guy thought often of Tony, with three, four, perhaps five years cut clean out of his young life just as those eight had been cut from his own.

Once on an evening of dense sea-mist a message came that the enemy were attacking with arsenical smoke. That was Apthorpe, momentarily left in charge at Headquarters. Guy took no action. An hour later a message came cancelling the alarm. That was Colonel Tickeridge, back at his post.

3

AT the end of August Guy was sitting in his company office in the hotel when two captains of a county regiment entered and saluted.

'We're A Company, 5th Loamshires.'

'Good morning. What can I do for you?'

'You're expecting us, aren't you?'

'No.'

'We've come to take over from you.'

'First I've heard of it.'

'Damn. I suppose we've come to the wrong place again. You aren't D Company, 2nd Halberdiers?'

'Yes.'

'That's all right then. I expect the orders will get through in time. My chaps are due to arrive this afternoon. Perhaps you wouldn't mind showing us round?'

For weeks they had waited for fifth columnists. Here they were at last.

There was a field telephone, which sometimes worked, connecting D Company with Battalion Headquarters. Guy, as he had seen done in the films, wrote on a piece of paper *Ask Bn. H.Q. if these chaps are genuine* and turned to Brent: 'Just attend to this will you, Bill? I'll see to our visitors,' and to the Loamshires: 'Come outside. It's rather a good billet, isn't it?'

They stepped out to the hotel terrace; bright blue overhead and before them; warm gravel underfoot; roses all round them; at his side, the enemy. Guy studied the two men. They were in service uniforms. They should have been in battle-dress. The junior had not yet spoken – a German accent perhaps; the senior was altogether too good to be true, clipped voice, clipped moustache, a Military Cross.

'You want to see my L.M.G. positions, I expect?'

'Well, I suppose we ought to some time. At the moment I'm more interested in accommodation and messing arrangements. Is the bathing good? How do you get down to the beach? As far as I'm concerned this is going to be my summer holidays. We'd no sooner got straightened out after Dunkirk than they put us on defence duty on the invasion coast.'

'Would you like a bathe now?'

'Sound scheme, eh, Jim?'

The junior officer gave a grunt which might have been Teutonic.

'We usually undress up here and go down in great-coats. I can fit you out.'

Brent joined them to say that he had not been able to get an answer from Headquarters.

'Never mind,' said Guy, 'I'll see to it. I want you now to take our visitors bathing. Show them up to my room. They'll leave their things there. Find them a couple of great-coats and towels.'

As soon as the Loamshires had gone Guy turned back and found Sergeant-Major Rawkes.

'Sergeant Major,' he said. 'Did you see anything odd about those two officers who came in just now?'

'We have never had much of an opinion of the Loamshires, sir.'

'I suspect them. They've just gone down to bathe with Mr Brent. I want you to relieve the man at the gun covering the bathing place.'

'Me, sir? At the gun?'

'Yes. This is a security matter. I can't trust anyone else. I want you to keep them covered all the time, on the way down, in the water, on the way up. If they try anything funny, fire.'

Sergeant Major Rawkes, who had in recent weeks formed a good opinion of Guy, looked at him with mild despair.

'Shoot Mr Brent, sir?'

'No, no. Those fellows who say they are in the Loamshires.'

'What exactly would you mean by funny, sir?'

'If they attack Mr Brent, try to drown him, or push him over the cliffs.'

Rawkes shook his head sadly. He had let himself be taken in. He should never have come near trusting a temporary officer.

'That's orders, sir?'

'Yes, of course. Get on with it quick.'

'Very good, sir.'

He walked slowly to the gun pit.

''Op it, you two,' he said to the men on duty. 'Don't ask me why. Just 'op it and be grateful.'

Then he lowered himself to the Bren, stiffly, in protest. But as he put the weapon to his shoulder, he relaxed a little. This was a rare sport, officer-shooting.

Guy ran to his room and examined the intruders' kit. One of them instead of a service revolver was carrying a Luger. Guy pocketed the cartridge-clips of both weapons. There was no other suspicious feature; everything else in their pockets was English including a very correct move-order. Guy tried to telephone again and got through to Sarum-Smith.

'I must speak to the C.O.'

'He's at a conference at Brigade.'

'Well, the second-in-command or the adjutant then.'

'They're out. There's only me and the quartermaster left.'

'Can you get a message through to the C.O. at Brigade?'

'I don't think so. Is it important?'

'Yes. Take it down.'

'Wait a jiffy till I get a pencil.'

There was a pause and then the voice of Apthorpe spoke. 'Hullo, old man, something up?'

'Yes, will you get off the line. I'm trying to pass a message to Sarum-Smith.'

'He's gone off to find a razor blade to sharpen his pencil.'

'Well, will you take it? Message begins: "D Coy to 2 Bn via Bde HQ." '

'I'm not sure that's the correct form.'

'Damn the correct form. Tell the C.O. that I've got two men here who claim to be Loamshires. They say they have orders to take over my positions. I want to know if they're genuine.'

'I say, old man, that sounds a bit hot. I'll come right over myself.'

'Don't do anything of the sort. Just get my message to the C.O.'

'I could be with you in twenty minutes on my motor-bike.'

'Just pass my message to the C.O., there's a good chap.'

Huffily: 'Well, if you don't want me, that's your look-out. But it seems to me far too serious a matter to settle single-handed.'

'I'm not single-handed. I've a hundred men here. Just pass the message.'

Very huffily: 'Here is Sarum-Smith. It's his pigeon to pass

messages. I'm very busy here, I can tell you, on pretty confidential business.'

Sarum-Smith, back at the telephone, took the message.

'Sure you've got it clear?'

'Yes. But I think there's an order that has some bearing on your query. It came just as the adjutant was leaving. He told me to pass it on but I've not got round to it. Wait a sec. It's somewhere here. Yes. Second Battalion will hand over their positions to Fifth Loamshires and concentrate forthwith at Brook Park with full stores and equipment. That's the place we first arrived at. Sorry for the delay.'

'Damn.'

'Do you want that message sent to the C.O.?'

'No.'

'It's all been rather a flap about nothing, hasn't it?'

As Guy rang off he saw the bathers return up the cliff under the sights of the entrenched Bren gun. They had enjoyed their swim, they said. They lunched with Guy, slept, and bathed again, then drove back to their unit. It would surprise them, Guy supposed, when they found their pistols unloaded. They would never know they had been as near death that sunny first day of their holidays as on the dunes at Dunkirk. One untimely piece of horse-play and they might have been goners.

Another series of jolts, buffer on buffer down the train.

The brigade assembled and went under canvas at Brook Park. 'Dispersal' was the prevailing fashion now. Instead of the dressed lines which had given Penkirk the airs and some of the graces of a Victorian colour-print, there was now a haphazard litter of tents, haunting the shadows round the solitary oaks of the park, or shrinking in the immature surrounding coverts. A great taboo fell on the making of tracks. Special sentries were posted to shout at men approaching Brigade Headquarters across the lawn, directing them to creep through the shrubberies.

The nature of Apthorpe's 'confidential business' was soon revealed. He had been helping the quartermaster arrange an unexpected consignment of tropical uniforms. In the first two days at Brook Park the Halberdiers paraded company by company and were issued with sun helmets and ill-fitting khaki drill. Few looked anything but absurd. The garments were then put away and nothing was said about them. They aroused little curiosity. In the past months they had moved so suddenly, so often and so purposelessly, they had been alternately provided with, deprived of, and reprovided with so many different military objects, that speculation about their future had become purely facetious.

'I suppose we're going to reconquer Somaliland' (which had just been precipitately abandoned), said de Souza.

'It's just part of a fully equipped Halberdier's normal kit,' said Brent.

However it produced one climax in the process which de Souza called 'the Languishing of Leonard'.

During their defence of the Cornish cliffs the Second Battalion had seen very little of one another. Now they were reunited and Guy found a sad change evident in Leonard. Mrs Leonard had planted herself and her baby in lodgings near him and she had worked hard on his divided loyalty. Bombs were beginning to fall in appreciable numbers. An invasion was confidently predicted for the middle of September. Mrs Leonard wanted a man about the house. When Leonard moved from the coast with his company, Mrs Leonard came too and settled in the village inn.

She asked Guy to dinner and explained her predicament.

'It's all right for you,' she said. 'You're an old bachelor. You'll make yourself very comfortable, I daresay, in India with native servants and all you want to eat. What's going to happen to me, that's what I'd like to know?'

'I don't think there's any prospect of our going to India,' said Guy.

'Then what's Jim's new hat for then?' asked Mrs Leonard. 'That's an Indian hat, isn't it? Don't you tell me they've given him that hat and those size six shorts to wear here in the winter.'

'It's just part of a fully equipped Halberdier's normal kit,' said Guy.

'D'you believe that?'

'No,' said Guy. 'Frankly, I don't.'

'Well then?' said Mrs Leonard triumphantly.

'Daisy won't understand it's what a soldier's wife has to put up with,' said Leonard. He had said this often obviously.

'I didn't marry a soldier,' said Mrs Leonard. 'If I'd known you were going to be a soldier I'd have married into the R.A.F. *Their* wives live comfortable and what's more they're the people who are winning the war. It says so on the wireless, doesn't it? It isn't as though it was only me; there's the baby to think of.'

'I don't think that in case of invasion, you could expect to have Jim expressly detailed for the defence of your baby, you know, Mrs Leonard.'

'I'd see he stayed around; anyway, he wouldn't go surf-bathing and lying about under palm trees and playing the ukulele.'

'I don't think those would be his duties if we went abroad.'

'Oh, come off the perch,' said Mrs Leonard. 'I've asked you here to help. You're in with the high-ups.'

'Lots of men have young babies, too.'

'But not *my* baby.'

'Daisy, you're being unreasonable. Do make her see sense, Uncle.'

'It isn't as though the whole army was going abroad. Why should they pick on Jim?'

'I suppose you *could* apply for transfer to barrack duties,' said Guy at last. 'There must be a lot of chaps there who'd be eager to come with us.'

'I bet there would,' said Mrs Leonard. 'It's just evacuation, that's what it is, sending you off thousands of miles from the war, with bearers and sahibs and chota pegs.'

It was a sad little party. As Leonard walked back to camp with Guy, he said: 'It's getting me down. I can't leave Daisy in the state she's in. Isn't it true women sometimes go off their heads for a bit just after having a baby?'

'So I've heard.'

'Perhaps that's the trouble with Daisy.'

Meanwhile the sun-helmets were laid aside and long, hot days were spent in biffing Brook House from every possible direction.

Some days later Leonard met Guy and said gloomily: 'I went to see the colonel this morning.'

'Yes.'

'About what Daisy has been saying.'

'Yes?'

'He was awfully sporting about it.'

'He's an awfully sporting man.'

'He's going to send my name in for transfer to the Training Depot. It may take some time, but he thinks it'll go through.'

'I hope your wife will feel relieved.'

'Uncle, do you think I'm behaving pretty poorly?'

'It's not my business.'

'I can see you do. Well, so do I.'

But he had not long in which to face whatever shame attached to his decision. That night, a warning-order arrived and everyone was sent on forty-eight hours embarkation leave.

4

Guy went for a day to Matchet. It was summer holidays for the school. He found his father busy with North and Hillard's *Latin Prose* and a pale blue *Xenophon* 'brushing up' for the coming term.

'I can't read a word of it unseen,' said Mr Crouchback almost gleefully. 'I bet the little blighters will catch me out. They did last term again and again, but they were very decent about it.'

Guy returned a day early to see that everything was well with his company's arrangements. Walking through the almost empty camp at dusk, he met the Brigadier.

'Crouchback,' he said, peering. 'Not a captain yet?'

'No, sir.'

'But you've got your company.'

They walked together some way.

'You've got the best command there is,' said the Brigadier. 'There's nothing in life like leading a company in action. Next best thing is doing a job on your own. Everything else is just bumf and telephones.' Under the trees, in the failing light, he was barely visible. 'It's not much of a show we're going to. I'm not supposed to tell you where, so I shall. Place called Dakar. I'd never heard of it till they started sending me 'Most Secret' intelligence reports, mostly about ground-nuts. A French town in West Africa. Probably all boulevards and brothels if I know the French colonies. We're in support. Worse really – we're in support of the supporting brigade. They're putting the Marines in before us, blast them. Anyway it's all froggy business. They think they'll get in without opposition. But it'll help training. Sorry I told you. They'd court-martial me if they found out. I'm getting too old for courts martial.'

He turned away abruptly and disappeared into the woodland.

Next day the move-order was issued to entrain for Liverpool. Leonard was left behind with the rear-party 'pending posting'. No one except Guy and the colonel knew why. Most supposed him ill. He had been looking like a ghost for some time.

Something of this kind had happened in Captain Truslove's regiment. A showy polo-player named Congreve sent in his papers when they were under orders for foreign service. The colonel announced at mess: 'Gentlemen, I must request that Captain Congreve's name shall never again be mentioned in my presence.' Congreve's fiancée returned his ring. From colonel to drummer-boy all felt tainted and many of their subsequent acts of heroism were prompted by the wish to restore the regiment's honour. (Not until the penultimate chapter did Congreve turn up again, elaborately disguised as an Afghan merchant with the keys of the Pathan fortress where Truslove himself awaited execution by torture.) But Guy had no shame about the defection of Leonard. It seemed, rather, as their train moved spasmodically towards Liverpool, that it was they who were deserting him. Their destination was not the Honolulu-Algiers-Quetta station of Mrs Leonard's film-clouded imagination, but it was a warm, highly coloured, well-found place far from bombs and gas and famine and enemy occupation; far from the lightless concentration-camp which all Europe had suddenly become.

Chaos in Liverpool. Quays and ships in absolute darkness. Bombs falling somewhere not far distant. Embarkation staff officers scanning nominal-rolls with dimmed torches. Guy and his company were ordered into one ship, ordered out again, stood-to on the dockside for an hour. An all-clear siren sounded and a few lamps glowed here and there. Embarkation officers who had gone to earth emerged and resumed their duties. At last, at dawn they numbly climbed on board and found their proper quarters. Guy saw them bedded down and went in search of his cabin.

This was in the first-class part of the ship, unchanged from peace time when it had been filled with affluent tourists. This was a chartered ship with the Merchant Marine crew. Already Goanese stewards were up and about in their freshly laundered white and red livery. They padded silently about their work, arranging ashtrays symmetrically in the lounges, drawing the curtains for another day. They were quite at peace. No one had told them about submarines and torpedoes.

But not all were at peace. Turning a corner in search of his cabin Guy found a kind of pugnacious dance being performed in and out of his cabin by Halberdier Glass and a Goanese of distinguished appearance – thin, elderly, with magnificent white moustaches spanning his tear-wet nut-brown face.

'Caught this black bastard in the very act, sir. Mucking about with your kit, sir.'

'Please, sir, I am the cabin boy, sir. I do not know this rude soldier.'

'That's all right, Glass. He's just doing his job. Now clear out both of you, I want to turn in.'

'You aren't surely going to have this native creeping round your quarters, sir?'

'I am no native, sir. I am a Christian Portuguese boy. Christian mama, Christian papa, six Christian children, sir.'

He produced from his starched blouse a gold medal, strung round his neck, much worn with the long swing and plunge of the ship rubbing it year by year to and fro on his hairless dark chest.

Guy's heart suddenly opened towards him. Here was his own kin. He yearned to show the medal he wore, Gervase's souvenir from Lourdes. There were men who would have done exactly that, better men than he ; who would perhaps have said 'Snap' and drawn a true laugh from the sullen Halberdier and so have made true peace between them.

But Guy, with all this in his mind to do, merely felt in his pocket for two half-crowns and said: 'Here. Will this make things better?'

'Oh yes, sir, thank you. Very much better, sir,' and the Goanese turned and went on his way rejoicing a little, but not as a fellow man at peace ; merely as a servant unexpectedly over-tipped.

To Glass Guy said: 'If I hear of you laying hands on the ship's company again, I'll send you to the guard room.'

'Sir,' said Glass, looking at Guy as though at Captain Congreve who let down the regiment.

The men were given a 'long lie' that morning. At eleven o'clock Guy paraded his company on deck. An unusually large and varied breakfast – the normal third-class fare of the line – had dissipated the annoyances of the night. They were in good heart. He handed them over to their platoon commanders to check stores and equipment and went to explore. The Second Battalion had done better than the others, who were close packed in the ship moored next to them. They had their transport to themselves except for Brigade Headquarters and a medley of strangers – Free French liaison officers, Marine gunners, a naval beach-party, chaplains, an expert on tropical hygiene and the rest. A small smoking-room was labelled OPERATIONAL PLANNING. OUT OF BOUNDS TO ALL RANKS.

Lying out in the stream might be descried the huge inelegant colourless bulk of an aircraft carrier. All contact with the shore was forbidden. Sentries stood at the gangways. Military police patrolled the quay. But the object of the expedition was not long kept secret for at midday an airman jauntily swinging a parcel charged '*Most Secret. By hand of officer only*' allowed it to fall asunder as he approached his launch and a light breeze caught, bore up and scattered abroad some thousands of blue, white and red leaves printed with the slogan:

FRANÇAIS DE DAKAR*!*
Joignez-vous à nous pour délivrer la France!
GENERAL DE GAULLE.

No one, except one of the chaplains who was new to military life, seriously expected that these preparations would bring anything about. The Halberdiers had been too much shifted, exhorted and disappointed during recent weeks. They accepted as part of their normal day the series of orders and cancellations and mishaps. Shore leave was given and then stopped; censorship of letters was raised and reimposed; the ship cast off, fouled an anchor, returned to the quayside; the stores were disembarked and re-embarked in 'tactical order'. And then quite suddenly one afternoon, they sailed. The last newspaper to come aboard told of heavier air-raids. De Souza called their transport 'the refugee ship'.

It seemed barely possible that they would not turn back but on they steamed into the Atlantic until they reached a rendez-vous where the whole wide circle of grey water was filled with shipping of every size from the carrier and the battleship *Barham*, to a little vessel named *Belgravia*, which was reputed to carry champagne and bath-salts and other comforts for the garrison of Dakar. Then the whole convoy altered course and sailed south, destroyers racing round them like terriers, an occasional, friendly aeroplane swooping overhead and gallant little *Belgravia* wallowing on behind.

They practised doubling to 'action stations' twice a day. They carried 'Mae West' life-belts wherever they went. But they took their tone from the smooth seas and the Goanese stewards who tinkled their musical gongs up and down the carpeted passages. All was peaceful and when the cruiser *Fiji* was torpedoed in full sight of them a mile or two ahead, and all the naval detachment became busy with depth-charges, the incident barely disturbed their Sunday afternoon repose.

Dunn and his signalmen had reappeared and were on board

with Brigade Headquarters, but Apthorpe ignored them, perhaps never was aware of their presence, so deep were his colloquies with the specialist on tropical medicine. The men did Physical Training and boxed and listened to lectures about Dakar and General de Gaulle and malaria and the importance of keeping clear of native women; they lay about on the forward deck and in the evenings the chaplains organized concerts for them.

Brigadier Ritchie-Hook, alone, was unhappy. His brigade had a minor and conditional role. It was thought that the Free French would find the town beflagged for them. The only opposition expected was from the battleship *Richelieu*. This the Royal Marines and a unit of unknown character called a 'commando' would deal with. The Halberdiers might not land at all; if they did it would be for 'cleaning up' and relieving the Marines on guard duty. Little biffing. In his chagrin he quarrelled with the ship's captain and was ordered off the bridge. He prowled about the decks alone, sometimes carrying a weapon like a hedging implement which he had found valuable in the previous war.

Presently the heat grew oppressive, the air stagnant and misty. There was an odd smell, identified as that of groundnuts, borne to them from the near but invisible coast. And word went round that they were at their destination. The Free French were said to be in parley with their enslaved compatriots. There was some firing somewhere in the mist. Then the convoy withdrew out of range and closed in. Launches went to and fro among the ships. A conference was held on the flagship from which Brigadier Ritchie-Hook returned grinning. He addressed the battalion, telling them that an opposed landing would take place next day, then went to the transport carrying his other battalions and gave them the stirring news. Maps were issued. The officers sat up all night studying their beaches, boundaries, second and third waves of advance. During the night the ships moved near inland and dawn disclosed a grey line of African coast across the steamy water. The battalion stood to, at their bomb-stations, bulging with ammunition and emergency rations. Hours passed. There was heavy firing ahead and a rumour that *Barham* was holed. A little Unfree French aeroplane droned out of the clouds and dropped a bomb very near them. The Brigadier was back on the bridge, on the best of terms with the captain. Then the convoy steamed out of range once more and at sundown another conference was called. The Brigadier returned in a rage and called the officers together.

'Gentlemen, it's all off. We are merely awaiting confirmation from the War Cabinet to withdraw. I'm sorry. Tell your men and keep their spirit up.'

There was little need for this order. Surprisingly a spirit of boisterous fun suddenly possessed the ship. Everyone had been a little more apprehensive than he had shown about the opposed landing. Troop decks and mess 'danced and skylarked'.

Immediately after dinner Guy was called to the room marked 'Out of Bounds to all Ranks'.

He found the Brigadier, the captain and Colonel Tickeridge all looking gleeful and curiously naughty. The Brigadier said: 'We are going to have a little bit of very unofficial fun. Are you interested?'

The question was so unexpected that Guy made no guess at the meaning and simply said: 'Yes, sir.'

'We tossed up between the companies. Yours won. Can you find a dozen good men for a reconnaissance patrol?'

'Yes, sir.'

'And a suitable officer to lead them?'

'Can I go myself, sir?' he said to Colonel Tickeridge.

This was true Truslove-style.

'Yes. Go off now and warn the men to be ready in an hour. Tell them it's an extra guard. Then come back here with a map and get your orders.'

When Guy returned he found the conspirators very cheerful.

'I've been having a little disagreement with the Force Commander,' said Ritchie-Hook. 'There was some discrepancy between the naval and military intelligence about Beach A. Got it marked?'

'Yes, sir.'

'In the final plan it was decided to leave Beach A alone.

Some damn fool had reported it wired and generally impractic-
able. My belief is that it's quite open. I won't go into the reasons. But you can see for yourself that if we got ashore on Beach
A we could have taken the frogs in the rear. They had some
damn fool photographs and pretended to see wire in them and
got windy. I saw no wire. The Force Commander said some
offensive things about two eyes being better than one with a
stereoscope. The discussion got a bit heated. The operation is
cancelled and we've all been made to look silly, but I'd just
like to make my point with the Force Commander. So I am
sending a patrol ashore just to make certain.'

'Yes, sir.'

'Very well, that is the intention of the operation. If you find
the place wired or get shot at come back quickly and we will
say no more about it. If it's open, as I think it is, you might
bring back some little souvenir that I can send the Force Commander. He's a suspicious fellow. Any little thing that will
make him feel foolish – a coco-nut or something like that. We
can't use the naval landing craft but the Captain here has
played up like a sportsman and is lending a launch for the
trip. Well, I'm turning in now. I shall be glad to hear your report in the morning. Settle the tactical details with your C.O.'

Ritchie-Hook left them. The captain explained the position
of the launch and the sally-port.

'Any other questions?' asked Colonel Tickeridge.

'No, sir,' said Guy. 'It all seems quite clear.'

5

Two hours later Guy's patrol paraded in the hold from which
the sally-port opened. They were dressed in rubber-soled shoes,
shorts, and tunic-shirts; no caps; no gas-masks; their equipment stripped down to the belt. Each had a couple of hand
grenades and his rifle, except for the Bren pair who would set
up their gun on the first suitable spot and be ready to cover
the retreat if they were opposed. All had blackened faces. Guy
carefully gave them their instructions. The sergeant would

board the boat first and land last, seeing everyone safely ashore. Guy would land first and the men fan out on either side. He would carry a torch stuffed with pink tissue paper which he would flash back from time to time to give the direction. Wire, if it existed, would be above high water. They would advance inland far enough to discover whether there was wire or not. The first man to come on wire was to pass the word up to him. They would investigate the extent of the wire. A single blast of his whistle meant withdrawal to the boat ... and so on.

'Remember,' he concluded, 'we're simply on reconnaissance. We aren't trying to conquer Africa. We only fire if we have to cover our withdrawal.'

Presently they heard the winch over their head and they knew that their boat was being lowered.

'There's an iron ladder outside. It'll be about six foot to the water level. See that the man before you has got into place before you start going down. All set?'

The lights were all turned off in the hold before the sally-port was opened by one of the crew. It revealed a faintly lighter square and a steamy breath of the sea.

'All set below?'

'Aye, aye, sir.'

'Then carry on, Sergeant.'

One by one the men filed from the darkness into the open night. Guy followed last and took his place in the bow. There was barely room to squat. Guy experienced the classic illusion of an unknown, unsought, companion among them. The sally-port shut noisily above them. A voice said: 'Any more for the *Skylark*?' Skylark was the *mot juste,* thought Guy. They cast off. The engine started with what seemed a great noise and the launch bounced gently away in the direction of Beach A.

It was nearly an hour's run for the beach lay on the north of the town in a position which, if captured, might have secured the landing to the south. The reek of the engine, the tropic night, the cramped bodies, the irregular smack of little waves on the bows. At last the man at the wheel said: 'We must be getting in now, sir.'

The engine slowed. The line of the shore was plain to see,

quite near them. The clearer eyes of the seamen searched and found the wide gap of the beach. The engine was shut down and in complete silence they drifted gently inshore under their momentum. Then they touched sand. Guy was standing with his hands on the gunwale, ready. He vaulted overboard and found himself breast-high in the tepid water. He stumbled straight ahead uphill, waist-deep, knee-deep, then clear of the sea on firm sand. He was filled by the most exhilarating sensation of his life; his first foothold on enemy soil. He flashed his torch behind him and heard splashing; the boat was drifting out again and the last men had to swim a few strokes to get into their depth. He saw shadowy figures emerge and spread out on either side of him. He gave the two flashes which meant 'Forward'. He could just see and hear the gun pair move off to the side flank to find a position. The patrol moved on uphill. First hard wet sand, then soft dry sand, then long spiky grass. They kept on quietly. Palm trunks rose suddenly immediately in front. The first thing he met was a fallen coco-nut. He picked it up and gave it to Halberdier Glass, next to him on the left.

'Take this back to the boat and wait for us there,' he whispered.

Halberdier Glass had shown signs of respect during the early stages of the expedition and an unwonted zeal.

'What me, sir? This here nut, sir? Back to the boat?'

'Yes, don't talk. Get on with it.'

He knew then that he had lost all interest in whether he held or forfeited Glass's esteem.

The second thing he met was wire, loosely tangled between the palm trunks. He gave the three flashes that meant: 'Go carefully. 'Ware wire.'

He heard stumbling on both sides of him and whispered messages came up to him: 'Wire on the left.' 'Wire on the right.'

Casting a dim light forward now, and exploring with hands and feet, he discovered a low, thin, ill-made defensive belt of wire. Then he was aware of a dark figure, four paces from him, plunging forward across it.

'Stand still, that man,' he said.

The figure continued forward, clear of the wire and noisily pushing through scrub and grass and thorn.

'Come back, damn you,' Guy shouted.

The man was out of sight but still audible. Guy blew his whistle. The men obediently turned about and made off downhill for the beach. Guy stood where he was, waiting for the delinquent. He had heard that men who ran amok had sometimes been brought to their senses by an automatic response to command.

'That half-file in front,' he shouted as though in the barrack square. 'About turn. Quick march.'

The only response, quite near to his left, was a challenge. 'Halte-là! Qui vive?' Then the explosion of a grenade. And then suddenly firing broke out on all sides, the full span of the beach; nothing formidable, a few ragged rifle shots whistling between the palms. At once his own Bren on the flank opened up with three bursts which fell alarmingly near him. It seemed to Guy rather likely that he would soon be killed. He repeated the words which are dignified by the name 'act' of contrition; words so familiar that he used them in dreams when falling from a height. But he also thought: what a preposterous way in which to get oneself killed!

He ran back to the beach. The boat was there, two men in the water held it in to the shore. The remainder of the patrol stood near it.

'Get aboard,' said Guy.

He ran across to the gunners and called them in.

There was still a lot of shouting in French and some wild shooting inland.

'All present and correct, sir,' reported the sergeant.

'No, there's a man adrift up there.'

'No, sir, I've counted them. All present. Jump in, sir, we'd better be off while we can.'

'Wait one minute. I must just have another look.'

The R.N.V.R. lieutenant in command of the boat said: 'My orders are to push off as soon as the operation is completed, or sooner if I think the boat is being put into excessive danger.'

'They haven't seen you yet. They're firing quite wild. Give me two minutes.'

Men, Guy knew, in the excitement of their first battle were liable to delusions. It would be highly convenient to suppose that he had imagined that dark, disappearing figure. But he went up the beach again and there saw his missing man crawling towards him.

Guy's one emotion was anger and his first words were: 'I'll have you court-martialled for this,' and then: 'Are you hit?'

'Of course I am,' said the crawling figure. 'Give me a hand.'

This was no German defence with searchlights and automatic weapons, but there had plainly been some reinforcement and the rifle shots were thicker. In his haste and anger Guy did not notice the man's odd tone. He pulled him up, no great weight, and staggered with him to the boat. The man was clutching something under his free arm. Not until they had both been hoisted aboard and the boat was running full speed out to sea did he give his attention to the wounded man. He turned his torch to the face and a single eye flashed back at him.

'Get my leg out straight,' said Brigadier Ritchie-Hook. 'And give me a field-dressing someone. It's nothing much but it hurts like the devil and it's bleeding too much. And take care of the coco-nut.'

Then Ritchie-Hook busied himself with his wound but not before he had laid in Guy's lap the wet, curly head of a Negro.

And Guy was so weary that he fell asleep, nursing the trophy. The whole patrol was asleep by the time they reached the ship. Only Ritchie-Hook groaned and swore sometimes in semi-coma.

6

'WOULD you want to be eating this nut now, sir, or later?'

Halberdier Hall looked down at Guy's bedside.

'What time is it?'

'Eleven sharp, sir, as was your orders.'

'Where are we?'

'Steaming along, sir, with the convoy, *not* towards home. Colonel wants to see you as soon as you're ready.'

'Leave the nut here. I'm taking it for a souvenir.'

Guy still felt weary. As he shaved he recalled the final events of the previous night.

He had woken much refreshed, bobbing under the high walls of the ship with the head of a Negro clasped in both hands.

'We've a wounded man here. Can you pass down a loop for hoisting?'

There was some delay above and then from the blind black door above a light flashed down.

'I'm the ship's surgeon. Will you come up and make way for me?'

Guy climbed aboard into the hold. The surgeon descended. He and two orderlies had a special apparatus for such occasions, a kind of cradle which was swung down, fastened to the Brigadier and tenderly drawn up again.

'Take him straight along to the sick bay and prepare him. Anyone else injured?'

'That's the only one.'

'No one warned me to expect wounded. Luckily we had everything ready this morning. No one told me to expect anything tonight,' the surgeon grumbled, out of sight and out of earshot behind the laden orderlies.

The men came aboard.

'You've all done jolly well,' said Guy. 'Fall out now. We'll talk about it tomorrow. Thanks, sailors. Good night.'

He woke Colonel Tickeridge to report.

'Reconnaissance successful, sir. One coco-nut' – and placed the head beside Colonel Tickeridge's ash-tray on the edge of his bunk.

Colonel Tickeridge came slowly awake.

'For Christ's sake what's that thing?'

'French colonial infantry, sir. No identifications.'

'Well for God's sake take it away. We'll talk about it in the morning. Everyone back safe?'

'All my patrol, sir. One supernumerary casualty. Stretcher case. He's been put in the sick bay.'

'What the devil do you mean by "supernumerary"?'

'The Brigadier, sir.'

'*What?*'

Guy had assumed that Colonel Tickeridge was in the secret; had been party to making him look a fool. Now he dropped something of his stiffness.

'Didn't you know he was coming, Colonel?'

'Of course I didn't.'

'He must have hidden in the hold and crashed the party in the dark, sir, with his face blacked.'

'The old devil. Is he badly hurt?'

'The leg.'

'That doesn't sound too bad.' Colonel Tickeridge, fully awake now, began to chuckle, then turned grave. 'I say, though, this is going to be the hell of a mess. Well, we'll talk about it tomorrow. Go to bed now.'

'And this?'

'For Christ's sake throw it in the drink.'

'Do you think I ought to, Colonel, without consulting the Brigadier?'

'Well, get it out of here.'

'Very good, sir. Good night.'

Guy took a firm grip of the wool and walked down the breathless corridor. He met a Goanese night steward and showed him the face. The man gave a squeal and fled. Guy was light-headed now. Apthorpe's cabin? No. He tried the door of the Operations Room. It was unlocked and unguarded. All the maps and confidential papers had been tidied away. He put his burden in the Brigadier's 'In' tray and, suddenly weary again, turned to his own cabin, threw down his bloody shirt, washed his bloody chest and hands, and fell deep asleep.

'How's the Brigadier, Colonel?' Guy asked when he reported to the orderly-room.

'Very cheerful. He's not been round from the chloroform long. He's asking for his coco-nut.'

'I left it on his desk.'

'You'd better take it to him. He wants to see you. From his

account you seem to have put up rather a good show last night. It's jolly bad luck.' This was not quite the form Guy had expected congratulations to take. 'Sit down, Uncle, you aren't on a charge – yet.'

Guy sat silent while Colonel Tickeridge paced the carpet.

'It's only once or twice in a chap's life he gets the chance of a gong. Some chaps never get it. You got yours last night and did all right. By all justice I ought now to be drafting a citation for your M.C. Instead of which we're in the hell of a fix. I can't think what possessed us last night. We can't even keep the thing quiet. If it was just the battalion involved we might conceivably have tried, but the ship's full of odds and sods and the thing just isn't on. If the Brigadier hadn't stopped one, we might have made you carry the can. "Over-zealous young officer ... mild reprimand", you know. But there'll have to be a medical report and an inquiry. You simply can't do things like that at his age and get away with it. If I'd had any idea what was in his head, I'd have refused cooperation. At least I think I should have done this morning. It won't look too good for the ship's captain either. It won't do you any good. Of course you were acting under orders. You're in the clear legally. But it'll be a black mark. For the rest of your life when your name comes up, someone is bound to say: "Isn't he the chap who blotted his copy-book at Dakar in 40?" Not, I suppose, that it matters to you. You'll be out of the Corps and your name won't crop up, will it? Come on, let's take the head to the Brig.'

They found him in the sick bay, alone in the officers' ward, his machette, freshly scoured, beside him.

'It wasn't a clean stroke,' he said. 'The silly fellow saw me first so I had to bung a grenade at him, then look for the head and trim it up tidy. Well, Crouchback, how d'you like having a brigadier under your command?'

'I found him most insubordinate, sir.'

'It was a potty little show, but you didn't do too badly for a first attempt. Did I hear you threaten me with a court-martial at one stage of the proceedings?'

'Yes, sir.'

'Never do that, Crouchback, particularly in the field, un-less you've got a prisoner's escort handy. I've known a prom-ising young officer shot with a Lee-Enfield for threatening things in the field. Where's my coco-nut?' Guy handed him the swaddled head. 'My word he's a beauty, isn't he? Look at his great teeth. Never saw a better. I'm damned if I give him to the Force Commander. I'll shrink and pickle him; it'll give me an interest while I'm laid up.'

When they left Guy asked: 'Does he know what you told me, Colonel? I mean about his being in for a row?'

'Of course he does. He's got out of more rows than anyone in the Service.'

'So you think he'll be all right this time?'

Colonel Tickeridge answered sadly and solemnly:

'He's the wrong age. You can be an *enfant terrible* or you can be a national figure no one dares touch. But the Brig's neither of those things. It's the end for him – at least he thinks it is and he ought to know.'

The convoy sailed down the coast and then began to break up, first one ship turning aside, then another. The men-o'-war steamed away to another rendezvous – all save the damaged ships who limped down to dry docks at Simonstown. The Free French pursued their mission of liberation elsewhere, the faith-ful little *Belgravia* with them. The two ships containing the Halberdier Brigade berthed at a British port. Since the night at Dakar a rare delicacy had kept everyone from questioning Guy. They knew something had happened, that all was not right. They pretended not to be curious. It was the same in the sergeants' mess and on the troop deck, Guy's sergeant told him. The Brigadier was carried ashore to hospital. The Brigade resumed its old duty of standing by for orders.

7

THREE weeks later the brigade was still standing by for orders. Their transports had steamed out to sea and they were in camp

on shore. The doctrine of 'dispersal' had not reached West
Africa. The tents stood in neat lines on a stretch of sandy
plain, five miles from the town, a few yards from the sea. The
expert on tropical diseases had flown away and the rigorous,
intolerably irksome hygienic precautions he had imposed fell
into desuetude. Local leave to up-country stations was given to
officers for sporting purposes. Apthorpe was one of the first to
go. The town was out of bounds to all ranks. No one wished
to go there. Later when he came to read *The Heart of the Matter* Guy reflected, fascinated, that at this very time 'Scobie' was
close at hand, demolishing partitions in native houses, still con-
scientiously interfering with neutral shipping. If they had not
the services of the new Catholic chaplain, Guy might have
gone to Father Rank to confess increasing sloth, one dismal
occasion of drunkenness, and the lingering resentment he felt
at the injustice he had suffered in the exploit to which he had
given the private name of 'Operation Truslove'.

Wireless news from England was all of air raids. Some of
the men were consumed with anxiety; most were consoled by
a rumour, quite baseless, which was travelling the whole world
in an untraceable manner, that the invasion had sailed and
been defeated, that the whole Channel was full of charred German corpses. The men paraded, marched, bathed, constructed
a rifle range and were quite without speculation about their
future. Some said they were to spend the rest of the war here
keeping fit, keeping up their morale, firing on the new range;
others said they were bound for Libya, round the Cape; others
that they were to forestall the German occupation of the
Azores.

Then, after three weeks, an aeroplane arrived bringing mail.
Most of it had been posted before the expedition even sailed
but there was a more recent, official bag. Leonard was still on
the strength of the Second Battalion, pending posting. It was
now announced that he was dead, killed by a bomb, on leave
in South London. There was also a move-order for Guy. His
presence was required at an inquiry into the doings on Beach
A, which was to be held in England as soon as Brigadier Ritchie-Hook was fit to move.

There was also a new Brigadier. He sent for Guy on the day of his arrival. He was a youngish, thick, mustachioed, naturally genial man, plainly ill at ease in the present case. Guy had not seen him before, but he would have recognized him as a Halberdier without studying his corps buttons.

'You're Captain Crouchback?'

'Lieutenant, sir.'

'Oh, I've got you down here as captain. I must look into it. Perhaps your promotion came through after you left U.K. Anyway it doesn't matter now. It was only an Acting Rank of course while you had a company. I'm afraid you'll be losing your company for the time being.'

'Does that mean I'm under arrest, sir?'

'Good God, no. At least not exactly. I mean to say this is simply an inquiry not a court-martial. The Force Commander made a great fuss about it. I don't suppose it'll ever come to a court-martial. The Navy are being rather stiff too, but they do things their own way. I should say myself you're in the clear – unofficially, mind. As far as I understand the case you were simply acting under orders. You'll be attached here at my headquarters for general duties. We'll get you all off as soon as Ben – your Brigadier, I mean – can move. I'm trying to get them to lay on a flying-boat. Meanwhile just hang about until you're wanted.'

Guy hung about. He had had his captaincy without knowing it, and had now lost it.

'That means six or seven pounds more pay, anyway,' said the staff captain. 'It shouldn't take long to straighten out. Or I'd take a chance and give it to you now if you're short.'

'Thanks awfully,' said Guy. 'I can manage.'

'Nothing much to spend money on here certainly. You can be sure of getting it somewhere, sometime. Army pay follows you up, like income tax.'

The battalion wanted to 'dine' him 'out', but Tickeridge forbade it.

'You'll be back with us in a day or two,' he said.

'Shall I?' Guy asked when they were alone.

'I wouldn't bet on it.'

Meanwhile there had been a series of disturbing bulletins from and about Apthorpe.

Messages from up-country passed by telephone from one semi-literate native telephonist to another. The first message was: *'Captain Apthorpe him very sorry off collar requests extension leaves.'*

Two days later there was a long and quite unintelligible message to the Senior Medical Officer demanding a number of drugs. After that was the request that the specialist in tropical diseases (who had left them some time before) should come up-country immediately. Then silence. At last a day or two before the mail arrived, Apthorpe appeared.

He was slung in a sheeted hammock between two bearers, looking like a Victorian woodcut from a book of exploration. They deposited him on the hospital steps and at once began an argument about their 'dash', they talking very loudly in Mende, Apthorpe feebly in Swahili. He was carried indoors protesting: 'They understand perfectly. They're only pretending. It's their lingua franca.'

The boys remained like vultures day after day, disputing over their 'dash' and admiring the passing pageant of metropolitan life.

Everyone in the brigade mess was particularly pleasant to Guy, even Dunn who was genuinely delighted to have the company of someone of more ignominious position than himself.

'Tell me all about it, old chap. Is it true you went off and started a battle on your own?'

'I'm not allowed to talk. The matter is *sub judice.*'

'Like that matter of the boot. You've heard the latest? That lunatic Apthorpe has taken refuge in the hospital. I bet he's shamming.'

'I don't think so. He looked pretty sick when he came back from his leave up-country.'

'But he's used to this climate. Anyway, we'll catch him when he comes out. If you ask me I'd say he was in worse trouble than you are.'

This talk of Apthorpe brought back tender memories of

Guy's early days in barracks. He asked permission of the brigade major to visit him.

'Take a car, Uncle.' Everyone was anxious to be agreeable. 'Take a bottle of whisky. I'll make it all right with the mess president.' (They were rationed to one bottle a month in this town.)

'Will that be all right with the hospital?'

'Very much all wrong, Uncle. That's your risk. But it's always done. Not worth while calling on a chap in hospital unless you bring a bottle. But don't say I told you. It's your responsibility if you're caught.'

Guy drove up the laterite road, past the Syrian stores and the vultures, noticing nothing except the dawdling natives who obstructed his way; later a few printed pages would create, not recall, the scene for him and make it forever memorable. People would say to him in eight years time: 'You were there during the war. Was it like that?' and he would answer: 'Yes. It *must* have been.'

Then out of the town by a steep road to the spacious, whitish hospital, where there was no wireless to aggravate the suffering, no bustle; fans swung to and fro, windows were shut and curtained against the heat of the sun.

He found Apthorpe alone in his room, in a bed near the window. When Guy entered he was lying doing nothing, staring at the sun-blind with his hands empty on the counterpane. He immediately began to fill and light a pipe.

'I came to see how you were.'

'Rotten, old man, rotten.'

'They don't seem to have given you much to do.'

'They don't realize how ill I am. They keep bringing me jigsaws and Ian Hay. A damn fool woman, wife of a box-wallah here, offered to teach me crochet. I ask you, old man, I just ask you.'

Guy produced the bottle he had been concealing in the pocket of his bush-shirt.

'I wondered if you'd like some whisky.'

'That's very thoughtful. In fact I would. Very much. They

235

bring us one medicine-glassful at sundown. It's not enough. Often one wants more. I told them so, pretty strongly, and they just laughed. They've treated my case all wrong from the very first. I know more about medicines than any of those young idiots. It's a wonder I've stayed alive as long as I have. Toughness. It takes some time to kill an old bush hand. But they'll do it. They wear one down. They exhaust the will to live and then – phut. You're a goner. I've seen it happen dozens of times.'

'Where shall I put the whisky?'

'Somewhere I can reach it. It'll get damned hot in the bed, but I think it's the best place.'

'How about the locker?'

'They're always prying in there. But they're slack about bed-making. They just pull the covers smooth before the doctor's round. Tuck it in at the bottom, there's a good chap.'

There was only a thin sheet and a thin cotton counterpane. Guy saw Apthorpe's large feet, bereft of their 'porpoises', peeling with fever. He tried to interest Apthorpe in the new brigadier and in his own obscure position, but Apthorpe said fretfully: 'Yes, yes, yes, yes. It's all another world to me, old man.'

He puffed at his pipe, let it go out, tried with a feeble hand to put it on the table beside him, dropped it, noisily in that quiet place, on the bare floor. Guy stooped to retrieve it but Apthorpe said: 'Leave it there, old man. I don't want it. I only tried to be companionable.'

When Guy looked up he saw tears on Apthorpe's colourless cheeks.

'I say, would you like me to go?'

'No, no. I'll feel better in a minute. Did you bring a corkscrew? Good man. I think I could do with a nip.'

Guy opened the bottle, poured out a tot, recorked and replaced the spirit under the sheet.

'Wash out the glass, old man, do you mind? I've been hoping you'd come – you especially. There's something worrying me.'

'Not the signalman's boot?'

236

'No, no, no, no. Do you suppose I'd let a little tick like Dunn worry me? No, it's something on my conscience.'

There was a pause during which the whisky seemed to perform its beneficient magic. Apthorpe shut his eyes and smiled. At last he looked up and said: 'Hullo, Crouchback, you here? That's lucky. There's something I wanted to say to you. Do you remember years ago, when we first joined, I mentioned my aunt?'

'You mentioned two.'

'*Exactly*. That's what I wanted to tell you. There's only one.'

'I *am* sorry.' All the talk lately had been about people killed by bombs. 'Was it an air-raid? Leonard caught one . . .'

'No, no, no: I mean, there never was more than one. The other was an invention. I suppose you might call it a little joke. Anyway, I've told you.'

After a pause Guy could not resist asking: 'Which did you invent, the one at Peterborough or the one at Tunbridge Wells?'

'The one at Peterborough, of course.'

'Then where did you hurt your knee?'

'At Tunbridge Wells.' Apthorpe giggled slightly at his cleverness like Mr Toad in *The Wind in the Willows*.

'You certainly took me in thoroughly.'

'Yes. It was a good joke, wasn't it? I say, I think I'd like a drop more whisky.'

'Sure it's good for you?'

'My dear fellow, I've been just as ill as this before and pulled through – simply by treating it with whisky.'

He sighed happily after this second glass. He really did seem altogether better and stronger.

'There's another point I want to talk about. My will.'

'You needn't start thinking about that for years yet.'

'I think about it *now*. A great deal. I haven't much. Just a few thousand in "gilt-edged" my father left me. I've left it all back to my aunt of course. It's family money, after all, and ought to go back. The one at Tunbridge Wells not' – roguishly – 'the good lady at Peterborough. But there's someone else.'

Guy thought: could this inscrutable man have a secret, irregular ménage? Little dusky Apthorpes, perhaps?

'Look here, Apthorpe, please don't go telling me anything about your private affairs. You'll be awfully embarrassed about it later, if you do. You're going to be perfectly fit again in a week or two.'

Apthorpe considered this.

'I'm tough,' he admitted. 'I'll take some killing. But it's all a question of the will to live. I must set everything in order just in case they wear me down. That's what keeps worrying me so.'

'All right. What is it?'

'It's my gear,' said Apthorpe. 'I don't want my aunt to get hold of it. Some of it's at the Commodore's at Southsand. The rest is at that place in Cornwall, where we last camped. I left it in Leonard's charge. He was a trustworthy sort of chap, I always thought.'

Guy wondered: should he make it plain about Leonard? Better leave it till later. He had probably left Apthorpe's treasure at the inn when they went to London. It might be traced eventually. This was no time to add to Apthorpe's anxieties.

'If my aunt's got it, I know exactly what she'd do. She'd hand the whole thing over to some High Church boy-scouts she's interested in. I don't want High Church boy-scouts playing the devil with my gear.'

'No. It would be most unsuitable.'

'Exactly. You remember Chatty Corner?'

'Vividly.'

'I want him to have it all. I haven't mentioned it in my will. I thought it might hurt my aunt's feelings. I don't suppose she really knows it exists. Now I want you to collect it and hand it over to Chatty on the quiet. I don't suppose it's strictly legal but it's quite safe. Even if she did get wind of it, my aunt is the last person to go to law. You'll do that for me, won't you, old man?'

'Very well. I'll try.'

'Then I can die happy – at least if anyone ever does die happy. Do you think they do?'

'We used to pray for it a lot at school. But for goodness' sake don't start thinking of dying *now*.'

'I'm a great deal nearer death now,' said Apthorpe, suddenly huffy, 'than you ever were at school.'

There was a rattle at the door and a nurse came in with a tray.

'Why! Visitors! You're the first he's had. I must say you seem to have cheered him up. We have been down in the dumps, haven't we?' she said to Apthorpe.

'You see, old man, they wear me down. Thanks for coming. Good-bye.'

'I smell something I shouldn't,' said the nurse.

'Just a drop of whisky I happened to have in my flask, nurse,' Guy answered.

'Well, don't let the doctor hear about it. It's the *very* worst thing. I ought really to report you to the S.M.O., really I ought.'

'Is the doctor anywhere about?' Guy asked. 'I'd rather like to speak to him.'

'Second door on the left. I shouldn't go in if I were you. He's in a horrid temper.'

But Guy found a weary, foolish man of his own age.

'Apthorpe? Yes. You're in the same regiment, I see. The Applejacks, eh?'

'Is he really pretty bad, doctor?'

'Of course he is. He wouldn't be here if he wasn't.'

'He talked a lot about dying.'

'Yes, he does to me, except when he's delirious. Then he seems worried about a bomb in the rears. Did he ever have any experience of the kind, do you know?'

'I rather think he did.'

'Well, that accounts for that. Queer bird, the mind. Hides things away and then out they pop. But I mustn't get too technical. It's a hobby horse of mine, the mind.'

'I wanted to know, is he on the danger list?'

'Well, I haven't actually put him there. No need to cause unnecessary alarm and despondency. His sort of trouble hangs on for weeks often and just when you think you've pulled them through, out they go, you know.

'Apthorpe's got the disadvantage of having lived in this God-forsaken country. You chaps who come out fresh from England have got stamina. Chaps who live here have got their blood full of every sort of infection. And then, of course, they poison themselves with whisky. They snuff out like babies. Still, we're doing the best for Apthorpe. Luckily we're rather empty at the moment so everyone can give him full attention.'

'Thank you, sir.'

The R.A.M.C. man was a colonel but he was seldom called 'sir' by anyone outside his own staff. 'Have a glass of whisky?' he said gratefully.

'Thanks awfully, but I must be off.'

'Any time you're passing.'

'By the way, sir, how is our Brigadier Ritchie-Hook?'

'He'll be out of here any day now. Between ourselves he's rather a difficult patient. He made one of my young officers pickle a Negro's head for him. Most unusual.'

'Was the pickling a success?'

'Must have been, I suppose. Anyway he keeps the thing by his bed grinning at him.'

8

NEXT morning at dawn a flying-boat landed at Freetown.

'That's for you,' said Colonel Tickeridge. 'They say the Brig. will be fit to move tomorrow.'

But there was other news that morning. Apthorpe was in a coma.

'They don't think he'll ever come out of it,' Colonel Tickeridge said. 'Poor old Uncle. Still there are worse ways of dying and he hasn't got a madam or children or anything.'

'Only an aunt,' said Guy.

'Two aunts, I think he told me.'

Guy did not correct him. Everyone at Brigade Headquarters remembered Apthorpe well. He had been a joke there. Now the mess was cast into gloom, less at the loss of Apthorpe than at the thought of death so near, so unexpected.

'We'll lay on full military honours for the funeral.'

'He'd have liked that.'

'A good opportunity to show the flag in the town.'

Dunn fussed about his boot.

'I don't see how I'll be able to recover now,' he said. 'It seems rather ghoulish somehow, applying to the next of kin.'

'How much is it?'

'Nine shillings.'

'I'll pay.'

'I say, that's very sporting of you. It'll keep my books in order.'

The new brigadier went to the hospital that morning to inform Ritchie-Hook of his imminent departure. He returned at lunch-time.

'Apthorpe is dead,' he said briefly. 'I want to talk to you, Crouchback, after lunch.'

Guy supposed the summons was connected with his move-order and went to the brigadier's office without alarm. He found both the brigadier and the brigade major there, one looking angrily at him, the other looking at the table.

'You heard that Apthorpe was dead?'

'Yes, sir.'

'There was an empty whisky bottle in his bed. Does that mean anything to you?'

Guy stood silent, aghast rather than ashamed.

'I asked: "Does that mean anything to you?" '

'Yes, sir. I took him a bottle yesterday afternoon.'

'You knew it was against orders?'

'Yes, sir.'

'Any excuse?'

'No, sir, except that I knew he liked it and I didn't realize it would do him any harm. Or that he'd finish it all at once.'

'He was half delirious, poor fellow. How old are you, Crouchback?'

'Thirty-six, sir.'

'Exactly. That's what makes everything so hopeless. If you were a young idiot of twenty-one I could understand it. Damn it, man, you're only a year or two younger than I am.'

241

Guy stood still saying nothing. He was curious how the brigadier would deal with the question.

'The S.M.O. of the hospital knows all about it. So do most
of his staff, I expect. You can imagine how he feels. I was with
him half the morning before I could get him to see sense. Yes,
I've begged you off, but please understand that what I've done
was purely for the Corps. You've committed too serious a
crime for me to deal with summarily. The choice was between hushing it up and sending you before a court martial.
There's nothing would give me more personal satisfaction than
to see you booted out of the army altogether. But we've one
sticky business on our hands already – in which incidentally you
are implicated. I persuaded the medico that we had no evidence. You were poor Apthorpe's only visitor but there are
orderlies and native porters in and out of the hospital who
might have sold him the stuff' (he spoke as though whisky,
which he regularly and moderately drank, were some noxious
distillation of Guy's own). 'Nothing's worse than a court martial that goes off half-cock. I also told him what a slur it would
be on poor Apthorpe's name. It would all have had to come
out. I gather he was practically a dipsomaniac and had two
aunts who think the world of him. Pretty gloomy for them to
hear the truth. So I got him to agree in the end. But don't thank
me, and, remember, I don't want to see you again ever. I shall
apply for your immediate posting out of the brigade as soon
as they've finished with you in England. The only hope I have
for you is that you're thoroughly ashamed of yourself. You
can fall out now.'

Guy left the office unashamed. He felt shaken, as though he
had seen a road accident in which he was not concerned. His
fingers shook but it was nerves not conscience which troubled
him; he was familiar with shame; this trembling, hopeless
sense of disaster was something of quite another order; something that would pass and leave no mark.

He stood in the ante-room sweating and motionless and was
presently aware of someone at his elbow.

'I see you aren't busy.'

He turned and saw Dunn. 'No.'

'Perhaps you wouldn't mind my mentioning it then? This morning you very kindly offered to settle that matter of the boot.'

'Yes, of course. How much was it? I forget. Nine pounds, wasn't it?'

'Good Lord, no. Nine shillings.'

'Of course. Nine shillings.' Guy did not want to show Dunn his trembling hands. 'I've no change now. Remind me to-morrow.'

'But you're off tomorrow, aren't you?'

'So I am. I forgot.'

His hands when he took them out of his pockets trembled less than he had feared. He counted out nine shillings.

'I'll make out the receipt in Apthorpe's name if it's all the same to you.'

'I don't want a receipt.'

'Must keep my books straight.'

Dunn left to put his books straight. Guy remained standing. Presently the brigade major came out of the office.

'I say, I'm awfully sorry about this business,' he said.

'It was a damned silly thing to do. I see that now.'

'I did say it was your responsibility.'

'Of course. Of course.'

'There was nothing I could possibly have said.'

'Of course not. Nothing.'

They took Ritchie-Hook out of the hospital before Apthorpe. Guy had half an hour to wait on the quay. The flying-boat lay out. All round the bum-boats floated selling fruit and nuts.

'Have you got my nut packed up safely, Glass?'

'Yes, sir.'

Halberdier Glass was in a black mood. Ritchie-Hook's servant was travelling home with his master. Glass had to stay behind.

Colonel Tickeridge had come down to the quay.

He said: 'I don't seem to bring luck to the officers I pick for promotion. First Leonard, then Apthorpe.'

'And now me, sir.'

'And now you.'

'Here comes the party.'

An ambulance drove up followed by the Brigadier's car. Ritchie-Hook, one leg huge, as though from elephantiasis, in plaster. The brigade major took his arm and led him to the edge of the quay.

'No prisoners' escort?' said Ritchie-Hook. 'Morning, Tickeridge. Morning, Crouchback. What's all this I hear about you poisoning one of my officers? The damn nurses couldn't stop talking about it all yesterday. Now jump to it. Junior officers into the boat first, out of it last.'

Guy jumped to it and sat as far as he could out of everyone's way. Presently they hoisted Ritchie-Hook down. Before the boat had reached the aircraft, the brigade car was honking its way through the listless, black crowds; they had run things pretty close for the funeral parade.

The flying-boat was a mail carrier. The after half of the cabin was piled high with bags among which the Halberdier servant luxuriously disposed himself for sleep. Guy remembered the immense boredom of censoring those letters home. Here and there one came across a man who through some oddity of upbringing had escaped the state schools. These wrote with wild phonetic mis-spellings straight from the heart. The rest strung together clichés which he supposed somehow communicated some exchange of affection and need. The old soldiers wrote SWALK on the envelope, meaning 'sealed with a loving kiss'. All these missives served as a couch for Ritchie-Hook's batman.

The flying-boat climbed in a great circle over the green land, then turned over the town. Already it was much cooler.

It had been the heat, Guy thought, all the false emotions of the past twenty-four hours. In England where winter would be giving its first hints of sharpness, where the leaves would be falling among the falling bombs, fire-gutted, shattered, where the bodies were nightly dragged half-clothed, clutching pets, from the rubble and glass splinters, – things would look very different in England.

The flying-boat made another turn over White Man's Grave and set its course across the ocean, bearing away the two men who had destroyed Apthorpe.

White Man's Grave. The European cemetery was conveniently near the hospital. Six months of changing stations and standing by for orders had not corroded the faultless balance of the Halberdier slow march. The Second Battalion had called a parade the moment the news of Apthorpe's death arrived and the regimental sergeant major had roared under the fiery sun and the boots had moved up and down the blistering road. This morning it was perfect. The coffin bearers were exactly sized. The bugles sounded Last Post in perfect unison. The rifles fired as one.

As a means of 'showing the flag' it was not greatly appreciated. The civil population were *aficionados* of funerals. They liked more spontaneity, more evident grief. But as a drill parade it was something that the Colony had never seen before. The flag-covered coffin descended without a hitch. The vital earth settled down. Two Halberdiers fainted, falling flat and rigid, and were left supine.

When it was all over Sarum-Smith, genuinely moved, said: 'It was like the burial of Sir John Moore at Corunna.'

'Sure you don't mean the Duke of Wellington at St Paul's?' said de Souza.

'Perhaps I do.'

Colonel Tickeridge asked the adjutant: 'Ought we to pass the cap round to put up a stone or something?'

'I imagine his relations in England will want to fix that.'

'They're well off?'

'Extremely, I believe. And High Church. They'd probably want something fancy.'

'Both Uncles gone the same day.'

'Funny, I was thinking the same. I rather preferred Crouchback on the whole.'

MORE ABOUT PENGUINS
AND PELICANS

For further information about books available from Penguins please write to Dept EP, Penguin Books Ltd, Harmondsworth, Middlesex UB7 0DA.

In the U.S.A.: For a complete list of books available from Penguins in the United States write to Dept CS, Penguin Books, 625 Madison Avenue, New York, New York 10022.

In Canada: For a complete list of books available from Penguins in Canada write to Penguin Books Canada Ltd, 2801 John Street, Markham, Ontario L3R 1B4.

In Australia: For a complete list of books available from Penguins in Australia write to the Marketing Department, Penguin Books Australia Ltd, P.O. Box 257, Ringwood, Victoria 3134.

MY UNCLE OSWALD
Roald Dahl

The long-awaited novel in which Uncle Oswald discovers the electrifying properties of the Sudanese Blister Beetle and the gorgeous Yasmin Howcomely – a girl absolutely soaked in sex – and arranges the seduction of all the great men of his time for his own wicked, irreverent reasons.

'Deliciously silly' – *Observer*
'Rollicking, raunchy, OUTRAGEOUS' – *Evening Standard*

SCHULTZ
J. P. Donleavy

Schultz, Sigmund Franz, impresario producer of flops in London's West End. He's a walking or sometimes chauffeur-driven and often boot-propelled disaster area. Which disasters are often indulgently plotted by his aristocratic partners His Amazing Grace Basil Nectarine and the languid Binky. But more frequently caused by Schultz's desperate need to seduce as many beautiful women as is humanly possible – and then more.

THE 400
Stephen Sheppard

'Looking at the Bank of England that night, George had become quiet and calm. His American voice spoke softly – "We'll take her." he said.'

So begins an adventure so daring, a scheme so breathtakingly elegant, a fraud so cheekily flamboyant that it defies the imagination . . . Stephen Sheppard's international bestseller, set in 1872 in London, Rio de Janeiro and Europe, is as full of verve and dash as his characters – four rascals you'll never forget.

'Could rival Forsyth' – *Now!*
'Blockbusting' – *Sunday Express*

BIRDY
William Wharton

One of the most extraordinary and affecting novels to be published for decades, *Birdy* has electrified the critics on both
sides of the Atlantic. Out of a young boy's need to escape and
his consuming obsession with birds and flight, William
Wharton has spun a story dazzlingly shot through with
humour, wisdom, tenderness, tragedy and longing.

'Wonderful' – Doris Lessing
'Wharton is exceptionally gifted' – John Fowles
'Will become a classic' – Patrick White

YOUR LOVER JUST CALLED
Stories of Joan and Richard Maple
John Updike

Joan and Richard Maple confess infidelities; join a Boston
civil rights march; take a trip to the in-laws, to the beach, to
Rome; and after twenty years – a million mundane moments
shared – attempt to explain to their four children why they
have decided to separate.

With astonishing power and tenderness, John Updike traces
the story of their marriage: a marriage that begins with love
and ends, irretrievably, with love.

DUBIN'S LIVES
Bernard Malamud

In William Dubin – a middle-aged, successful biographer
seeking love, increased accomplishment and his secret self –
the author has created one of his best characters: his novel is
a compassionate and wry tragicomedy of a man torn between
two women, living by discipline, love, honour, fidelity and his
passion for work.

'Masterly and hypnotic' – *Observer*

OFFICERS AND GENTLEMEN

Officers and Gentlemen follows *Men At Arms* in Evelyn Waugh's trilogy about the Second World War, described by Cyril Connolly in the *Sunday Times* as 'unquestionably the finest novel to have come out of the war'.

Guy Crouchback's first year in the army ended with an escapade – planned by Brigadier Ben Ritchie-Hook – that temporarily blotted both men's Halberdier copybooks. As a result Guy became attached to a Commando unit undergoing training on the Hebridean Isle of Mugg, where whisky flowed freely and H.M. forces had to show deferential respect to the omnipotent Laird.

But the high comedy of Mugg was followed, only a few months later, by the bitterness of Crete. Guy landed with defeat already imminent, and experienced all the chaos and indignity of a total withdrawal or surrender.

UNCONDITIONAL SURRENDER

The Crouchback who soldiers on in *Unconditional Surrender* has lost his Halberdier idealism but gained in human sympathy. Two years at the London H.Q. of Hazardous Offensive Operations are neither hazardous nor offensive, but they offer Guy the chance of reconciliation with his former wife. Then, sent to Jugoslavia, Guy the Catholic finds himself officially aiding the Communist take-over, but unofficially ministering to a ragged little group of Jews.

Moments of farce recur, but with a sharper edge. The reader, like Guy himself, discovers that the action and comedy of Crouchback's war have given way to a sober awareness of its ultimate futility and harshness.

THE HOUSEHOLDER
Ruth Prawer Jhabvala

Ruth Prawer Jhabvala has been compared with Jane Austen, E. M. Forster and Chekhov; from her pages rise the heat, the smells, the flashing iridescent colours and the ceaseless rhythms of Indian life. And such is the strength of her humorous and perceptive pen that this appealing story of a young schoolteacher trying to come to terms with marriage and maturity becomes more than a highly comic vignette of a particular society – it becomes a reflection of a universal experience.

'A writer of genius ; ; ; a writer of world class – a master story-teller' – *Sunday Times*

WOOLWORTH MADONNA
Elizabeth Troop

'She was very ordinary, a sort of Woolworth madonna, there must be millions like her.' Elizabeth Troop's heroine is more than that though. Faced with the demolition of her house, the slow sliding of hopes and dreams into middle age, the onset of high-rise living and flabby flesh, she still remains a force to be reckoned with – a force that is truly and unbeatably feminine and unforgettable.

'A rare discovery' – *New Statesman*

VOYAGE IN THE DARK
Jean Rhys

A chorus girl of eighteen in a fit-up touring company, Anna's brief liaison with a kindly but unimaginative man leads her to abandon the theatre and drift into the demi-monde of Edwardian London: red-plush dinners in private rooms 'up West'; ragtime, champagne and whisky back at the flat; these, and the discreet tinkle of sovereigns in the small hours, pave the way to disaster ...

MY MUSIC
Steve Race

Here are the ripest plums – the outrageous puns, the nonsense, the sparkling repartee – from thirteen glorious years of the internationally famous BBC Radio and Television quiz game, starring Frank Muir, Denis Norden, John Amis and Ian Wallace and chaired by Steve Race.

THE BEST OF JAZZ
Humphrey Lyttelton

'A kaleidoscope of anecdote, analysis, history, interpretation and background colour which should please beginner and expert alike . . . a smashing book' – Miles Kington in *Punch*

Crammed with anecdote, wit and erudition, here is a complete run-down on the history, the personalities – Louis Armstrong, Sidney Bechet, Jelly Roll Morton, Bessie Smith, Bix Beiderbecke – and the masterpieces which have bedecked a music whose golden notes and subtle rhythms have found a permanent home in modern culture.

THE Q ANNUAL
Spike Milligan

If you've seen Spike Milligan's hilarious Q Series on television, you'll enjoy this book . . .

In glorious black and white Spike sings his evening dress to sleep; measures Napoleon for half a coffin; impersonates John Hanson in 'On the Buses'; speaks out on behalf of oppressed minorities from the Royal Family to the Lone Ranger. There is a rare photograph of Ivan's wife Mrs Ethel Terrible, and dramatic new evidence on the liquefaction of Harry Secombe, Princess Anne's birthday, the electric banana . . .